LIVES OF THE SAINTS

Also by David Slavitt

FICTION

Salazar Blinks *1988*
The Hussar *1987*
The Agent, *with Bill Adler, 1986*
Alice at 80 *1984*
Ringer *1982*
Cold Comfort *1980*
Jo Stern *1978*
King of Hearts *1976*
The Killing of the King *1974*
The Outer Mongolian *1973*
ABCD *1972*
Anagrams *1970*
Feel Free *1968*
Rochelle, or Virtue Rewarded *1967*

NONFICTION

Physicians Observed *1987*
Understanding Social Psychology,
with P. Secord and C. Backman, 1976

POETRY

Ovid's Poetry of Exile *1989*
Equinox *1989*
The Tristia of Ovid *1986*
The Walls of Thebes *1986*
The Elegies to Delia of Albius Tibullus *1985*
Big Nose *1983*
Dozens *1981*
Rounding the Horn *1978*
Vital Signs: New and Selected Poems *1975*
The Eclogues and the Georgics of Virgil *1972*
Child's Play *1972*
The Eclogues of Virgil *1971*
Day Sailing *1968*
The Carnivore *1965*
Suits for the Dead *1961*

LIVES
OF THE
SAINTS

David R. Slavitt

Atheneum · New York
1989

Atheneum
Macmillan Publishing Company
866 Third Avenue, New York, NY 10022
Collier Macmillan Canada, Inc.

This is a work of fiction. Names, characters, places, and incidents either
are the product of the author's imagination or are used fictitiously. Any
resemblance to actual events or persons, living or dead, is entirely
coincidental.

Library of Congress Cataloging-in-Publication Data
Slavitt, David R., 1935–
Lives of the saints / David Slavitt.
p. cm.
ISBN 0-689-12079-6
I. Title.
PS3569.L3L5 1989
813'.54—dc20   89-17587   CIP

10 9 8 7 6 5 4 3 2 1

Printed in the United States of America

For Frannie and Henry Taylor

Acknowledgements

I have relied for much of the hagiographical information in this novel upon *Butler's Lives of the Saints* (1956), H. Thurston and D. Attwater, eds.; Donald Attwater's *Dictionary of Saints* (1965); and John J. Delanye's *Dictionary of Saints* (1980). For the helpful comment upon the thought of Nicolas Malebranche I have consulted Daisie Rodner's *Malebranche* (1978); Michael E. Hobart's *Science and Religion in the Thought of Nicolas Malebranche* (1982); and Charles J. McCracken's *Malebranche and British Philosophy* (1983). I have looked to Wu-chi Liu and Irving Yucheng Lo's anthology, *Sunflower Splendor* (1975), for information about Chinese poetry and, in particular, that of Yüan Chen. And for details about Iran and Sufism, I have consulted Roy Mottahedeh's *The Mantle of the Prophet* (1985).

LIVES OF THE SAINTS

Proem

I USED to be proud that there is no sainthood in Judaism. I took it as evidence that we were less primitive, more rational and civilized than Christians. The Hassidic wonder rabbis, had I known about them, would have been only a minor embarrassment to me. After all, my family weren't Hassids and therefore could not be held accountable for the excesses of a bunch of mystics, those wrong-way Corrigans of the Enlightenment. I know better now.

Saint Barbara is one of those martyr saints to whom I am now drawn. That her martyrdom was ridiculous only makes it more compelling. The principle she defended, even unto death, was perfectly absurd—that a privy should have three windows in its door, in honor of the Trinity. Not one or two. Or four.

For this she suffered and died. Which is to say for no reason at all.

Her father, a sophisticated citizen of Heliopolis, was so enraged by her pious foolishness that he beheaded her. With his own two hands. He, in turn, was immediately struck down by lightning.

One need not be absolutely primitive to read into such a peculiar set of circumstances a certain significance. The astonished Heliopolitans took it as God's judgment, and Barbara assumed her place in the hagiography.

Unless she has been demoted now, like Saint Christopher. "Mr. Christopher, be my guide"?

Suppose he had not beheaded her. Suppose, instead, that he had slapped his forehead with his open palm, exclaimed only half-facetiously, "Jesus Christ!" and fallen upon his knees. Suppose he had in perfect seriousness, either moved by the bizarre piety of his daughter or for whatever other extraneous circumstance, decided to cut that third hole in the privy door. Would the thunderstorm not have come? Would the lightning bolt have landed elsewhere? Or, if it had hit him, would the martyrdom have been his?

I am not being perverse. These are childish questions but only because children still have the innocence necessary to address serious issues and to ask about what we have learned to take for granted.

Can the father's beheading of his daughter be said in any sense to have caused the lightning bolt to strike him?

Father Malebranche denied that there is any such thing as cause and effect. The bold thrust of *De la recherche de la verité*, which he published anonymously in 1674, was to deny not only the logic of cause and effect but the epistemology of common sense, the innocent belief most of us have in the evidence of our senses. As far as he was concerned, that kind of empiricism was a mistake, or, even worse, our punishment for the Fall.

A nut! A gibbering idiot, right?

But you never know who is going to have something useful and relevant to say. Theoretical physicists, the intellectual heavyweights of our day—or the intellectual bullies—are generally agreed that at the subatomic level, cause and effect don't seem to have much relevance. Even at the atomic level, there are phenomena that are difficult to explain if one tries to be faithful to usual logical models.

The half-life of uranium 238, for example, is 4×10^9 years. Which means that, in a purely statistical way, half the atoms in any given piece of uranium will have decayed within that time. And in the next 4×10^9 years, half the remainder will have decayed. And so on. From a purely statistical point of view, there is no problem at all. But if you consider any particular atom, there are serious problems. How, for example, does any given atom know when to deteriorate? And, more perplexing, how does any particular atom know what the other atoms are doing or have done? How many of the rest of them have deteriorated? How do they coordinate this—which is what they'd have to do in any reasonable scheme?

The Malebranchian answer is that they don't coordinate. They don't have to—because there is no reasonable scheme.

Each atom has its own destiny.

Or, to put it another way, each atom is a manifestation of the Divine Logos with its own relationship to God. This is what the physicists find themselves forced to retreat to, although they are unhappy about it. This also happens to be what Nicolas Malebranche wrote in the last part of the seventeenth century, a thirty-six-year-old priest in the Congregation of the Oratory in Paris on the Rue St. Honoré.

St. Honoré was one of those chic saints. There are a number of them. They have, presumably, their own elegant enclave in Heaven, St. Honoré and his pals, Moritz and Tropez and Regis. And Remo.

And San Carlo, the opera buff.

And San Souci, the blithe layabout?

Disappointing to report, Honoré was one of those boring saints with an almost soporific entry in *Lives of the Saints*. A bishop of Amiens, he is responsible for several unspecified miracle cures. For reasons that are not even suggested, he is the patron of bakers, confectioners, corn chandlers, and all trades that deal with flour. His emblem in art is a baker's peel, which is about as much fun to carry around as an oar or a winnowing fan.

It is the other Honoré who ought to have a fashionable Rue and an elegant Faubourg named after him. That other Honoré lived in the fifth century as a hermit, which sounds somewhat gloomy except that his hermitage was on the Côte d'Azur on a tiny island off Antibes that must have been pleasant even then. Less frantic, in season, surely. By dint of his fervent prayers there, he managed to convert his sister Margaret from paganism to Christianity and to persuade her that she, too, should live an anchorite's life—on another island but close to his own. He promised that he would come to visit her once a year and did, regularly, late in the summer when the mimosas bloomed. And then, one year, when she was distressed and afflicted, depressed we might say today, either troubled with doubts or perhaps, and just as plausibly, disturbed by a return of her sanity, she grew impatient, could no longer wait for him, and forced some mimosas so that she could send him the blossoms. These he interpreted, correctly, as a signal that she needed him.

He arrived to comfort her and buttress her faith. It was their last meeting. She died that winter.

It was the kind of thing Ronald Firbank would have adored.

At any event, it is more interesting than the other Honoré with his crowd of corn chandlers and *confisseurs*, lugging that baker's peel about with him all over Amiens.

In one hand, his bishop's crozier, and in the other hand, the peel? Or both together?

Or did he have a special gizmo made up, a peel with a hook at one end, good for catching stray sheep and also getting loaves of bread out of ovens?

One ought not make fun of him. It was his destiny. He couldn't help it. And if the details of his life, those interesting miracle cures, have been obliterated by the passage of time, that makes them no less miraculous or praiseworthy.

The martyrdom of Barbara was there all along, waiting to express itself. Her father was her agent, her tool, as much as her executioner. He attended upon her as the mimosas attended Honoré, or those bakers the other Honoré.

It is a difficult doctrine. But are other doctrines less difficult? Can we bear the thought of the innocent girl cut down by her angry parent? Can we imagine his moment of remorse in that instant between her death and the lightening bolt—the thunderclap of which he could never have heard?

Between heartlessness and foolishness, who can choose?

Less remotely, a loony with a rifle makes an appearance at a shopping mall. Whatever has at last upset him is of only clinical interest. He had "bad thoughts," which he is even likely to have discussed with some therapist or other. Until today, these thoughts have been merely annoying, like a radio playing somewhere but not tuned in to any station. Mostly, there is static, but every so often, as the atomspherics do whatever they do, there is an intelligible signal drifting in for a few moments and then fading. Sometimes there are two such signals, which can produce amusing effects—as if at a concert hall there were, up in one of the loges, a jazz drummer doing his thing even as the string quartet on the stage below saws away at their instruments (and the audience conspires to pretend that nothing untoward is happening).

Not bad art but different art, what they called some years ago "a happening." Performance art.

An attempt to test the limits of context.

Or crazy.

Anyway, there it has been, for weeks or months, blaring away in the head of this poor son of a bitch. And nobody takes him seriously. Why should they? But one day, quite unpredictably, there is another of those dirty tricks the atmosphere plays on him, and the signal clears, steadies, and remains intelligible, even inescapable, for minutes, for days on end. It tells him what to do. It blares at him, in what he takes to be the absolute authority of the President of the United States of America.

Or John Wayne.

Or God Almighty.

So he fetches the rifle—there is always a rifle around somewhere—and he goes to the parking lot of the mall, and he blasts six people as they're coming out of the Piggly Wiggly.

They run like ants. Brains splatter on the pavement and blood, or perhaps the incarnadine mess is tomato sauce?

Both, probably. And nastily mixed.

Police cars converge, their sirens blaring, their lights flashing. The loony is bemused by the pretty colors and the shrill sounds. The blaring in his head is gone. He puts down the rifle, raises his hands, and stands there, stupid and helpless, waiting to be led away.

But is he the interesting figure? Has his life gobbled the lives of those six people he has just killed? Did his mental state, or the negligent gun laws, or the deficiencies in the mental health delivery system in that catchment area or all of these together cause the deaths?

Father Malebranche would say not. He would tell us that the lives of those six people were completed and fulfilled, that each of them was a center of attention, that the poor loony was no more than an attendant, destiny's gadget—as he himself would have maintained.

The Roman soldiers were not in charge. They were only obeying orders, and not Pilate's orders either but God's.

It was Jesus' crucifixion, not theirs.

1

WHAT Amanda Hapgood's life was really like is, of course, unknowable, as any life is unknowable at its heart. And yet, we make our unwarranted but mostly reliable guesses and assumptions all the time, leaping blithely across the chasms of our ignorance to the easiest conclusions. Thus we manage to construct plausible and even useful fictions.

But any fiction, no matter how absurd, can be useful if an editor like Lansberg is willing to authorize payment for it—as better editors in less objectionable enterprises have been reluctant to do.

In the face of such contrariness, one does what one must. Or perhaps one does what it is anyway one's destiny to do.

And Lansberg, too, is acting out of necessity, conforming to his destiny. It may be contemptible, but it is not what he would have chosen, if he had had a choice. Which he didn't.

None of us does.

Astonishingly, Hapgood agrees to this intrusion I have proposed to him—at Lansberg's direction and insistence, of course. In Hapgood's place, I shouldn't want some stranger rummaging around in what non-Malebranchians call "the effects" of the departed.

There are, according to Malebranche, two ideas of how nature works. In one, nature is a dynamic storehouse of causes and forces with their implied effects and consequences. This is the widespread but false view. The other possible idea is simpler, clearer, less widespread but nonetheless true—that there is only the temporal relation of *before* and *after*. What we think of as causality has nothing to do with any earlier events but is solely the will of God.

The loony in the parking lot pulling the trigger was hardly responsible for the appearance at that particular moment of those particular people. There were fifty or sixty individuals in view at that instant, and he could have picked out—and picked off—any of them. He could very well have aimed at one and hit another—indeed, it is likely that he may have done so. The trajectories have not been traced out by the police. There was no need. Everyone saw him firing. There was no possible requirement for that kind of forensic investigation. A bullet, though, had it been aimed at A, might easily have missed, hit a post, a wall, or the side of an automobile, and then ricocheted to hit B, either killing him or merely wounding him according to God's will. Or his destiny.

Or luck. Whatever we agree to call what we do not understand.

Each of these sad objects has its own career. And apparently, that includes the business of testifying about the existence of the dead woman.

The house, first of all. A single-story dwelling on a standard plot, it has a clump of tatterdemalion banana trees off to one side. These are supposed to look tropical and exotic, but mostly are just messy. The family is from—elsewhere? Most families are, so that's a safe enough assumption. Or perhaps they have a special fondness for fresh Cavendish bananas. Or had.

The garage has been turned into a family room. Or nonfamily room, more likely than not. When there are teenagers who like different music, different television programs, different friends with different topics of conversation, there is the perceived need for another room where they can go, either to claim it as their own or just to keep out of the way.

Among the predictable commercial posters on the living room wall, one announces that "War Is Not Good for Children and Other Growing Things." Apparently, it has been there for some time. Moved off the perpendicular, it reveals a discernible dust line describing a rectangle in the paint on the wall.

After a certain moment, they didn't see it anymore. The poster just disappeared.

Things do that.

The philosophy of Father Malebranche, I admit immediately, is extreme and may seem deranged, but it is appropriate for situations that are extreme and deranging. What it does is displace, redefine, refocus, and reorder the usual connections. . . .

How else can one endure the griefs of these objects? There is a baleful look to these abandoned articles of clothing, the dresses and blouses hanging in her closet, and an overwhelming poignancy to the orphaned pills and tampons and cosmetics in the bathroom. And there is her toothbrush, a green Oral-B 40, still hanging in its holder. It is intimately hers, something she put into her mouth every morning, hardly thinking about it. Be true to your teeth and they will never be false to you. The endless fight against periodontal disease! All beside the point now.

Fascinated, unable to believe what I am doing, happy to have Lansberg's directive as a kind of justification, I rummage through her underwear and pantyhose in the dresser drawers in her bedroom. She was slight, slender, scarcely burdening the ground she trod. A 32-A bra. And there are size-eight dresses hanging in the closet like felons on a gallows. And all those pairs of shoes so neatly arranged in the pockets of one of those space-saving shoe-holders fastened to the wall are a dainty 6-AA.

In the kitchen, one can learn a fair amount from her pots and pans, mostly Wearever aluminum but with a well-seasoned set of cast-iron skillets and a good Dutch oven in Calphalon. She had ordinary stainless flatware and nothing in the way of silver or crystal. On a wall shelf there is a small collection of popular cookbooks, and if I go through them, letting them open where they will, they show the pages to which she habitually turned. Her favorite recipes? Or her second favorite, the ones she made for company perhaps but had to consult each time. There are even confirming stains of batter or tomato sauce a chemist or an archaeologist might analyze, samples of those dishes she used to prepare. There are also her emendations in pencil that show her departures from the instructions of Mr. Claiborne or Ms. Child.

Other books in the shelves in the living room and bedroom give other sorts of testimony about her intellect and spirit. An English major in college, evidently, she kept several of the standard anthologies that are in use as college texts, or were back then. And a few books of poetry she apparently must have felt obliged to buy thereafter: Merrill, Clampitt, Nemerov, Rich.

In the smaller bookcase in the bedroom, though, her more current interests seem to have been *Principles of Accounting* and *The Joy of Sensuous Massage.*

All that cleverness, all those poems and recipes are gone, obliterated by the absolutely meaningless coincidence of her having decided to go to the health spa in the morning and to the Piggly Wiggly in the afternoon. Had she decided the other way, she'd still be alive, using her toothbrush in the morning. And at night, perhaps after she had mastered another tricky principle of accounting, sensuously massaging herself with the battery-operated vibrator I found in a shoe box up on the shelf in the closet.

A gift from a lover? A parting shot from her ex-husband when he moved out? A present from some female pal meant, not entirely, as a joke? A toy she bought herself?

The batteries, in any event, are fresh enough so that, if I turn the base, the motor comes to life with its ribald hum.

On top of the dresser, in a double frame in brushed aluminum, are two photographs, one of Greg, her son, who is nineteen now, and one of Cheryl, who is seventeen. In the photographs, they look to be maybe fourteen and twelve.

There are photographs of Ronald, the ex-husband, in the middle right-hand drawer of the desk. He was no longer on display but she hadn't thrown his pictures away either.

Saving them for her children, or for her grandchildren? Or for herself?

He is wearing aviator photo-grays and looking jaunty. His grin displays the expensive dental work that marked the beginning of his series of entertainments with younger women. There is a possible utility to the shining teeth. The radiance of the smile, especially in the gloom of some of the singles bars, may have given him some slight advantage, even if only psychological. Self-confidence in these matters is an invaluable asset.

It is easy to disapprove of Ronald, now that Amanda is dead. One wishes that, if her life were going to be so short, it might have been happier. And had Ron been other than he was, less restless or more devoted, or more self-restrained, or simply lazier, she might have been saved a certain measure of distress.

But that can't be the point. The loony's bullet cannot be said to have been a benefit, saving her from her distress.

That certainly wasn't what he intended. But intention would have nothing to do with the case if it was simply his destiny to appear when he did, aim as he did, or even miss as he might have, squeezing the trigger at that instant and that angle.

And Ronny now can claim to be a widower, which will earn him more sympathy than just being separated, and he'll probably get even more ass than he did with just the flashy dental work.

These are considerations somewhat beyond the limits of my assignment. What Lansberg and I had agreed on—as an experiment, a new kind of sob story but also a huge intellectual joke, was that I should go and interview objects. The *nouveau roman* of Alain Robbe-Grillet and Nathalie Sarraute is not one of the more pressing concerns of our lip-moving readers, but there are suggestive possibilities in the method, even for our poor slobs.

My suggestion, simply put, was that I should go and do a

piece about the objects, trying to translate their mute testimony into our semisensational prose.

The joke within the joke is that, according to Malebranche, there is no way of knowing objects. He is as rigorous as Bishop Berkeley—whom he greatly influenced—in his skepticism about the external world.

There is no reliable way to get from those shoes in their neat pockets to my brain except through God.

What was brilliant about Malebranche was the way in which he combined Descartes and St. Augustine. Descartes said, "*Cogito, ergo sum.*" And yet, in *De trinitate*, Augustine had long ago written it truer and better: "*Si fallor, sum.*"

If I am deceived, I am. If I doubt, I am.

I doubt. And doubting, I find St. Augustine a comfort.

One cannot simply confront a closet, a bureau, a bookcase, a medicine cabinet. One must make arrangements, which means that one must talk to these people, beguile them or cajole or ingratiate or bribe or do whatever is required to gain their trust.

Which one intends, of course, to betray.

I have learned about old Ronny's philanderings. And about Greg's general disgust. A druggie and a dropout, he was a bright boy before he set about obliterating himself.

As Cheryl was an intelligent and attractive girl before she undertook to eat herself into immenseness and thereby avoid those strenuous sexual sweepstakes of which she had been the reluctant observer.

It didn't work. What she couldn't imagine and therefore had failed to allow for was that some men like fatties.

Malebranchians, perhaps—who understand that they cannot know any external body but figure that a larger body may be easier to guess at.

I shouldn't joke, but what else is there to do?

Okay. There is more and worse. There is also Amanda's brother. Her mother had died about two years before, which left her brother needing to be cared for, a brother in his early or middle thirties whose name I don't know. He is retarded and emotionally unstable, was manageable enough at home when his mother was looking after him, but then needed institutionalization. And Amanda, who could not take him in herself, felt guilty about that.

And finally—as Ron confides in me, offering this juicy tidbit in the hope that I will not be too severe in my judgment of his behavior—she was having an affair with the accountant she was working for, a Mr. Fallyck.

I believe him. Who would make up such a name? What is the point of inventing stuff when the real world offers such *bizarrerie*?

But Malebranche is there with his curious consolation: *What real world?*

Where Ron was living was certainly not the real world.

There is a part of the Grove where the serious money hunkers down behind high walls and electronic surveillance systems, where sprinklers turn themselves on and rainbirds come to life spraying arcs of diamonds that could be real on lawns that might just as well be made of shredded dollar bills. Ron has found himself a playmate, a woman almost young enough to be his own daughter who is in fact the daughter of the man who thought up the idea of dipping the ends of bobby pins in plastic. Some invention! But it generated several millions of dollars and has made Babs one of the more fortunate young women of the republic. Or one of the more fortunate snow bunnies. She is forever flying off to Vail or Chamonix, or whatever the latest fashionable town in the Andes is, to repeat that feeling of exhilaration she gets from the rapid descent of a dazzling mountainside. Ron, as he was not shy about explaining, was only a casual pickup in one of the local bars, but he was a convenient fellow to have around, someone she could trust while she was away on these frequent jaunts, a cheap caretaker and a fellow whose company and attentions she could enjoy if she was in the mood, or decline if she wasn't.

Very modern, very up front.

I ask him about Amanda. He lays out the complicated pattern

for me as if it were some elaborate problem in geometry, interesting primarily because of its difficulty. I ask him if he thought Amanda had taken Fallyck at all seriously.

"Well, she was his employee. He was her boss. That's serious."

"Did she ever think about marrying him?"

"I don't know. She might have. She might have thought of that. But Fallyck's wife wouldn't let him go. Amanda would never have been interested in him if it hadn't been for the trouble we'd been having with the kids. And the trouble she'd been having with her brother up in that terrible state hospital. And with me, too, I guess."

We are out on the patio next to Babs's pool. The pool filter is making those rude, almost bodily noises that children make with straws when they get down to the bottom of the glass.

I ask him what he will do now. He can't very well bring Cheryl here to help him caretake the estate while Babs is traveling or making herself as scarce as it is possible for someone of her size to do while he performs his other duties when Babs is in residence. Or Greg, if Greg ever gets furloughed from the substance abuse treatment center where he is trying yet again to get straight.

"I don't know," he says. "I keep thinking about it. What I may have to do is go home again. Back there. I never thought I would. But you never know. It was always possible—before, when Amanda was alive. And now that she's dead, now that it doesn't make any sense at all, I may have to do just that."

The telephone rings a couple of times. Babs's machine answers.

"You want a beer?" Ronny offers. "There's all kinds of imported beer. Canadian, German, Australian, Mexican . . ."

"No, no, thanks."

"It's still hard to believe," he says.

"I'm sure," I tell him.

So, go figure it. She may have begun the affair to try to balance her husband's infidelities, so that she could forgive him if the occasion ever arose. So that, if he ever felt like coming back, she could, without feeling utterly defeated and humiliated, allow him to do that. Or maybe it was to defy her mother's ghost. Or because she was horny. Or to escape, so that she wouldn't feel so terrible about her brother and his bleak future. Or perhaps it was for her complexion, no more or less serious than the way she worked out at the health club a couple of times a week.

Or, as Malebranche would iterate, it could have been for no reason at all. It was her destiny, as she somehow perceived, which explains the odd passivity with which she lived her life. There was almost a fatalism, a sense that it wasn't worth fighting about and that she just didn't care.

It might simply have seemed to her to be less trouble to give in and get laid every once in a while than to keep saying no in the face of Fallyck's dopey insistence.

2

FROM the first premise—that I should try to elicit the mute testimony of these relics—it follows logically enough that I should persist in my intrusions. There is no way to argue that those things she left in her own home fall legitimately within my purview while others that happen to have been strewn elsewhere—with Mr. Fallyck, for instance—don't.

All Fallyck can do is yell at me in perfectly justifiable outrage. Lansberg can quietly fire me. Or, still worse, he can assign me to stories even more distressing than this one. He can try to force me to quit and, just for the pure sport of it, see whether he can drive me crazy enough to sacrifice my unemployment benefits.

I have my own mute objects to contemplate, cans of soup in the cupboard, baggies of food in the refrigerator and in the freezer, tubes of shaving cream and toothpaste and rolls of toilet paper in the bathroom. I have clothing that is being held for ransom at the cleaner's. All those things call out in their need and require not only my money but my attention. My allegiance. Which I begrudge. How long has it been since I've vacuumed? Or even picked up? There is a tendency of stuff to return to a wild state, and, more or less consciously, I have been allowing that to happen. I cannot be too much troubled

Lives of the Saints

then about Amanda Hapgood's poor leavings. Let them fend for themselves.

For Fallyck I don't have much concern either. He deserves whatever he gets. He was a married man and if he wanted to play around a little, that's okay by me. But there are risks to that game, no matter how cautiously one tries to play it. Dumb things happen. A guy is driving along in perfect innocence— except that he isn't innocent at all and neither is the woman with him, or the couple of hours they've just spent in the beachfront condo of some friend who is up in Vermont for a week of skiing—and whammo! A brass band is suddenly blaring away while balloons float dreamily up into the sky, and newspaper photographers are snapping pictures and television crews are pointing their camera lenses at him to catch his appalled expression as the beaming politician presents the poor fucker with a certificate for a dinner for two at some fancy restaurant because he is the ten millionth person to drive across this particular causeway.

His wife sues him for all he's got. His mother's angina gets worse and she goes into the hospital. His two daughters don't speak to him for the next four years.

How can one respond except with laughter?

The philanderer thinks it was just a piece of rotten luck, and in a way that's what it was—except that it was his rotten luck from the moment he was born. It was all there, waiting for him all these years, as surely as the color of his eyes and the texture of his hair had been waiting, curled up in the double helixes of his DNA—his whole future, like a cobra coiled to strike.

As Amanda Hapgood was waiting for me. And Clarence Fallyck, too, for that matter. Clarence Barton Fallyck. He likes to be called "C.B."

It is a matter of some delicacy, I tell him on the telephone. He was Amanda Hapgood's employer and friend? I tell him that I too am a friend of Amanda's—as indeed I sometimes persuade myself I have become, or might have become had she not died.

Friendships are possible after death, aren't they?

Isn't that the whole idea of sainthood?

Surely, it is the main idea. Where people go wrong, I think, is in their attribution of special power to the deceased. It is we, the living, who have the power of recollection or imagination. We have the power to keep them alive with us.

Those upon whom we choose to call, to cry out to or just to chat with, they are the saints.

I had expected C.B. to have some raffish charm. At the very least, he ought to have had a pencil mustache, some visible mark of the narcissism that drives many adulterers. What they are looking for is someone to agree with them about how wonderfully attractive and even irresistible they are.

There is no suggestion of that. On the contrary, C.B. is one of those people whose clothing is always at war, the tie twisting about, the shirt struggling for freedom from the belt and trousers, the socks falling down on the job. His hair is thin on top and he combs what he can from the thatch on one side of his head to cross the skull and cover the bare spot, a tactic that never works very well. But his hair has a will of its own and refuses to do his bidding.

My immediate reaction is that I had it wrong. Amanda was at least as much using as used. In the face of her husband's infidelity, she got even by going to bed with the nearest—and the most unprepossessing—man she could find.

Or not even to bed. To desk. They did it in the office after hours. On his desk.

He could hardly believe it. It was a piece of good fortune that had fallen into his lap. Or a piece of lap that turned out to be his good fortune.

She got herself back together and disappeared out into the parking lot, leaving him way behind, sitting in his chair and staring at the Rorschach test they had left on his blotter.

Or maybe she picked him out because she knew him well enough to have gathered that he, too, was being deceived. Or being cheated on. His wife was not even troubling to show him the cruel courtesy of deceit. Amanda may have been moved to some mordant pity by this circumstance. She may, at the very least, have taken it into account.

The Principles of Accounting are sometimes more complicated than one might have supposed.

I think of St. Hubert, one of those silly saints who is all the more engaging for his silliness. A hunter, he was out in the woods one day and he saw a stag with antlers that had grown in such a way as to suggest by a crossing of their points the emblem of Christ. Hubert spared the stag and for this was rewarded with sainthood. He is, reasonably enough, the patron saint of hunters.

The horns of cuckolds are also, at least in theory, capable of some iconographic confusion or semiotic pun.

Amanda showed her love for C. B. Fallyck in as direct a way as Hubert showed his mercy to the stag. It was as if his wife's infidelity had transformed him, arbitrarily enriching him and making him a more humane, more sympathetic person. As if his suffering—and there must have been some kind of suffering—brought him out of himself and ennobled him.

It is not very likely. But then the truth of Hubert's vision was never the point. The stag was just like any other stag, except for the irregularity of its antlers. The miracle was not in the stag but in the eye and perhaps the heart of the hunter.

It was not easy going. I had to scare him into our first meeting, identifying myself as a friend of Amanda's but leaving it open as to whether my intentions toward him were friendly or hostile, comforting or threatening. And then, when we did finally meet, I had to contrive an identity that might encourage his confidence. And confidences.

I became one of Amanda's admirers, a rejected suitor who had in some ridiculous fashion remained faithful, a *cavaliere servente*.

Eventually, we got to that moment for which I had been working all along even without knowing it—when he brought me to his office to show me the desk where she had worked.

And in an inner room, his rather larger desk, where, when they had closed the door, they had sported like naughty children, playing forbidden games that were even more delightful because of the drab earnestness of the setting. On the wall, one of those insurance company calendars showed three months on each large yellow page. The page had not yet been turned from the one she would have seen had she looked up from the desk where she was . . . sitting? Or perhaps lying down with her legs in the air and resting on C.B.'s shoulders?

"You never went anywhere else? Never spent time together, on a business trip perhaps, where you could be in a motel?" I asked.

He had suggested it many times, he told me. And she had held out the hope that one day they might manage a night together. Or even a whole weekend. "It would have been nice," he said, shaking his head sadly.

Her desk had been cleaned out and turned over to a new employee. I asked him what she'd left behind. The usual things—a spare pair of pantyhose, a box of tampons, a box of Kleenex, a bottle of cuticle remover, a bottle of clear nail polish, a bottle of Tylenol, and a plastic bag of green eucalyptus candies. From the bulk food section of the Piggly Wiggly.

Fallyck offered me one, which I accepted, not knowing what else to do. It was an oddly intimate gesture.

We went to a bar across the street from his building. He told me that his wife was not going to divorce him. Is not now and would not then. Oh, no. Nothing so simple and relatively painless as that. She has decided calmly and rationally that the best course for her would be to continue to enjoy whatever benefits there are in the marriage. She likes the way things are, likes the house, her car, her charge accounts, her sense of herself as a woman with a family. She likes keeping the children in an unbroken home. On the other hand, she also likes not being bound to him in anything. She has declared that she will not be questioned about where she might be when she goes out but will go where she pleases, when she chooses, with whomever she likes.

He might as well have been a member of the Japanese surrender party explaining the terms of the instrument he had signed.

"Was it worth it, then?" I asked.

"Amanda? She would have been worth it, yes. If she had been the issue. But she had nothing to do with Caroline's declarations. What she is saying now is what she was saying before—or what she was doing before anyway without talking about it. But I knew."

"Had you ever thought of marrying Amanda?"

He shook his head no.

"Why not?"

"She wouldn't have had me," he said.

True? Not true? Did he really think so? Or had it merely been easier for him to suppose this, so as not to have to make any deeper commitment to her?

I asked him if he knew about Amanda's brother. He didn't.

So she had not confided in him. Or, possibly, she had not told him how desperate she was, how depressed, how much likelier she might have been to accept a proposal from him than he had ever dared imagine. Either selfishly and cautiously or, quite conceivably, from generous impulses. She had been using him and did not want to presume too far or disturb his life any further.

Had she either clung to him tighter or let him go, she might have been worse off. As she might have been more and more uncomfortable about her brother, no matter which way she had decided—taking him in herself or letting him go to the institution. As she might have been more and more miserable with Ron, either letting the marriage drift along or breaking it off once and for all.

It is a terrible thing to think, but it is quite possible that, had she been one of those atoms of uranium, her time to decompose was at hand.

Surely, it is difficult to imagine a happy solution to any of her problems, or even a tolerable extrication.

"When I see one ball strike another," Malebranche says in his *De la recherche de la verité*, "my eyes tell me, or seem to tell me, that the one is truly the cause of the motion it impresses on the other, for the true cause that moves bodies does not appear to my eyes."

Scary, almost. But with his peculiar Cartesian pietism, Malebranche may have shown us the right way to look at certain phenomena. If it were God's will, the second ball might shatter. Or change from red to green. Or turn into a chicken. It is only through God's will that the ball even persists from moment to moment without changing color or turning into something else.

Think of the poor kid who was walking home one evening from a friend's house, hitting fence posts and fire hydrants and telephone poles with his stick as little boys will. And as he struck a telephone pole, the streetlight overhead went out. The whole block was out. The whole town.

He believed he'd caused the great power outage that knocked out everything from Maine to New York City.

In New York, one dithery lady said she thought they were dimming the lights in honor of Dorothy Kilgallen, the newspaperwoman and *What's My Line?* star who had died recently.

Who is to say that these witnesses were any further from the truth than you and I?

Did Caroline Fallyck's peculiar interpretation of feminism have anything to do with C.B.'s behavior? Or Amanda's? Or is it any less extravagant to suggest that Ronny's philanderings on the one side and Caroline's on the other somehow produced Amanda's display of pity or caused her gesture of consolation or whatever that transaction was in Fallyck's office after hours? Or did these three things just happen, each of them a discrete (if not quite discreet) event?

There are, in mathematics, certain problems that are impossible to solve unless you throw out some of the information. You can find an answer only if you ignore some of the data. You have to pretend to be stupider than you are to avoid paralyzing yourself.

In philosophy that can also happen. And in life.

*   *   *

Lansberg is delighted.

This is dreadful news indeed. I had hoped he might be merely satisfied. A grudging acceptance would have been ideal. The piece would have run, more because he needed it to fill up empty space than because he actually liked it. I'd have been paid and allowed to go free. Or my bondage would at least have been different.

But he is tickled pink. He insists that, from my piece, he knows Amanda Hapgood. I don't like quarreling with my editor over philosophical issues, but I tell him he's wrong. I don't know her. How can he know her?

"How can anyone know anyone? Or anything?" he asks. "If we worry about those kinds of questions, we have to shut down the paper. The illusion of knowing—that'll do. The shoes in their holders! That's fine stuff. Do you know that whenever Flaubert wants to make Emma physically present for us, he describes her shoes or her feet?"

I hate it when he demonstrates that he's civilized. A barbarian in his job would be bad enough, but a fellow of some refinement and culture? It's awful. We are here in these chairs at these desks like randomly distributed steel balls in some enormous Pachinko game. I keep telling myself that. It's not his fault. It's not my fault. Fault assumes cause and effect, assumes a rational universe, and, as Joe Orton said, "You can't be a rationalist in an irrational world. It isn't rational."

I return my attention to Lansberg and the here and now. He wants more of these pieces, a whole series—which is difficult not to resent. There were other victims, and there are other objects waiting to be interviewed and exploited. More confidences to be prized out of the hurts these people have suffered.

What I am doing is turning these people, the dead and their survivors too, into objects. That's what our paper does anyway. It is what all papers do.

But I seem to have contrived a way of doing it more blatantly. Which is, in Sidney Lansberg's view, a step forward. What he cannot imagine is that one day his own toys and totems, that little Tiffany clock on his desk, his letter opener with the jade handle, the photograph on the wall behind his desk showing him smiling with the mayor on his right and the governor on his left, may all be called upon to testify against him. Or even on his behalf, his grotesque and violent death having catapulted him into one of the lesser spheres of veneration:

SEA-WORLD SHARKS

DEVOUR EDITOR:

WAS HE PUSHED?

Still, I'm getting a raise—from my chum.

Sidney is the elided form of St. Denis.

Denis was a bishop who went to convert the Gauls and was martyred near Paris. An abbey, built on the spot where he died, was under the protection of the counts of Paris, so that, when they dethroned the sons of Charlemagne and became the kings of France, Denis got lucky and became the patron of the country. The oriflamme, the banner of the convent, became the national battle flag.

Denis is also a form of the older name Dionysus. As in the tyrant of Syracuse.

I wonder whether Sidney Lansberg knows any of this. Or cares.

3

I HAVE spent the morning in the morgue.

No, not that kind of morgue. I was going through old newspaper clippings. But it was every bit as macabre as if I had put in the time in some dank depository with a tile floor and excessive lighting where real corpses were stacked in large drawers. I assume they look that way. They do in movies.

These newspaper morgues are sufficiently disagreeable, dusty and acrid, so that I keep feeling that I am about to sneeze. But it was worth a little discomfort. I turned up some interesting information. For instance, I have established that John Babcock, lethal and crazy though he may have been, hardly qualifies as a major figure in the annals of mass murder. In first place in that sordid sweepstakes, with twenty-one victims at the San Ysidro, California, McDonald's on July 18, 1984, is James Huberty. He is comfortably ahead of Charles Whitman, the bell-tower sniper at the University of Texas at Austin in 1966, who is the silver medalist with fourteen victims, including an infant in the womb of a woman who survived. Whitman wounded thirty-one others. He had also killed his wife and mother the night before, so that one can figure his total at sixteen.

It makes no practical difference (except of course to the actual victims) because Patrick Henry Sherill remains in any event in third place, having killed fourteen post office workers in Edmond, Oklahoma, on August 20, 1986. (He then killed himself with a bullet to the head, but the death of the killer, whether by suicide or at the hands of the police, doesn't really count.)

Then the field gets crowded. On February 19, 1983, two Hong Kong immigrants named Mak and Ng shot thirteen Chinese-Americans to death in a Seattle gambling club. (That's only six-and-a-half deaths apiece, but each of them was found guilty on all thirteen counts of murder.) And the year before, on September 25, 1982, George Banks, a prison guard in Wilkes-Barre, had shot four girlfriends, the five children they had borne him, the mother of one of his girlfriends and one of her children, the second child of another girlfriend, and a man who just happened to be standing on the street—for a total of thirteen. And Howard Unruh, a World War II veteran, went berserk in Camden, New Jersey, and killed thirteen people, no details of which incident were in the morgue clips. There was only a reference in one of the other mass murder stories. Finally, James Ruppert of Hamilton, Ohio, killed his mother, brother, sister-in-law, and eight nieces and two nephews to reach the same unlucky total of thirteen and therefore qualify for that five-way tie.

At a certain point, the real newspapers are indistinguishable from our kind.

John Babcock was a nonentity. Not even by his altogether meaningless killing spree could he avoid the woeful mediocrity that was his nature and destiny all the days of his life.

Taking a leaf from Lansberg's book—or rag—I drove past the house in which Babcock lived to see whether it could tell me anything. It was unimpressive, an ordinary lower-middle-class bungalow in stucco with brown trim and an overhanging flat roof. The lawn was brown and looked to have chinch bugs in it. And there was a dusty clump of Spanish bayonet at the side of the garage.

If the lawn had been anything special, or if it had shown any signs that Babcock had invested time and effort in its upkeep, there might have been some stupid logic to what he'd done. The reports are that some of the youngsters in the neighborhood had been walking on his grass on their way home, cutting across his corner lot to save themselves a few steps. It was impossible for them to have done any damage to the lawn. The only possible injury they could have inflicted was psychic, aggravating the mysterious wounds Babcock's spirit already bore. From inside those walls, then, he watched them, peering out and cursing at their infringement on his property and his space.

He yelled at them. They ignored him. He came out and stood on his doorstep with a shotgun that he fired into the air.

That stopped their trespasses. For a while.

But then, it became fun to torment the loony. To see if he could be lured outside again to shout more curses or fire his gun. There were dares given and taken.

Nobody ever imagined he'd actually kill anyone. It was always conceivable of course that he might hit somebody by accident. But that long-odds possibility only gave their games a little extra thrill.

What he ought to have done was planted more Spanish bayonet. Its spiny leaves can tear a person apart. That would have kept them off his land.

But that would have been too sensible, too rational for him. And it would have taken too long.

What he finally did was to lose patience—not just with the youngsters but with the whole world, with the entire human condition. Had he wanted merely to kill one or two of those annoying boys, he could almost certainly have done so. But that wouldn't have been enough for him. It was too specific, too petty and limited. He wanted to make a more general response, spewing destruction, extending the effects of his rage to include the entire universe. Beyond revenge and mere murder, he aspired to terrorism. It was a political and even theological statement he wanted to make. He wasn't aiming at a handful of kids; he wanted to kill everyone.

And where does one find vast numbers of people? A generation or so ago, one would have gone downtown. But Main Street is an unsuccessful urban renewal project, and there isn't any downtown anymore. There are only malls now.

So he went to the nearest large mall. The one he knew and had shopped at himself.

One can, in this way, offer an almost plausible account, which is, of course, outrageous. What earthly sense is there in this progression? A few schoolchildren cut across the corner of Babcock's nonlawn. Therefore, he gets into his car with a loaded shotgun, drives to the Piggly Wiggly, and kills Amanda Hapgood.

And kills Hafiz Kezemi. Who had come from Teheran because it was dangerous there, to the United States, where it was safer. Twenty-two years old, a civil engineering student, he had hoped to go back to Iran one day when the troubles subsided and help rebuild the country, or so his sister told reporters. He might just as well have remained there, taking crazy risks and working to overthrow the Ayatollah.

And kills Roger Stratton, associate professor of English and author of a book of poems, who had elected early retirement from his teaching job and had taught his last class the day before Babcock blew him away. He was going to live modestly on his pension and spend his time writing more poems and putting together another book.

And kills Laura Bowers, 49, divorced, mother of two, co-owner with her sister, Felicity, of the Happy Times Travel Agency.

And kills Ambrosio Márquez Martínez, formerly of Managua, Nicaragua, and described in most of the reports as either a "businessman" or an "importer" although it is unspecified what business he was in or what he might have been importing. In such cases, readers are invited to speculate as to whether he might have been more involved with weaponry or illicit pharmacology. Guns or drugs, take your pick. Or both, as likely as not.

And kills Edward Springer, three years old.

It defies reason. It turns reasoning itself into a joke.

Nicolas Malebranche understood this and proclaimed it three hundred years ago, demonstrating a skepticism so rigorous as to be indistinguishable from faith.

Put it another way. In hospitals, there are some patients who try to take charge of their treatments, who attempt to collaborate with their doctors and nurses, wanting to know what is going on and what is likely to happen next, hoping that their intellectual participation may in some way improve their chances for recovery. Other patients lie back and accept what is happening or simply switching off, putting their trust in God and His deputies. Psychologists have studied these two contrasting styles to see whether they have any effect on the outcomes for the different groups of patients.

There is only a slight but still statistically significant difference—and that second group, those who switch their minds off and try to float along, accepting their destinies with serenity, do a little better than the ones in the first group, who try to maintain control. These people in the second group, whether they know it or not, are Malebranchians.

These kinds of speculations have no place in a paper like ours. It can be plausibly maintained, however, that the whole tendency of our paper and of others like it, with their crazy headlines and absurdist stories, is the defiance of reason.

Our readers are excited by such headlines as these:

BOY, ELEVEN, MAKES FIVE BABYSITTERS PREGNANT

or

MOM DELIVERS FOUR-POUND PEARL

or, one of my favorites,

DID LIBERACE'S DOGS HAVE AIDS?

What do these stories mean—if anything? They must mean something! It can't be that huge numbers of people in this age of polyurethane are devotees of surrealism or Dadaism, or whatever the right label is for the passion to make the grotesque chic. Is it not rather the case that these ridiculous stories are demonstrations, every one of them, that all things are possible? And are they not also suggestions that it is therefore pointless to try to fathom the mind of God?

It is an intellectual nihilism, one of the odd consequences of which is that the stupidest person you know is suddenly promoted to be the equal of the smartest. There is, at the checkout lines of every supermarket in America, an assertion of a new kind of democracy, the democracy of intellect, for if nothing makes sense, then the thoughtful person's ability to make some sense of some things is only a useless and irrelevant game. Or, worse, a fatal delusion.

What good is intelligence in the face of such declarations as

HIPPO EATS CIRCUS DWARF

where there is no possible reply except "Wow!"?

What bothers me about Lansberg is his good qualities.

In an enterprise like ours, sleaziness and vulgarity are predictable enough. Indeed, they are essential, a part of everyone's professional equipment. And it would be reasonable to expect the editor to have the surest instincts for whatever is sensational and outrageous. He represents the readers, after all, and it is his job to be as stupid and flighty as they are, to know their limits of attention and comprehension, and never to allow any of us to approach too close to those very restrictive boundaries.

It is a dismal kind of job he has, and I shouldn't object to it—or to him—so strenuously if he did it naturally, if his performance in it were an authentic expression of his mind and spirit. But it isn't. He is much smarter, much better, than what we are doing. He knows music and art and dance and theater. He is well read—probably better read than I am.

What this means is that Lansberg is the model for our disgrace. We can see in him an exaggeration of our own catastrophes. Do we betray our best selves? Of course we do, but never so aggressively as he. Are we traitors to our intellects and violators of our own standards of taste? Surely, but not with the ruthlessness he displays. He is his own Visigoth, pitching his rude camp in the ruins of what was once an impressive forum of civilization. And we are, every one of us, his followers. His horde.

What sometimes consoles me is the possibility that we may make him as uneasy as he makes us. It is reasonable to suppose that there must have been stages in his progression—or retrogression—to the intellectual squalor that is a prerequisite even for any serious candidacy for his job. And it would be a persuasive guess that at any point on this continuum, all other points must be threatening to one's psychic poise. Each of us must maintain that his is the correct or at least the most tolerable accommodation to the insane demands of the publisher, and it follows that all other accommodations are not only incorrect but intolerable—that anyone who is more fastidious than I am is too prissy, contemptible in his innocence, a mere child. On the other hand, anyone who is less fastidious is corrupt and depraved.

It is rather like the comparisons one makes of degrees of sexual sophistication in which either more or less than one's own is bad.

In those terms, Lansberg is a quadrisexual, which is a person willing to do anything with anyone for a quarter.

There is also a public, an audience, out there whom it is frightening to imagine. I have sometimes actually glimpsed them in the checkout lines that are their natural habitat. But it is perilous to extrapolate from such brief encounters.

Biologists in China, tracking the spoor of giant pandas, figured out how much bamboo they had to be eating and at what rate in order to sustain themselves. To do this, they had to calculate the ratio of excretion, which they knew, to ingestion, which they were assuming. They extrapolated it and published their findings, very proud of themselves for having learned the secrets of an odd and almost extinct species. But one of the reviewers correlated their figures with those of some other studies and suggested that there were inconsistencies. It was extremely unlikely that pandas eat twenty-six hours a day and defecate rather more than they eat.

Our readers quite likely do both.

You see how far I have already followed Lansberg's pioneering path.

I refuse, at any rate, to generalize from the few gum-chewing behemoths in pastel polyester I have occasionally seen purchasing our paper.

I prefer the better class of reader, who scans it quickly, surreptitiously, and ashamedly, while waiting in line. These readers almost always replace the paper neatly in its rack and then set about transferring canned goods from their carts to the checker's conveyor belt.

The only real reader is perhaps our publisher himself, Alexander B. Cosgrove III, proprietor of ABC Publications. A man I have never glimpsed at all.

There is an office with his name on the door, but I've never actually caught anyone going in or coming out. It is, in that regard, like a Christian Science Reading Room.

He may be a figment. And the readers may be figments of his.

A vertiginous possibility that Malebranche would have understood at once.

Lansberg's rationale for his peculiar career is quite generous and noble, at least at first blush. The idea is that he is sacrificing himself in order to support Pearl, his wife, who is an artist. He believes in her talent. She needs a studio, household help, clothing, the freedom to entertain and move about comfortably and on terms of equality in the world of wealth and privilege where her audience and her customers are to be found.

At first blush, noble. But nothing Lansberg does is straightforward. He did not believe in his own talents as a writer and a journalist, but was that modesty and humility or merely cowardice? And was his decision to take more lucrative and more contemptible work an accurate and natural expression of his character and intellect that he only blames on his wife so as to avoid taking responsibility, himself, for what he has done? And does this not put her under an enormous obligation to redeem him, no matter what he does, no matter how shabbily he behaves, even though she may never have asked him to do it?

You see this in colleges and universities all the time. Failed scholars become deans, have their salaries increased, move to larger and more elaborately finished offices, and expect their former colleagues to be grateful for the sacrifices they have made of their negligible talents for the general good of the university.

Then they devote themselves to pursuit of that general good, which means that they figure out ways of hiring more part-time instructors who don't get health insurance or pension benefits and can be underpaid so that various department budgets can be cut.

And those part-time instructors are replaced every now and then in order to keep them from worming their way into the various departments whose chairmen and chairwomen weaken or show some human decency or even mere pity. . . .

Or from organizing.

Those are not the reasons I work for Lansberg, though. There are no reasons. It was my destiny not to stay on in teaching. It was my destiny to come here, to be one of Lansberg's victims. The only reasons are in the mind of God, says Malebranche, and the mind of God is unknowable.

We are free, nonetheless, to speculate. To suppose, *par exemple*, that the universe is an elaborate machine for the exchange of torments and that each of us represents someone else's agony. Suppose, further, that each of us is burdened by his own talent and that the discomfort each feels is exquisitely calibrated to the level of the talent he has betrayed.

Sidney Lansberg tortures Pearl, who tortures him.

And in the same way, Lansberg tortures us, his employees, while we torment him with our innocence.

What is appealing about such a construction is its mathematical tendency. Ratio and proportion mean order and reason. And in our terror of the darkness, we run toward the light, even as moths to the candle flame.

Malebranche adored mathematics, saw in it a security and comfort, an order, he could associate only with the mind of God. He lay on his bed on St. Honoré's Rue and considered the infinity of God. And then, quite reasonably, he considered the idea of infinity. Or ideas of infinity.

How a series of numbers can extend indefinitely. Infinite extrapolability.

Or how, between any two whole numbers, one can divide endlessly, in infinite intrapolability.

$$\infty$$

Those of us who are less clever just count things. Sheep, for instance.

All we like sheep.

All, *oui*, like sheep.

We're all like sheep. Bah!

I have asked to be excused from this assignment.

Lansberg knows perfectly well why I am the least likely candidate among his desperate dependents to be sent out on this ghoulish duty. But he insists. He may have wanted only the satisfaction of hearing me say it aloud, as I refused to do.

It is also possible that he views what I take to be a disqualification as my best credential. It gives me an insight that no one else on the staff could bring to the subject.

What is most unfair is that he is correct.

Correct, but not right.

My private life is my own. Or it ought to be. But that is exactly what he's hiring, he tells me. Not just my eyes and my fingers but my brain and my heart.

He talks about hearts a lot. The new cardiac journalism. Our readers, every last one of them, have hearts. And while minds may be unequal, hearts are all the same. The Jacobinism of the emotions.

It's just not true. As Descartes and Malebranche both struggled to demonstrate, there is a connection between body and spirit, and between minds and hearts too, so that the refinement of the one conditions the responses of the other.

Those who have witnessed terrible things are changed forever. According to one theory, their brain chemistry is actually altered.

One concentration camp survivor said: "If you could lick my heart, you would be poisoned."

My claim is smaller than his. But I knew what he was talking about. I have known ever since my wife and daughter were killed.

In a car crash. Their lives were just erased, as if they had been pictures on a Magic Slate. And mine was transformed. Deformed.

It was raining. The other driver was drunk.

But those are not reasons. There are no reasons.

As Father Malebranche says.

4

FOR a long time, I thought of it as something that son of a bitch had done. He did this. Of course he did it. Nobody had forced him to get drunk and then drive. He thought it was fun, a sporty thing to do. He had done it before, too, putting people's lives at risk. Not just his own entirely worthless existence, but other people's.

I wanted to find him and kill him. I still do, I suppose. But I know I'm not likely to do that. It would not do Pam or Leah any good. And I'd be at considerable risk. I'd be the first guy the police would look for.

And it's tough to hire a killer, or it is if you aren't tough enough to do the job yourself. You have to work it so that the guy you hire is afraid of you and therefore unlikely to take your money and then walk away. After all, you can't sue him. Only if you're the kind of guy who might very well kill him can you deal with any confidence.

But in that case, you didn't need him in the first place, did you?

I used to think about these kinds of things a lot. I don't worry about them so much anymore.

I don't worry much about that son of a bitch, either. I think of him as a bug, a microscopic organism that floats around, doing its damage at random.

This is a Malebranchian view, a friend of mine told me. Which is when I started reading Malebranche, the guide for our times. More than Maimonides, Malebranche is a guide for the perplexed.

There are no reasons for anything.

If Pam and Leah hadn't been killed on the highway, they might have made it safely to their destination, which could perfectly well have been a shopping mall.

Where some other son of a bitch could have shot them dead.

Or, to put it more precisely, where they could have met their fates in another manner. The killer, in any case, is of little importance. It is only sensational papers like ours that pretend to find reasons in the childhoods of these creeps.

Ours and the *New York Times* and the *Washington Post* and the *Chicago Tribune*, and the *Los Angeles Times*, and whatever else you happen to read.

Malebranche raises his eyes to a farther horizon. Or closes them and soars higher still, considering an infinity of destinies. In so doing, he restores to primacy the sufferings of each victim. He makes them martyrs, witnesses to the awful majesty of God.

I don't know that I believe as serenely as Malebranche. But I think I understand his curious leap from the soothing intricacies of mathematics to the lucidity and perfection of a divinity. Or, looking at the question from another angle, it is possible that what he means by "God" is nothing more than an insistence that life is serious, that existence is significant, that the choices aren't between God and no God, but between meaning and meaninglessness.

It is also true that, at times of great stress, mathematics is a way of keeping a grip on one's sanity.

Going to sleep is difficult. Waking up is also difficult. I have nightmares that I cannot remember and wake up in the morning feeling as though I have been pummeled. My body aches and my spirit's wounds are also renewed, as tender as when they were first inflicted. I bear bruises upon bruises.

It takes me most of the morning to climb out of the deep

hole in which I find myself in that unwelcome first light of dawn.

I go to work, partly for the money, of course, but also to hide. To stay home would be torture. I have to go out, go somewhere and do something.

And there is also a curiosity I have. Lansberg may be disastrous, and ABC may be a cruel and stupid joke, but the people I go to talk to are real, crazy often, but real. I have the hope that they may be able to instruct me. They may at least be able to point me toward the answers I need to the stupid questions disaster always brings:

How can I bear this? And why should I?

Is it only supersitition and fear that keep people from killing themselves?

Is there a God? Is there any purpose to life? Or sense?

Malebranche supposed that there was a tendency toward "the undetermined and general good" that God had somehow built into the will of mankind. He believed in the inevitability of progress toward *le bien en général,* which was not an altogether bizarre idea in the Renaissance. From the point of view of our century, it seems more innocent than stupid, but there was no need for him to have waited this long. Within a hundred years of his death, the Terror had come with its mob, its tumbrels carrying thousands to the guillotine, and with all those busy vandals defacing the carvings of churches all over France. I cannot take this idea seriously. I am not even convinced that Malebranche would try to maintain it today.

Meanwhile, the poor souls I talk to are looking for answers, scanning the skies for UFOs, hoping that little green men will step out of their strange craft and amaze us all with the solutions to those perplexities. Or that the evidence of a two-headed turtle, a three-legged duck, and other such anomalies are miracles that show us the workings of the hand of God still evident at least at moments, still able to work the controls.

It is so desperate as to be deserving of respect. Such distortions of reason are like the twisted metal in those pictures of buildings that have collapsed in tornadoes or been knocked down by earthquakes. One gets some sense of the force to which those structures were subjected.

And their television stars? Their vulgar fascination with the love lives and diets and illnesses of actors and actresses and game-show hosts?

Even for those, I can persuade myself into a degree of indulgence. These show-biz figures are our latter-day saints, paracletes and exemplars to whom the rest of us look for instruction in those same difficult subjects. Is there a God? Is there any purpose to life or any sense? Is there a pattern to good fortune, or a penalty that the beneficiary must always pay in one way or another? In the Renaissance, it was assumed that cardinals were damned, all of them. Parish priests might be saintly, but bishops were in jeopardy and cardinals, gorging and swilling and fornicating in their sumptuous palaces, were all presumptively going to hell.

Not good news for Christie Brinkley and Vanna White.

Our readers may not look like much. And the subjects of our reports may often seem gullible or even crazed. But their experience has a primitive authenticity. The delusions we report are, in one way or another, real.

What I especially like about Malebranche is the odd way in which he combines skepticism and faith, denying on the one hand any possibility of cause and effect and yet with a catch— that spectacular shoestring catch—"save in the mind of God."

The deaths of children are the hardest to bear. The slaughter of the innocents. The massacre of the thousand virgins.

It happens in nature all the time, with millions of tiny fish being spawned for each one that reaches maturity. But in human terms, it seems hard to be deprived of the richness of life's experience, the satisfactions and delights of earthly bliss.

What earthly bliss? Am I happy? Do I know anyone who calls himself happy?

I will go talk to the parents of the little boy later. Last.

If then.

I will look at the room they will not yet have had the heart to touch, the room they will have kept as a shrine. And my eyes will fill with tears in the blur of which I will see not his room but Pam's. And Pam's toys. And Pam's little dresses still on their hangers in the closet.

What difference is there between the deplorable relics in their grotesque containers in the crypts of those churches in France and Italy where I used to go with such disdain and these? What is the difference between those holy places and our own? An innocent is martyred. The place doesn't merely persist, unchanged. It may look the same—that corner past which I never drive looks just as it did a year ago, with a dry cleaner and a tropical fish store and, across the street, a low red-brick professional building three dentists own, renting out the second floor to an insurance brokerage. It is perfectly ordinary, but not ordinary at all.

For me, to go to that corner is like visiting the Coliseum. Or Dachau.

In certain countries in Europe, wherever there has been a fatal automobile accident, they put up little shrines by the side of the road. A cross maybe, with a pot of flowers someone freshens every now and then.

Or, more precisely, they are markers, showing that the places have become shrines.

To the ends of lives. To sacrifices to the gods of mobility. Or of bad weather. Or of drunkenness.

If that is primitive supersision, we are becoming more and more superstitious every day as we sit in front of the television screens and watch the late news with the minicam shots of the burned house in which a mother and four children died. Or the shots of the twisted metal of the shells that remain of the seven cars that the jackknifed trailer rig destroyed on the interstate. Or the shattered plate-glass window of the drugstore into which the runaway concrete truck plowed when its brakes failed, killing three and injuring two more.

Every night. Every damned night. I used to look at these things as if they were irrelevant to me, as if they could only have taken place on the dark side of the moon. Or in Peru. But these are real people. And the landmarks behind those disaster sites are the familiar ones we see every day.

What are they telling us? What are we supposed to be learning from these endlessly repeated lessons? What kinds of places to avoid? Where disasters like to strike? Are there signs and portents I have somehow missed?

Are there reasons?

Only in the mind of God.

The professor is the one Lansberg will like the least. If I'm lucky, Lansberg will so hate the professor that he'll kill the piece and end the series. I can go back to my regular beat and report more sightings of glowing objects in the summer skies, or houses haunted as the films of last season still flicker in the imaginations of their audiences.

Supernature, friend to the subnormal.

But this professor is going to unsay all of Lansberg's credos and undo all the damage our paper tries to do. Lansberg will suspect that I've made the man up, just to give him a hard time. And to some extent, as far as I can manage it, that may be the truth.

Professors don't appear much in our pages. There was a crazy math teacher who thought he had figured out a system for beating the roulette table in Reno and gambled away his school's sports budget for the year. But that's quite different.

To write about a professor without belittling him, without trying to make him look like a pompous ass or a jerk . . .

Unheard of!

And a nice angle to it, too. A real tearjerker! Poor son of a bitch works away for all those years looking forward to his retirement, and then, just as he's about to cash in his chips and sit down to write his poems, along comes Babcock and blam, blam, blam . . .

In the parking lot of the Piggly Wiggly.

Vague academic puffball that he was, he may not even have noticed the noises. Or if he did, he may have supposed that they were the sounds of an engine backfiring.

A lot of people thought that. Until they saw the first fallen bodies. And Professor Roger Stratton's was one of the first of those bodies.

Which was, to a degree, fortunate. He probably never knew what hit him. And therefore he may never have experienced the terror most of the survivors talk about and some of the later victims must have felt.

That assumes, as many people do, that it isn't death we ought to fear but dying.

The reports—unreliable except that they sell papers—are of a glowing light, sometimes golden, sometimes rosy, and a feeling of amazing peacefulness.

MAN DIES, REVIVES, 16 TIMES

As if your ordinary bozo who has croaked, seen Heaven, and returned only once or twice weren't enough. He's just a casual visitor. But after sixteen times, this fellow must have been an old-timer, maybe even a member of Welcome Wagon, greeting the newly dead and showing them around.

On the other hand, in the following issue, we had the other kind of piece:

WOMAN CELEBRATES 133RD BIRTHDAY

which suggests a certain lack of confidence in our frequent flyer's reassurances. Maybe she was just too stupid to die and couldn't get the hang of it. She didn't look like much. We ran a picture that showed a wrinkled, apelike creature who looked grumpy.

But Lansberg is quite right. The great issues don't need to be vulgarized. They are vulgar, for they are exactly those things that everybody worries about.

But uselessly. It is like watching a chicken trying to solve an intellectual puzzle. The fence is too high. There is a box next to the fence. The chicken could jump up to the box and from there jump over the fence, but the farmer needn't worry. No chicken is likely to figure out how to go from ground to box to fence top. Not even if he has a flock of thousands upon thousands of chickens.

And each chicken might be correct in thinking—assuming it could think at all—that reasons are not its business. Reasons are only in the mind of the farmer.

Who is, himself, not so very bright a cluck.

That, of course, is the tack I shall have to take with the Stratton piece. The suggestion will be that even a man like that, a writer and a college professor, is no better equipped to deal with the uncertainties of life and death than the least of our readers. The huge questions that stare us all in the face outfaced him too.

For all his learning, what did he know?

I am dismayed to have thought of this. And I am all but sickened by my certainty that Lansberg will be delighted with this way of avoiding any snobbishness that might be implicit in our decision to write about an "intellectual."

Not that there is anything so intellectual about getting shot to death in a parking mall, but we must watch ourselves. Our audience is dumb but they're mean. And they don't like any uncomfortable and impolite allusions to their limitations.

Which they know, well enough.

I am only lately beginning to learn about my own.

5

WHEN counting sheep does no good, there is always the car—
the new car the insurance company provided. It is the kind of
car I'd never have trusted Leah and Pam in. They were driving
a safe car. I cruise around late at night in a convertible that is
obviously dangerous. Flip over in one of these and your head
cracks like an eggshell.

Safe cars ought to be safe, right? That's why we buy them.
And use seat belts. All the sensible precautions! But those only
work in that imaginary world in which cause and effect are
operating. In the real world, things just happen. And then other
things happen.

Charlie Chaplin is walking along and a truck with one of
those oversized loads comes by, and as it turns the corner the
red warning flag falls off the logs that are sticking out in back.
Chaplin, a decent fellow, picks up the flag and starts after the
truck. And a Communist demonstration comes parading behind him from the cross street.

He gets arrested as a red. I think it's in *Modern Times*.

The implications are not un-Malebranchian, I think.

Late at night, with the tape deck going, Mozart usually, I go
tearing along the expressways with the top down, feeling the
rivers of chilled air from the air-conditioning ducts sluicing
into the ocean of warmer muggier air like fresh water pouring

into salt. The music plays and the stars overhead twinkle indifferently. And I have a sense of interplanetary travel as my speck of light and noise wanders randomly through the empty spaces that intimidated Pascal.

Another Frenchman drunk on infinity. They seem to have a weakness for it.

These late-night jaunts don't actually make me feel better. More accurately, they make me feel a little less bad. It is possible in the expanses of space and at high speeds and with the intricacies of Mozart's cadenzas in the later piano concertos to feel numbed if not actually overwhelmed. And without a hangover the next morning!

Not that hangovers are so terrible. They can, with the stupid immediacy of the physical, take one's mind off larger troubles.

Stratton's widow is named Stephanie. For the proto-martyr. Stoned to death, I believe.

Of course, there are seven other saints bearing that name, among them a king of Hungary. And one of the sons of Thucydides was named Stephanos. But the likelihood is that the connection is with the obvious Stephen, who has not only his own day, on which good King Wenceslaus looked out, but also the third of August, which celebrates "the invention of St. Stephen's relics." A Jewish doctor appeared in a dream to a priest of Caphargamala in 415 and showed him where the bones were. The reality of the discovery was confirmed by the miraculous recovery of sixty-three persons who had been suffering from an assortment of ailments and by the coming of rain to end a severe drought.

I doubt that Stephanie Stratton will be much interested in any of this, even if she was married to a professor. But I find it comfortably distracting.

What I have ignored up until now is the question of free will. If each of us has his destiny and everything is foreordained, what is the point of our striving to be good?

None, perhaps. Or one could go further and maintain that it isn't even a very interesting question. Those of us who are good, whose destiny it is to be good, will exert themselves, thinking of other people and criticizing their own actions, as if it were their free choice to be doing these things. And the others will do what they do without thinking about it, which is more or less what one might have expected.

What brings the subject to mind is my resolution not to trade tragedies with Stephanie Stratton. It is tempting to think of doing so. Here is a person who has suffered a sudden and brutal loss, as I have. And it is pleasant to suppose that we might be able at least to exchange information about how to get through the days and nights. Or, uselessly but humanely, just exchange sympathy, the shared understanding of the magnitude of the random undoing of a life.

With Amanda's people, her wounded children, her crazy ex-husband, or her hangdog lover, I felt no connection. But with Stephanie Stratton, I could well find myself talking to a plausible human being. And in that case, I might find myself in an interesting ethical dilemma. If I keep my own life to myself and carry on like a disinterested reporter, I shall be treating her with less than total honesty, getting her story from her for my own purposes and offering her nothing in return. If, on the other hand, I am forthcoming, exchanging grief for grief, then I shall be trading on Pam's and Leah's deaths, using them . . .

And not even for my own purposes, which would be sufficiently unattractive, but for Lansberg's! Which is an intolerable idea.

It is an ethical problem I can wrestle with if I want to. But what's the point? I know that whatever I do will be a decision arising from my mood of the moment, from my sense of what's comfortable, from cues I get from her.

In other words, it is out of my hands. But neither is it up to her. She can have no idea what I'm thinking about.

The mind of God, then?

Of course that's absurd, but what isn't?

Oddly enough, she lives only a couple of moments' drive from an exit I pass several times during the week in my nocturnal wanderings. So do several hundred thousand other people, I suppose. Still, we respond to these coincidences, try to read some of them as omens and auguries. I had driven up this same expressway only a few hours before, and the repetition of the trip seemed peculiar, the light different, the landscape brighter and less real. The semitropical sunshine gives a peculiar look to cars and buildings here, makes everything shimmer. Or look as though it has been painted in acrylic by a maniacal giant on some tricky backdrop. A malevolent giant, as a matter of fact, because the result of such painstaking attention to sordid details goes beyond social realism to satire. There is, for instance, a cemetery one passes with its decorative pond scooped out of the clay and stocked with a couple of pairs of ducks. It looks almost real at night. In the daytime, though, it looks like what it is—an artifactual thing. And despite myself, I generally count the ducks, for there are stray dogs that live in the cemetery and prey upon the hapless fowl, so that they have to keep restocking the pond.

But the same exit as the one I generally use to turn around and head home? It resonates. And Stephanie Stratton is more challenging than I expected.

I keep thinking of the paper and of Lansberg and of ABC III as my destiny, my appropriate torture. What I often forget is that other people don't seem to feel that need of punishment. Simply and rightly, they despise our kind of sensationalism.

I show her my ID. She looks at it, looks at me, and barks out a single slice of a laugh. "You've got to be kidding!"

"I'm afraid not."

"It's the last thing in the world I need, to talk to a vulture like you."

"I understand. I quite agree," I said. "I won't require a word."

"Then what do you want?" she asks, her head cocked in a warning that I am unlikely to get whatever it is.

"Just to look at your late husband's room. The desk where he worked. To see if the objects he left behind tell me anything. It's a piece on relics, actually."

"Relics? Like saints have? Are you crazy?" she asks. She is a pretty woman, a little past it, her face tanned and outdoorsy from the golf course or the tennis courts. A trim figure, which

47

she doesn't mind showing off. But what is most attractive is her expression of amused incredulity. She looks like a young girl reacting to an off-color story that is funnier than she's comfortable admitting.

I think of pointing out to her that her name is not unconnected with saints and relics. "I don't know," I say, in answer to her question. "I stopped trying to figure that one out a long time ago."

She stands there in the doorway, not inviting me in but not dismissing me. I stand there watching the fluctuations of her mental teeter-totter.

And my own.

It is not much, but it is as far as I have come since the accident.

Consciously or not, she may have intuited my surprise at my awareness of her. She may even have responded to it. Just as certain parts of the body keep on growing after death, the hair and the fingernails in particular working busily away, so there may be parts of one's emotional equipment that continue to function in some low-level way, on the off-chance that life may go on.

For whatever reason, or for no reason at all, she invites me inside, letting me know, however, that it is only grudgingly: "What the hell, come on in then."

"Thank you," I say, balefully, for it is not my victory but Lansberg's. (On the other hand, it would have been my defeat if she had sent me away.)

A comfortable house with lots of books, which is what I look for first. What I am doing is what we all do, reading bookcases and medicine chests in the houses of our acquaintances. As I explain to her, when she asks me to tell her again what nonsense I have come to bother her with.

She listens, not too patiently, and after a while cuts me off. "Why? What earthly reason would I have for putting up with such a thing?"

"None, really," I acknowledge. "Except perhaps to share your feelings. Other people are hurting. They want to know how to bear their lives. They're not very bright, maybe, but they are our readers, and their questions may be legitimate. Maybe more pressing than you and I might suppose, because their resources are so much more meager."

"A nice enough speech," she says. "Do you believe it?"

"I don't know. It's what I tell myself."

"You make it tough for me to kick you the hell out, which is what I obviously ought to do. Isn't it?"

"That's up to you, of course. You'd be within your rights."

"Which you can admit because you guess that I'm not going to do that."

"That's what I'm hoping," I tell her.

"You're a terrible bastard, you know that? Coming around like this—like a goddamn crow for the easy pickings you can get from corpses!"

"Crows have to live. They serve a function in nature."

"Listen," she says. "He was fifty-six years old. For maybe the last ten years he had been looking forward to early retirement so he could get away from teaching composition classes and get back to his real work. You think I need smart remarks about crows?"

"I'm sorry," I say.

"It's not your fault. You didn't kill him. You want some coffee?"

"If it's not too much trouble."

"If it was too much trouble, I wouldn't have offered. I've got one of those Thermos things, so it stays hot. I got it so he could have coffee when he was home writing, and not have to heat it up each time . . ." She stops, fights against breaking down, wins, and then gets up to fetch the coffee.

I am sorely tempted to tell her how much we have in common. She is numb. I am numb. We could at least acknowledge one another's pain. How can I not tell her? But I remember my resolution not to play on Leah's and Pam's deaths for Lansberg's frivolous purposes.

Not that it matters. I can hardly be doing any further damage to my wife and daughter. They are beyond hurt, which is a fairly stupid thing to say about the dead but not totally devoid of meaning. Think of those poor crazed bastards who blow their

wives and children away and then either call the police or try
to shoot themselves but miss, some subversive neurons having
somehow interfered so that the cells in the hair folicles and at
the base of the fingernails can keep on flourishing and dividing
a little longer. And what those who can still talk invariably
explain to the bewildered sergeant is some version or other
about wanting to protect the ones they've killed.

To put them beyond harm.

I look up. She is looking at me.

"Well, I'll give you credit," she says. "You look about as
miserable as you ought to feel, considering what you've come
for."

"I'll take that as a compliment."

She has misunderstood my gloomy look. She has attributed
it to my presence here, to my intrusion on her grief. So that
now, whether I tell her about Pam and Leah or not, I am ben-
efiting from their deaths, or Lansberg is. I can clear up her
misapprehension or let it stand, and either way ABC III stands
to gain.

On the other hand, when she comes back from the kitchen
with the two mugs of coffee, she lets me in on her motives,
which are, as I'd suspected, complicated.

"It's not such a terrible thing to do," she says. "I don't think
he'd have minded. I try to imagine what he'd have thought,
and it's very hard. He was a poet, you know. He hadn't published a book in fifteen years but he'd been writing. Especially
in the last year or so, looking forward to this early-retirement
setup. And I figure that a piece about him, even in a paper like
yours . . . the exposure might be helpful. There are almost
enough poems for a new book, enough at least to make a section
in a book if they included the old poems, which are out of print
now anyway. So, you see, I really shouldn't be putting you
down. I hadn't intended to. But I couldn't help it. I may not be
able to help it, even now. But at least you'll know why I'm
being nasty. It's a bad conscience."

"That's where I live," I tell her. "Born and bred in the briar
patch."

"Will you mention the poems? Will you do what you can?"

"Sure," I say, wondering which of us is crazy. How many readers of poetry also read our paper? Wouldn't she do better to tack up a small sign on a tree in the middle of the woods? But I am not going to throw away an advantage. "You'll lend me a copy of his book?" I ask.

She hesitates. Is she one of those people who just hate to lend books? Or does her uncertainty come from something more specific? Does she, for example, distrust my motives, which are mixed? "It's out of print and they're hard to come by," she says.

"I understand," I tell her. "I promise to get it back to you."

The decision gets made. She nods. Then she shows me his desk, a Door Store arrangement of a flat board on a couple of filing cabinets. It is just the way he left it. The pencils are still arranged on the blotter, all lined up and sharpened, ready to go.

"May I?" I ask, pointing to the chair.

"Sure," she says.

I sit in his chair. I put my elbows on his desk.

She turns away. Unable to bear it? Or to allow me to communicate with the least possible interference or distraction with whatever of his spirit remains in these mute, intimate objects?

This time, I do not pay particular attention to the books. I could, I suppose, but what would any of the titles of those slender volumes mean to our nonreaders? The thicker book on the desk was more central to his life, anyway—*The Random House Handbook*—for the bonehead English classes to which Stratton devoted most of his life. The poetry may have been his ambition, but he never got there. It was a goal, a sort of magnetic north pole to which he referred, hardly even imagining its glittering icy grandeur as he slogged through the swamps and bogs of remedial composition.

I did some of it myself, once. It is not dishonorable work, teaching basic language skills to those who are desperately in need. It is more useful, or could be, than sitting around in some comfortable seminar room with intelligent, literate students to chat knowledgeably about Hawthorne and Poe. But the reality is that these composition courses are closer to intellectual triage. The admissions offices let in anyone at all and then leave it to the English department menials to do the nasty sorting out of the quick from the brain dead. Those who fail bonehead English never make it to sophomore status, let alone to their diplomas. Which means that they can spend quite a bit of time and money, fooling themselves that they're going to graduate someday and get one of those good jobs in middle management. They are not, after all, the very brightest of human beings.

Which is one reason these colleges treat them so badly. Faculties hate them. The administrations see them as prey and, in a grotesque variation of Robin Hood, steal from the stupid for the benefit of the smart. It may be a way of hard-pressed institutions to survive but it is unattractive.

Sour grapes? I admit it. But that doesn't make them any sweeter.

Not that Stratton and I were ever actually colleagues. He was at the larger and handsomer South Campus of the college. My association with it was brief, only two terms, and I was at the North Campus, an inner-city operation housed in what had once been a brewery and, on rainy days, still smelled strongly of beer.

It is a terrible indictment of the life I've been leading that I can't say I'm well rid of it, better off now that I'm out of that dismal business.

But the way things work out, it's a safe bet that poor Stratton supposed the grass was greener anywhere but on his side of the fence. Even allowing that he could have been shrewd enough to see some of the injustices that were a part of the institution and built into his job, and even conceding that he put up with them without acquiring the protective blindness that was the adaptation of most of his colleagues, one is still not driven to conclude that he had come to accept them. He might have hated every damned day there and yet been afraid to leave, afraid of winding up in an even worse pickle—like mine, *par exemple*.

I can't blame him too severely. I tend to feel sorry for the man, not only because he is dead but because of the way he lined up these pencils on his desk pad. Not just a random handful, but an even dozen. And all of them sharpened to beautiful conical points.

Which suggests that writing didn't come easily to him.

So he hated the job. (He took early retirement and one can draw certain inferences from that.) He wanted, as Stephanie has told me, to put his teaching behind him and devote himself to his art. But the desk suggests a pencil sharpener rather than any demoniac maker of sentences.

Mastery of *The Random House Handbook* does not guarantee frequent visits from the Muse—even if one has taken early retirement to be accommodating for her and to make one's life inviting.

I am doing it again, or trying to. I am making him lucky to have been blown away by the loony. A kind of promotion from this vale of tears to some better place? Not that, necessarily, but perhaps a better and more merciful conclusion than what might have happened to him otherwise. Than what he would have experienced, himself. A destiny that had been lurking in wait all this time, since the day he showed up in first grade with his brand-new pencil box. One of those bright plastic things in the shape of a large pencil, the trick being that the eraser comes off and inside there are these pencils in all different colors, and a ruler, and maybe a protractor (which must puzzle kids young enough to have pencil boxes).

And as long as he lived, those matched pencils represented to him the heart of the intellectual life, the real emblem of the artist and the thinker. The smell of cedar shavings, the funny little sharpeners in those boxes, and the orderliness of how every object fitted in. The pencil was to Stratton as the peel was to Honoré.

It is the orderliness that is pitiable. The outrageous possibility that these terrible events we live through are not just random bits of a welter is what wrings one's heart. That, I believe, was Malebranche's vision, the awesome and vertiginous glimpse of pattern and sense that could make him feel as giddy as if he were drunk. And it was not a simple cause-and-effect relationship either, but a richer, higher, deeper, more wonderful, and more terrifying set of connections among events that he wanted to call our attention to. That our breath should be taken away, even as his was.

What he must have meant by "The Mind of God."

Sometimes, I have the sinking feeling that Malebranche was just another nut. I sit up late at night reading him because philosophy is supposed to be soporific.

I am afraid of sleeping pills. If I had sleeping pills in the house, I might begin to think about how enough of them could help, could get me beyond the torments I wake to every morning. I think about such things even without the actual bottle of pills on the shelf.

Instead, I study Malebranche and, like a novice chess player trying to understand mysterious moves in the games of the masters, I puzzle through some of his disputes. As for instance how he believes that Spinoza may have confused the idea with its *ideatum*. With its idea-ed thing. Or, bluntly, what Malebranche is suggesting is that Spinoza failed to distinguish between six as an abstract concept and six apples.

But Malebranche even argues with himself. In the *Recherche*, for instance, he claims a primacy for algebra over geometry, because algebra is more abstract and purer. The equations float in a clearer ether than that in which the polygons and circles dip and soar. In the *Entretiens*, however, he is clear about including geometry within "the sphere of intelligible extension," which is to say that he was going back to agree with Descartes.

But who gives a shit? At two in the morning, having tried with brandy to dull just a little the electric jangle of my nerves so that a last drive into the velvety heart of the night is a tempting but insane idea, Malebranche seems as reasonable an option as any. To open the familiar heavy tome and perform its mental calisthenics may be to invite torpor and stupor—who are my friends, guests I have invited and who may perhaps drop by. Like Fafnir and Fastolf, but less imposing.

And shyer.

Sometimes, when I get into it, I can almost believe this stuff makes some sense, that those numbers and figures are wheeling and tumbling just as Malebranche believed—in the mind of God, lovely and eternal and safe.

He may have been a nut but he wasn't a fool. He never married. He never had a daughter. He loved algebra and geometry and logic, to which nothing could happen. Which could never be taken away from him. The worst he had to fear was that he might die, that his brain would lose its grip upon the majesty of these things. But even that was tolerable, for they would persist anyway, undiminished, untouched and untouchable.

And in these things, he thought he saw God, where idea and *ideatum* join at last.

Sometimes, running his syllogisms and thinking his thoughts, I can persuade myself that the elaborate complexity of the system he devised is not merely delusionary but evidence of some truth. I don't believe, but I can imagine belief.

Or, just as likely, the book merely grows heavy in my hands, my eyes blur and my lids sag. Consciousness, my jailer and tormentor, decides to take a break. And for a time, I am untroubled, sitting in my chair but dead to the world, as the saying goes.

I wish.

I got a solicitation from a university library a week or so ago, which I glanced at, almost threw away, and then looked at again because of its illustration. What had caught my eye was a representation of a bookplate of the twenties that showed a bearded fellow whose skinny body protruded from the window of a stylized tower. The caption explained that the figure in the bookplate was that of St. Basil, protector of books and libraries. So instead of throwing it into the wastebasket, I put it on the pile of odd items on my desk that demand or invite further consideration.

My kind of fellow, after all. A lot closer to me, surely, than that joker wandering around France with his baker's peel. I looked St. Basil up—the Great, that is, for there are a number of saints of that name. He was bishop of Neo-Caesarea (New Jersey?) and the founder of Eastern communal monasticism. He provisioned an estate that included dwelling houses, a church, a hospital for the sick, and a hospice for travelers, and he was a beloved and admired fellow at whose funeral vast crowds came out to mourn. His name is popular in the Eastern church, especially in Russia, where the initial declines to a V. And where the diminutive becomes the name for male cats. What in English is a Tom, in Russian is a Vaschka. (Maschka is a female cat, which is, in English, what?)

More impressive—and depressing—is the bland announcement that the Order of St. Basil has produced 14 popes, 1,805 bishops, 3,010 abbots, and 11,085 martyrs.

A fearsome number. And fearsome that at that level the names are subsumed, forgotten, or reduced to mere integers in the running tally.

Another Basil is Basil the Blessed, who was one of those holy fools who pop up from time to time—especially in Russia—wandering around half naked, shamming stupidity, and courting humiliation. And every now and then getting themselves canonized by the Russian church. Basil began as an apprentice to a shoemaker but he kept giving the shoes away to poor people, which is not the way to succeed in the world of business. By the time he died, he'd managed to make such a nuisance of himself that he'd attracted the notice—not favorable, one hardly need observe—of Ivan the Terrible.

"More coffee?" Stephanie Stratton stands in the doorway pretending to be the attentive hostess. It is not unlikely though that there are other motives that have brought her into the room. She wants to see someone other than her husband sitting in that chair at that desk in that room. She had seen me sit down. She went away. Now she wanted to come back and find me there, confirming for herself that I had persisted through time, that this was no aberration but the primary reality to which she would eventually have to adjust.

Her coming in to take a sudden look this way suggests that the adjustment has not yet been perfected. I know how that is.

We all know the phrase about one's heart going out to someone. It is not quite accurate. The sensation is in the upper chest, but it involves the lungs and the stomach. It is as if all one's organs had been turned to metal and then a strong magnet were brought into the room.

I realize that there is no further advantage I can expect for Lansberg and the paper, and that therefore nothing now prevents me from confiding in her. I can let her know that we have something in common and that, when I told her that I understood what she was feeling, it was no mere empty phrase.

I get up and follow her into the living room, where she will not have to consult her emotions moment by moment to determine how much more she can stand.

"A month or so ago, there was a story we got off the wire," I tell her, "about a couple who checked into a hotel for their honeymoon and never came out. The groom was the heir to a winery, so money was no problem. They've been living on room service for twenty-one years."

She looks at me as if I am crazy and I suppose she may be right. I certainly hadn't intended to begin this way. But having committed myself, there is no choice but to continue.

"We ran it on the front page," I tell her.

"So?"

"I'm wondering why. I mean, it was the editor's decision, but I don't think he knows why he decides the way he does. It's instinct. Those of us who don't have that instinct have to try to work out reasons. If there are reasons, that is. And I think it's a story with a double-barreled appeal. For the young, it's sexual. Twenty-one years in a honeymoon suite! There is a naughty suggestion of twenty-one years of sexual excess. On the other hand, for the rest of us, for those who are a little older and have been beat up a little more, there is the fantasy of twenty-one years of safety. Of protection. The agoraphobe's dream."

"Maybe," she says. And then, "Why are you telling me this?"

"I don't know," I say. And then, "Yes, yes, I do. I'm trying to offer you the only comfort I know. That life is full of risks. And the alternative to risk isn't safety but nonlife. A cocoon. Twenty-one years in a bridal suite."

She looks at me blankly. Defiantly. Who am I to be telling her such things? And what am I telling her, anyway? I certainly haven't been very clear.

"I know what it is," I say.

"Do you?"

"I do. My wife and daughter were killed, four months ago. In a car crash with a drunk driver. It was another kind of senseless killing, another kind of killer, but . . . close enough."

She looks at me without much expression. She isn't doubting me. She isn't rejecting what I've said. But she isn't reacting much either. On the other hand, what did I expect?

"I had promised myself I wouldn't bother you with this. But as a kind of credential . . . So you'll know that I really do understand a little of what you're going through . . ."

"Thank you," she says, nodding once. There is not a quiver in her voice, not a tremor of lip or eyelid.

What had I expected? I ask myself once again. Gratitude? Sympathy?

She takes my coffee cup. His cup, maybe.

Back at the office, where I go to transcribe my notes into a draft of the piece, I find a young man waiting for me, another recent journalism graduate who, after some months of looking at more reputable publications, has discovered that there are very few jobs out there and that the degree for which he had paid so much, and maybe even worked so hard, is something of a joke. It is like having a certificate as a trolley car driver. Or an armor repairer. There aren't a whole lot of openings.

Lansberg likes these youngsters. He can train them to do just what he wants, let them knock themselves out for a year or so, squeeze them dry, and then let them go, running and screaming as often as not, to positions in corporate publicity departments—that pay better and are only slightly more disagreeable. Our lies are at least random and not calculated to enrich any company at the expense of other companies and the general public. Even our ads are harmless. One I like that runs regularly is for the most powerful amulet ever created. It has Solomon's Seal and the Holy Cross, the Japanese Crane of Good Fortune, the Pyramids, the Yin and Yang sign, the Crescent and Star, the Four-Leaf Clover and the Eternal Circle of Life (whatever in hell that is). And their claim is difficult to argue with in that no one is likely ever to have created a more powerful amulet. In pewter finish, copper or gold tone. My bet is that they sell a lot of the copper ones because people figure that they may prevent arthritis as well as bringing good luck in money, love, and happiness as the copy offers.

And into these squalid purlieus of scrivener's hell come these desperate candidates for employment, whom Lansberg likes to refer to me. It is a complicated piece of sadism, for he knows that I am likely to tell them the truth and that by so doing I will be confessing to a perfect stranger that my life has been a disaster. I am warning them, and yet we all know—I, the candidates, and Lansberg as well—that nothing I say will deter them from accepting an offer. Furthermore, Lansberg also understands how I am likely to pick the best possible candidates, those who are exactly the ones he most wants to torture and humiliate.

Not that it makes any difference. They will come here or not come here according to whatever plan has been fashioned for each of them, no matter what I tell them. In which case, and for the sheer mischief of it, I might as well praise our operation, paint it in the best possible light, as if I were hoping to attract a valuable prospect to a worthwhile enterprise. I decide to try this, not just to be perverse but to conform to the perversity I have perceived in Roger Stratton's life. And Amanda Hapgood's, too.

This morning's applicant is a Princeton graduate, an English major, a published author. Three of his short stories have appeared in second-line quarterlies. In better times, he might have been grist for Henry Luce's mill or Katherine Graham's. But *Time* and *Newsweek* are cutting back, and all those victims of the CBS economy drive are out on the street, available and even desperate. Cheap! Mr. William T. Harris from Princeton with his stories in *Persiflage, Rhodomontade,* and *The Texas Review* cannot compete.

Why not buck him up a little? I have him sit down in my guest chair and offer him coffee. I think of St. Basil the Blessed, whom Princeton's security force would not have tolerated much better than Ivan's did, and I call this young man's attention to a headline in our current issue, the teaser of a piece I didn't happen to write but could have.

DIETER GOES BERSERK,

TRIES TO EAT DWARF

"What," I ask, "do you make of that?"

"Well, it's funny."

"Yes, that's true. What else?"

"I don't know. I don't take it very seriously."

"Ah, but we do. It's a headline on the front page. That's serious!"

"It sells papers, you mean," he says, not quite belligerently but with his back up a bit.

"It sells papers, yes, but only because it speaks to something in our audience. It answers some need or touches them in some tender place. In this instance, I'd imagine, it evokes an old fear."

"Of being eaten?" he asks. "Is there a lot of that? People are worried about cannibalism?"

"Sure, they are. We all are, if only we can admit it. Weren't there people in your family who loomed over you and swooped down into your stroller to coo and tell you what a sweet baby you were? And didn't they say, 'Oh, I'm going to eat you up'? People remember that kind of thing. Didn't they teach you about Freud at Princeton? One of our greatest poets!"

He is afraid I am making fun of him. And rightly so. "You have lots of stories about dwarfs getting eaten?" he asks.

"Whenever we can. Dwarfs are little people, the way you and I were, the way everybody was. Little people who are helpless and vulnerable. And the risks are very great that they could get eaten at any time. In our paper, I'd say it happens four or five times a year."

"You mean that's true? That happened?"

"Nutty things happen all the time. Not always in good taste. Not always in conformity with Aristotle's poetics. But there are other poetics, and it's up to us to discover them as we go along. The fear of being eaten is deep enough and widespread enough to sell papers."

He opens the paper and reads the story. He smiles. "This doesn't seem terribly frightening," he says.

Not a bad kid, I think. In his place, I would be uncomfortable. I wouldn't have the vaguest idea of what to say either. He has, after all, mixed feelings about having come here. We weren't his first-choice place. On the other hand, to get turned down by a place like this will be that much tougher for him to take. What can he tell the *Texas Review* crowd?

"It's a funny piece," I tell him. "But it's soothing. The ridiculousness of the story is what is comforting. The chances of a thing like that actually happening are fairly slim. As the baker was not."

The joke is primitive. The story is of a baker in the south of France who decided to lose 130 pounds in order to attract the notice of a girl he liked. Or to prompt her to imagine him as the plausible human being he believed he really was, underneath all that fat. So he lived for fourteen months on vegetables and cottage cheese. And he went nuts, hallucinated, so that it suddenly seemed to him that an old friend of his—who wasn't really a dwarf but was pretty short—was a chicken. And the baker took off after him with a cleaver, thinking he'd butcher him and eat him. The shouts of rage and fear from his short friend actually began to resemble the cries of a terrified chicken—which was what got the story into some local paper in Arles. From which it got onto the wire services. Where we found it and saw that it was pure gold.

"Do you think you could do this kind of thing?" I ask him.

"I think I could learn," he says, which is either cautious or modest. Probably cautious. But it gives me an idea.

"I think you probably could learn. If you didn't have contempt for it, and if you weren't fighting yourself about it all the time, you probably could. This is no place for intellectual snobs, though. We need people who are confident enough to be here without going through an identity crisis about it every morning."

"I understand," he says.

Does he? Can he see the warning I've given him?

"Well, why don't we see what you can do?" I suggest. "Why don't you take some of those clips, pick four or five from that basket, and go over to the Xerox machine and make copies. Take them home, think about them, pick one out, and do us a piece. In clear simple sentences. It's not as easy as it looks. Come back on Thursday and I'll see how you've done. Fair enough?"

"I appreciate it!" he says.

I looked down at his résumé. "See you on Thursday, then, Mr. Harris. And good luck to you!"

"Thank you very much."

From across the room, I watch him make copies at the Xerox machine. He wants to work here, to take his place at one of these gray metal desks, and sit in an ergonomic chair that Cosgrove bought in order to get more work out of each of us. The look is innocuously high-tech but the designer's bright colors and glossy finishes cannot blot out the squalor that swims just under the surface.

All he sees is that I've turned it into a competition in which, if he wins, he gets a job here. This room is the prize! This building, way out in the swamps where the land was cheap and where there is nowhere for employees to go for long lunches. This terrible concrete box that could just as well have been a medium-security corrections center is what he wants.

It's what I wanted once, angry at having been let go at that terrible college. It seemed at that moment that illiteracy was taking over the world, and if I couldn't beat it, the smart thing would be to join it.

I know better now. I know that it is Lansberg who has won. Twice in one morning now. And without even knowing he was involved, either time.

6

WHAT got to Lansberg were the pencils. He had been worrying about the series, fearful that it might be getting too highbrow. He is fearful all the time on that score, but he needn't be. ABC III doesn't read. That's the secret of successful publishing in America—never to look at your product. Which is not a mistake Big Al Cosgrove is likely to make. For one thing, he's never in his office. For another, he may not even know how to read. It's those of us who were in the fast group in the first grade—the bluebirds?—who wind up like this, clicking away at a VDT. That kid, Harris, was a bluebird too, no question.

But ABC was a dodo. He was one of those dolts whose books got warped and mangled by the beginning of the second week from the sessions of inelegant wrestling he had not yet figured out how to avoid. Now he knows better. He can hire people like Lansberg to read for him. And people like me to write what Lansberg has to read.

Lansberg distrusts us, worries that we're always trying to sneak quality into the paper, get recondite and smart-ass, alienate readers, and enrage Cosgrove. As he would do himself if he were in our shoes and at our desks. As he almost certainly did at one time. So he is suspicious of this relic series as potentially highbrow and reads it with a gimlet eye. Still, the bit about the pencils and their testimony was too lively even for him to dismiss. He cut the piece way down but he ran it. He even left in the name of Stratton's book of poems, *Eclectic Lights*, probably because he could rely on our contemptible readers to find it contemptible.

What is uncomfortable for me is that those readers who notice and react with the little sneer Lansberg has in mind for them will probably be right. In agreement, that is, with my own opinion—which is that the poems are virtually worthless. Conventional academic surrealism, not incompetently done but not worth doing. Modish stuff, written to formula almost as sedulously as what we do here.

Have I done poor Stephanie a disservice? I rather doubt it. Nothing my troubled conscience and jangled nerves can't contrive to deal with. It is difficult, at any rate, to imagine publishers combing our pages for suggestions for books, especially those publishers who do poetry. So I have hardly spoiled her golden opportunity.

Let Stephanie Stratton continue to hope. At least the piece is running.

Which means, of course, that I am a prisoner of my success and have to keep on with the project.

It would be easier if I didn't believe in it, if I had Harris's brashness or Lansberg's not-quite-elegant distaste with which to distance myself. But I can go home and open one of Leah's bureau drawers, stare at the contents, and feel the tears brimming up. Or, worse, I might feel nothing. In which case I would be doubly bereaved, for that would be the death of grief, for which it is still possible to grieve.

One of these days, I shall clean out the drawers and closets. It is an awesome task to face, painful and depressing. But it is also painful to live with these objects, to have them around, mournful and irrelevant, without the lives that were their context.

* * *

Those old Christians were not stupid. Crazy, maybe, but not stupid. The relics of their saints were promptings to the contemplation and maybe even emulation of the virtues they had displayed in living. All those martyrs and contemplatives, mystics and eccentrics. Whose lives I read because I am distracted, because I cannot concentrate on anything longer than a paragraph, or anything as demanding as a poem. These lives of the saints are short reports of wonders and disasters, much like those we print every week in our deplorable rag but with the respectability distance and time can supply.

Sometimes the stories are miraculous. But there are times when the modesty and piety of the saint was undeniable but altogether unsensational, the kind of thing that could never make our paper. Then the miracle is that such simple goodness was noticed and remembered. St. Notburga, a domestic servant in the Tirol, for instance, was caught giving to the poor some of the scraps she had been directed to feed the pigs. She was dismissed from the service of her employer, Count Henry, and found a place with a modest farmer at Eben. There she continued her benefactions, stinting herself for the benefit of others. She was later recalled to the castle—that may have been the real miracle—where she spent the rest of her life piously and decently busy in the kitchen. Her emblem is a sickle hanging in the air above her, because she had refused, when she was in the farmer's employ, to reap on a Sunday.

The sickle is also the emblem of St. Isidore, who spent his whole life on a farm at Torrelaguna, outside of Madrid, and whose life was even less eventful. Neither he nor his wife, Mary, who is also popularly regarded as a saint in Spain, ever did anything of note. He was a model worker, a kind neighbor, and a devout Christian.

Is that enough?

Knowing by how much most people fall short of even that modest goal, it may well be more than enough.

Did Stephanie Stratton know this? Did she care more for Roger's character, or even for his vague and gentle smile, than for his deplorable verses?

Of course she did. And it is not any deep commitment to poetry that prompts her to try to get some posthumous publication for his poems. It is loyalty to him, to his memory.

To which of these other disasters shall I turn my attention? The little boy I shall leave for the last. The Iranian then? The Nicaraguan? One is a mild sufferer, the other at least possibly a villain. I hope he is a villain. I want a bad guy in this somewhere. If everybody is likable, what I turn out to be doing is a rewrite of Thornton Wilder's *Bridge of San Luis Rey*. Which was okay, but too sweet, too upbeat for my taste. He softened the impact of his disaster by setting it in seventeenth-century Peru, so that all his people would have died anyway. Their losses were a convention of absurd adventure movies, moreover, those rope bridges being foreign to the experience of most of the members of the Book-of-the-Month Club. Put the characters on a less picturesque bridge, the one over the Mianus River, for instance, over which Wilder would have driven on his way from New Haven to New York, and the picture changes, all those delicate pastels turning into a nightmare palette of fresh and drying blood.

I don't much care which step I do first, the Managua mambo or the Teheran twist, for either way, I am on firm ground with some version or other of the appointment in Samarra—not the O'Hara novel but the story in its not altogether appropriate epigraph. The poor bastard leaves Managua, say, and comes to decency and democracy and civil order here in sunny Florida. Where Death is waiting for him. Dressed up in a loud Hawaiian shirt, maybe, and wearing sunglasses and a cute hat, but underneath the foolery it's the familiar grim guy with the scythe come down to catch the water skiers at Cypress Gardens and the porpoises at Sea World between assignments.

Why the hell not? The Nicaraguan it shall be.

But having arrived at that decision, I am enmired. My hand strays from the address of Señor Martinez and I find myself looking up that of the Happy Times Travel Agency.

It is a dismal name. I imagine grief-stricken people calling to book a flight for some funeral. I can't decide whether their revulsion at this mindless cheerfulness sends them to another name in the ample listing in the Yellow Pages, or they put up with it, suffering yet another small blow, hearing a voice chirp, "Happy Times." Or something a little trickier and more self-conscious, like "Happy Times from Happy Times."

But then I look at my notes and it comes clear. Felicity Bowers is the surviving sister. She has put up with her name for all those years? She will ram it back down the world's retching throat, any way she can.

I dial and ask for Felicity Bowers.

"May I tell her who is calling?"

I identify myself. Honestly, for a change, with the name of the paper rather than with the loftier "ABC Publications" we usually use. For those who don't know about us, it doesn't matter. Those who do know who we are are likely to be put off, so that the parent corporation is a convenient subterfuge. But I am almost defiant. "The *Star*," I say, forthrightly.

The snort suggests that she has seen our paper. "This is Felicity Bowers," she says, not even bothering to disguise the fact that it has been she, all along.

I make an appointment to see her, not by charm but by sheer force of will. It is clearly a decision she is making against her better judgment. Or certainly against her inclination. But then, what good are inclinations? Where do reasons get you? I had decided to call Señor Martinez, hadn't I?

Malebranche is persuasive about volition. He talks about how our volitions are inadequate and ineffective unless they are the expressions of God's volition. Indeed, he maintains that our volitions are the results of His. Consider how a paralyzed person cannot will his arm to move. He remembers what he used to do and he imagines the movement of his arm, but nothing happens.

Meanwhile, in another body, without any particular thought, a man thinks, imagining the motion of his arm, and apparently as a consequence of his thought, the arm moves.

So? Does this prove anything? Probably not. But the idea of God's will making itself manifest in the events of our lives is widespread. All those who take the Bible seriously, who believe in God and who suppose that in the history of a small people in the Middle East there is some evidence of a divine presence or intention, or even a distorted and one-sided dialogue with such a presence, are paddling in treacherous waters. Each logical step leads to the thundering falls, at the brink of which Malebranche and his blind pietism overhang sublime madness. If it was God's intention to smite the first-born of all the Egyptians—who had not been the primary persecutors of the Jews, after all—then anything is possible.

The prohibition against the mixing of linen and wool cannot be absurd in a world in which everything is absurd, arbitrary, and unknowable.

My mind orders my hand to dial the number of Señor Martínez, but another volition intervenes.

The telephone turns into a chicken, clucks a couple of times, and hops off my desk. The desk shakes itself, sprouts a tail, moos, and ambles off to find a more congenial and appropriate meadow. At any moment, these things could happen, and would if God willed them.

Our doubts on the matter are nothing but evidences of our diminished capacity for love and trust that is the curse of fallen man. Before the Fall, Adam understood that God was more excellent than himself and he could, without effort, trust and love God more than himself. After the Fall, instead of being united to the body, the soul came to be subjected, dominated.

In other words, your rational objections and interpositions are merely snares and delusions of the serpent. Pay them no mind.

Intricate and clever and sneaky and a little childish? Yes, all of those things. But also evidence of a mind driven to extremities, pushed and battered to the limits of what is tolerable and beyond. Dazed, crazed, grief-stricken, turning inward upon itself, unable to make the simplest decisions—should I have the Corn Flakes or the Special K?—one stands paralyzed in the pantry and wonders about volition. It is the intelligent person's nervous breakdown.

Fortunately for an Oratorian on the Rue St. Honoré, there

weren't a whole lot of choices to make. The monastic day is more regulated than most. There was a proper vessel to contain the volatility of the distraught mind and bruised feelings. He sat at his escritoire and scribbled away, a kind of therapy as arduous and respectable as any contemporary practitioner has to offer, and his brethren recognized him as a valuable fellow.

Take away his escritoire and put him instead at a VDT with Lansberg filling in for the abbot, and what has changed?

The source is the same, the trembling, the edge of tears, the inability to decide things, the irrelevance of decisions of apparent simplicity that he thought he'd puzzled out. But what a coming down there is!

I have been ignoring one of the more amiable aspects of this saint business—the way in which these figures make a family for anyone who believes in them. It isn't just the idea of intercession, the model of Heaven as a huge Renaissance court where it is all but hopeless to try to approach the king directly and one must go through various intermediaries who may have influence. That's the discouraging part of it, perhaps, the remoteness of divine help. Which is one way of accounting for the fact that most prayers seem to go unanswered. On the other hand, the intricacy and variety of the relationships is pleasant. There may not be help but there can be comfort in having so many spirits around is which to confide, from which one may expect companionship if not miracles.

You have your namesake saint, whose day you celebrate instead of your own birthday. You have your business or trade or craft. A baker would turn to Honoré, a metal worker to Eloi, a gardener to Fiacre, or a soldier to Michael the Archangel. You can also approach the saint who might conceivably have some interest in your predicament. A traveler might apply to St. Christopher, for instance. Jude likes to intercede in desperate cases, which means either that he is particularly kind or—as I sometimes think—something of a show-off.

For those who are alone and friendless, there is an extended family, a gang of imaginary friends and playmates of the kind that young children invent for themselves, but with the sanction of a respectable religion that is rich in tradition as well as real estate. In other words, no matter how absurd this all may be, they can't lock you up as a loony for believing it.

And if they do? You call upon St. Léonard of Limoges, patron saint of prisoners. He may not be able to do much for you, but if you believe in him, he will listen.

On the way up there, I realized why my candor about my association with the *Star* had worked so well. Felicity Bowers wasn't trying to peddle a hopeless collection of poems; she was running a business. And publicity—even in our not so estimable pages—might be of actual value to her. It certainly couldn't hurt. That room in the Sheraton in Clearwater in which the Reverend Bakker and his buddy had their way with the poor secretary was booked for two years solid by bizarre thrill seekers, unbelievers but those who were troubled by their unbelief. Doubting Thomases in reverse, they needed to come to the actual room and lie down on the actual bed where it happened in order to sever their bonds with Praise the Lord.

Whatever Felicity Bowers felt about her sister's death, a mention in a publication with a circulation as large as ours might make the phone ring more frequently and produce the more significant jinglings of the cash box.

Am I being unfair?

It would be unfair to print such a thing. But I am free to think it, at least to wonder about it as a possibility.

It is possibly what I want. Anything, rather than Stephanie Stratton's mute, moist grief. Which I despise—because it is too much like my own.

She was way up the coast, so that it made sense for me to take the skyway. I'd driven that route before but without really noticing how weird it is. There you are, barreling along in midair with nothing on either side of you but other cars and, down below, thick palmetto scrub clutching at the concrete pylons, ready to gobble them up and retake the roadway. Behind you, quite arbitrarily, the city looms, a wall of buildings, some of them gleaming white, others in outrageous pastels, and still others in a bright mirror finish that, at the right time of day, can be dazzling. The construction is as unreal as the palmetto wastes. And together, they are incongruous and intensify one another's grotesqueness.

Meanwhile, there are icy blasts from your air conditioner so that you are practically freezing, but you've got your windows closed because otherwise you'd be stewing in the subtropical heat. The radio blares out over the air conditioner, the roar of the engine, and the whine of tires, yours and those of other motorists.

You look beside you at a passing car with another guy, just like you, with his air conditioner blasting and his radio or tape deck blaring—except that while he's flying through midair in his German sports car, he's also talking on the telephone.

It isn't any violation of nature. The only violation of nature here would be to stop all the cars, get out, and descend the forty feet or so to the palmetto scrub and the heat. There, you'd be eaten alive in no time by the bugs and rodents and amphibious monsters, not to mention the alligators and snakes, the poisonous toads and the walking fish.

Nature here is unnatural. It is the artifactual world that offers us the only chance we have of survival.

Go and ask some astronaut whether he feels uncomfortable or worries about how he looks in his space suit. Ask him, when he's hanging out there in space, connected to the mother ship by a frail umbilicus, or supported by some complicated backpack, what his views are on the subject of nature. You think he'll know what you're talking about?

Not here, either. The city is the edifice we have thrown up to hold back the awful appetites of the jungle and mangrove and palmetto scrub you can sometimes actually hear at night, snapping and rustling and making rude digestive sounds. And then an air conditioner or a sprinkler system switches on, thank God, to make an antiphon of civilization's relatively puny power.

On the other hand, the ravages of nature are natural. We may feel grief but cannot be outraged at what nature does—to individuals by means of bacteria or showier lightning bolts, or to whole towns with tidal waves or tornadoes, with their curious predilection for the inhabitants of trailer camps. Even so, these people have perished naturally. It is the unnatural death—of the widow bludgeoned by a burglar, or the child molested by some madman, or the mother and child hit by a drunk driver—that is anomalous. And the survivors translate back to what they know or can stand, treating the burglar or the sex offender or the drunk driver as if he were not human at all but an embodiment of some force of brute nature.

As Malebranche says every one of us is.

She is not quite the grieving sister I had expected to encounter.

"She was a thief and a bitch and I'm glad she's dead" is what Felicity Bowers tells me, even before I can pick something appropriate from the array of conventional condolences I keep filed away in my mind for my work on this series.

"I see," I say. "Then it wouldn't bother you too much if I were to look at her things," I say, my eyes on the prize.

"Her things? What things?" the surviving sister asks. She is a woman of some substance, maybe a size sixteen, but well coiffed and well groomed. Her fingernails, carefully lacquered in blood red, are especially impressive. Her hair is steel gray. She looks at me with an expression that suggests both curiosity and severity.

I explain, as well as it is possible to explain about relics, a notion that I ascribe, in what I recognize as cowardice, to my editor.

She laughs. "And you believe that?"

"I believe in my paycheck," I tell her. "But it is possible, aesthetically. Why else do we go to see Roosevelt's desk at Hyde Park? Or Washington's plantation? Or Monticello? The objects tell us something."

"But those were great men. My sister never did anything interesting, except to embezzle twenty-eight thousand dollars and change from this business. To turn me virtually into a pauper. Which is the thanks I got for taking her in when her husband dropped her for somebody younger. I knew at the time I was sticking my neck out. I just didn't know how far."

"I'm sorry to hear this."

"And you know what's worst?"

"I give up," I say.

She looks at me, clearly wondering whether I am all right and then deciding that it doesn't much matter, that I am probably not dangerous. "It's as bad as if she'd been a wonderful sister and I was really sorry to lose her. I mean, this way, there's guilt. Nightmares. The whole thing." She holds her hands clasped together before her as if in prayer.

"I am sorry," I say, sorry now that I was flippant before.

She shrugs. Meaning, perhaps, that it wasn't my fault. Or meaning that I can't possibly understand what she is talking about. Or meaning nothing except perhaps her inability to comprehend any of it.

"Was it as simple as that?" I ask. "Your sister's husband just threw her over for a younger woman?"

"It happens," she says.

"Oh, yes. But did he throw her out? Or did she leave him?"

Felicity smiles. "You're right. She walked out on him—out of pride. To show him she wasn't absolutely dependent on him, as of course she was. Or would have been, except for me, because I had this little business and an apartment and could take her in."

"As you did, being the good sister," I prompt.

She nods.

"Older or younger?" I ask.

"I was the younger one," she tells me. "Which she resented, too. That she should have to come to me for help."

A striking woman, she is not easy to like. She is, in her size and with her careful grooming and maquillage, forbidding, almost intimidating. Or her anger is. And her pain.

"What I need is to look at her room, her closet, her dresser . . ."

"I can't leave here," she tells me. "But some evening, maybe.

Or on a Saturday. It'd be better on Saturday. I don't get out of here until six-thirty or seven, and by the time I get home, I'm bushed."

"Saturday's fine. Late in the afternoon, maybe, this Saturday? Then we can go out for a drink or something, on the paper."

"That's not necessary," she says, as if I'd made a pass. But something else is troubling her. "You won't find anything interesting. What she's left behind doesn't say anything. It's just . . . stuff!"

"It can't hurt to try," I tell her. "At the worst, I'll be wasting my time. I get paid either way."

"You'll mention the name of the agency?"

"Absolutely, I promise."

7

I N a way, the fact that Laura was anything but saintly is interesting to me. If there is any sense at all in these sentimental and exploitative rummagings through the orts and leavings of these dead people, if they do indeed speak in some way, then Laura's personal effects should speak differently from those of Amanda Hapgood or Roger Stratton. It would have been better if Felicity Bowers had not influenced me, if I could have walked into the bedroom, opened Laura's closet, stared at her dresses and her shoes, and somehow intuited from them the selfishness or indifference or whatever it was that made her behave badly to her sister.

Better? How better? More persuasive? Do I really care whether this is true or not?

Truths come in all sorts of configurations. To want to know whether the events in a novel are true, whether the author has based his characters on real people or used events in his own life to construct his fiction is a vulgar and contemptible concern. Such curiosity betrays an inability to appreciate the loftier truths of coherence, and a gossipy fascination with truths of mere correspondence. And if the distinction should hold for novels and poetry, why not for newspaper stories? Am I to be so rigidly bound by fussy academic distinctions among the different genres? Have the academics treated me so handsomely that I should care very much what they think?

Still, in an abstract and scientific way, it would be entertaining to demonstrate that what I have been assuming is at least plausible and possible. To fling in the faces of those very same, very smug academicians vulgar gobbets of truth they must find altogether indigestible.

Which is one of the things I look for in my readings at night, during those hours when I am courting exhaustion and oblivion—indigestibility. Or call it unacceptability, or vulgarity, or whatever you will. Consider, for instance, Blessed Lydwina, whose story is so grotesque that even Lansberg would have difficulty in reading it without bursting into gales of scornful laughter.

This young woman, one of nine children of a Dutch workman, was injured in a skating accident in 1396. She was sixteen years old at the time. She became an invalid, suffering intensely but offering up her pain as reparation for the sins of others. After an interval of eleven years, during which she either purified her soul or absolutely lost her last connection with what we'd call reason, she began to experience ecstasies and visions, having conversations with saints and visiting purgatory and heaven. During the last nineteen years of her life (that would be from 1414 to 1433) she is said to have taken no sustenance except Communion and to have slept little if at all during the last seven years—during which time she had also become almost completely blind. Predictably enough, these extraordinary sufferings and deprivations attracted a certain amount of local attention. A parish priest newly assigned to her town decided that her example was dangerous and her visitations and ecstasies suspicious, and he accused her of hypocrisy and charlatanism. But the townsfolk of Schiedam—ancestors no doubt of some of our readers—threatened to drive him from his pulpit and the district. Her cult—she is only Blessed—was approved only in 1890. And she is patroness of . . .

Ice-skating! What else?

I put the book on top of the already precarious pile on the dresser. I live in the same house that we lived in together, or anyway at the same address. The house is different now. Much messier and mostly closed up. I almost never go into Pammy's room. Or the living room or dining room for that matter. The garage, the kitchen, the bedroom, and the bathroom are my haunts now, and they are regressing to a kind of undergraduate squalor that comports with my mood. It is, at any rate, my own, doesn't remind me of anything painful, but rather implies a certain low level of activity, some elemental sort of life— even if only that of the colorful molds I've been finding on the skins of elderly oranges too long forgotten and left to their own devices in the fruit keeper of the refrigerator.

It is nearly two in the morning. I am hoping that my fatigue will be rewarded with a few hours of oblivion. More likely than not, though, grotesque dreams will plague my sleep, will torment me as if I had been somehow at fault. Or as if my sufferings could do any good. The whole idea of pain is to discourage us from keeping our hands too long on hot things or from grasping sharp things too tightly so that we could do ourselves injury. Not to feel pain is a grave and perilous condition. But pain that comes entirely after the fact, pain that serves no minatory function . . . What good is that?

This is the very question poor Lydwina must have asked herself. If it wasn't to keep her from hurting herself further, could it have been absolutely without purpose?

It is only a short step and a little skip and jump from that question to the answer she arrived at—that her sufferings must have some use in the general scheme of things, must be of some help to others if not to herself, perhaps as reparation for their sins.

Crazed and desperate girl! Or lucky girl, to live in an age of faith when she could get a whole town to believe this fairy tale along with her, to keep her company and help her in her moments of doubt.

Locke had great difficulty with Malebranche's distinction between "ideas" and "sensations," but it puzzles me why this should have been so. Locke's own philosophy distinguishes between primary and secondary qualities. The mind, in Locke's view, when it perceives a rose's shape, perceives an object distinct from itself, but when it perceives a rose's color or smell, it operates differently, color and smell being sensations, and involving what he calls direct modifications of the soul. Compared with that kind of framework, Malebranche is actually quite easy to understand. Imagine some rapt believer, one who supposes himself to be in perfect harmony with his creator. Each perception, each sensation, whether internal or external, arises directly from God, not as an effect of God's volition but as an immediate part of God's intention. Inspiration, exhalation, heartbeat, the cool of stone, the warmth of wood, the light filtering through the colors of stained-glass windows . . . all this is exactly as God means it to be at that very instant! And could not be, except for God's intention. Would fall inward or fly apart, losing color, texture, odor, and substantiality—as well as purpose and order.

It is also a quick and easy solution to the problem of how we get ideas in our heads of the bodies out there—God puts them into our minds. We see all things in God (*nous voyons toutes choses en Dieu*). "We should know furthermore, that through His presence God is in close union with our minds, such that He might be said to be the place of minds as space is, in a sense, the place of bodies."

It is a beautiful if perhaps childish comfort to believe in this way. But for Lydwina, her pain, also a part of God's intention, must have been all the more troublesome. Why had He picked on her? Why was he persecuting her? But it was as easy to say that he had picked her *out*, that he was not persecuting but blessing her, that he was using her innocence and her pain in some transaction in the complicated economy of pain and pleasure, sin and redemption of which she had heard in church but which she did not pretend to understand.

It is late enough for me to risk turning out the light. Let the monsters come, their images of pain and loss and helplessness restored by fanatical curators who busy themselves during the daylight hours, preparing and refurbishing their exhibit of horrors for the next night's showing.

What do they do at night though? I suppose they go to the refrigerator to work on the oranges.

Could they have conspired with her, that priest perhaps whose capitulation she had managed and maybe others in the church as well? Could they have consecrated rather more substantial hosts than their customary and insubstantial wafers? Aren't there more nourishing varieties of *boulangerie* that can be used, huge dark pumpernickels, doughy boules, those Italian moon breads perhaps, baguettes, kaiser rolls, raisin bread, bagels even . . .

All the works of Honoré's devotees.

No, let her be real. And let her sufferings help us who need whatever help we can get.

8

THIS morning, I found a poem on my desk. From Lansberg, with his scrawled "FYI" over a large set of grease-pencil initials that look like the random scrawl of a kindergarten child. The poem is by one Yüan Chen, and a portion is highlighted in Day-Glo yellow.

> One by one, I have given away your dresses,
> but I keep meeting them, your ghosts in the marketplace,
> or in the evenings surprising me
> by the riverbank. Your sewing box remains
> just where you left it. I can't bear to touch it,
> knowing how sharp are its needles.

The poem is not irrelevant to my series. But surely he doesn't expect me to use it, to refer *en passant* to this well-known passage of Yüan Chen. I had a hell of a time finding out who he was. One must distinguish among Ch'ü Yüan (343?–278 B.C.), Yüan Chieh (719–772), and Yüan Chen (779–831). Our boy—or Lansberg's—is famous for his poems about his dead wife and then for his poems about drunkenness.

All very interesting, but the real message is that Lansberg sits around in the evenings reading Chinese poetry. That he is as refined and intelligent as anybody on the staff, including me obviously, because I was the recipient of these photocopied verses. Which of course implies that if he can stand it, I can stand it.

On the other hand, and without unsaying any of that, there may also be a friendly gesture, an acknowledgment that what I am doing is difficult, that life has always been hard to bear, and that good old Sid Lansberg feels for me.

Why am I more comfortable with my first inference than my second?

In the library, I swotted up the scholars' gossipy details. Yüan Chen married a Miss Wei in 802. Their only child was Fan-tzu, a daughter. In 809, Yüan Chen was sent to a remote and unimportant post in Chiang-ling (in modern Hupeh), where he went, leaving his daughter behind, to serve until 813, when things got even worse, and he was posted to remote Szechwan, virtually an exile.

With what simplicity and restraint does he complain!

Is it only a question of the aesthetics of pain and suffering or is this a matter of character, a test not merely of taste but of the soul?

I'm not sure I want to know.

On Saturday afternoon, I went up to Felicity Bowers's condo, a unit in a large new development of townhouses. Not that there are any of these one could call venerable, but the latest seem to have an aggressiveness to them, with even gaudier plantings and more fanciful decorative touches than whatever had gone before. This ought to mean larger rooms, better construction, some actual advantage for the finicky consumer, but of course it doesn't. In buildings as with journalism, it's all flash and dazzle. The security system in this one uses television cameras so that the residents can turn to an otherwise vacant channel on their television sets to see who is at the door. And the doors are impressive—burglarproof steel but with some sort of plastic overlay that is supposed to resemble wood planks and blend in with the Spanish motif—both the Alhambra and the Alamo having been included in the architect's *hommage.*

An architect, I daresay, not altogether unlike myself.

Felicity Bowers doesn't bother with the television option. Unlike the normative resident, she doesn't have her television set on. She looks through the spyhole, then opens the door.

"I don't know," she says. "I must have thought a dozen times of calling you to cancel this, to let you know I'd changed my mind. I should have."

"It won't take me fifteen minutes," I promise her. "And then I'll go away if that's what you want. But I had been looking forward to dinner."

"Dinner isn't the point, is it? I mean, it's Laura's things you want to paw through."

"Look at, I'd say. But I won't quibble. You're feeling guilty, I suppose. But this can't hurt her. Whatever you did or didn't do, this won't affect her at all one way or the other."

"It will affect me," she insists.

"Why don't we talk about it a little," I suggest. "We can go to a coffee shop or something, if you'd feel more comfortable."

"I don't want to talk about it. I don't want to think about it! Can't you understand that?"

"I can see that you're uncomfortable. I might be able to help a little—not as a reporter, but just as one human being to another."

"You don't seriously believe that, do you?" she asks me.

For that, I start to like her. "I don't know what I believe, frankly. But it's possible. Anything's possible. In fact, that could very well be a motto of our paper."

"I've been looking at your paper. I'd never read it before, but I went out and got a copy," she says, pointing behind her but without turning her head, as though the wants to avoid something that smells bad.

On the coffee table, a large rectangular slab of glass resting on a couple of polished cypress knobs, I see the headline of our current issue:

PARACHUTIST MOM

GIVES BIRTH

IN FREE FALL

"Well, you see? Doesn't that prove what I said? Anything's possible!"

"How can you work for such a paper? How can you write such garbage?"

"How can you live in a place like this?" I ask.

She stares at me for perhaps thirty seconds, then smiles, then starts to laugh. "Okay, come on in," she says.

Triumph, right? I have yet again transcended Lansberg's vulgarity and Cosgrove's crassness. I ought to feel good, but I don't. I have a sour awareness of disappointment, almost of betrayal. If she knew what kind of paper I was representing, why did she invite me in? What can she possibly hope to gain from letting me—in her own words—paw through her sister's effects? Even if she hated her sister, and even if she supposed that a piece in our paper might help her to book a few airplane seats or sell a couple of cruises to the ghouls and lunatics who make up a certain share of the market, shouldn't her principles, her sense of propriety, or simply her taste be enough to prevent this lapse? I gave her the appropriate signal, a reasonable cue to slam the door in my face. And all she did was laugh and invite me in.

The devil must feel just such distress every time he negotiates the purchase of a soul, a surface satisfaction that cannot quite mask the deeper ache.

And the satisfaction is not at all in his own cleverness but rather in the fresh confirmation each experience provides of his view of the world—that he is not crazy or merely depressed but that weakness and venality and evil and hatred are really out there, not just figments of his wounded heart but active and lively forces in the daily lives of men and women everywhere.

When Felicity Bowers invited me in, I felt the same leadenness as when Stephanie Stratton offered me coffee.

To some degree, I am perhaps blaming them for not having spared me from the dismal duty Lansberg had assigned me. If either of them had stood firm, the necessary consequence of their decisions would have been my having to report back at the office that, despite my best efforts, the survivors had refused to cooperate and unless we were to offer some sort of payment there was nothing left to do but drop the series.

They don't like to offer payment, not unless they absolutely have to. It is enough at any rate to make them think again about how much they want the story. And as likely as not Lansberg himself would then get involved in the negotiations, which would leave me on the sidelines—cheering for the other team, but no longer responsible, no longer a part of it.

But a minimal display of charm, a little joke, a few signs of trivial distress and they give me whatever I want. I am—like Don Giovanni, like Lothario or Casanova—torn between amazement and chagrin at how easy it is.

Every damned time.

The furniture is that crudely carved dark wood, more or less Mexican, that goes along with the Hispanic motif of the whole development, either in dumb assent or with some sort of ironic edge. There is a double bed, a dresser with a small television on it, a pair of night stands each of which sports a large wrought-iron lamp, and a big squarish chair in that same dark wood and dark brown leather. The rug is geometric, brightly colored, possibly suggesting the Maya. The room looks as though it has been lifted as a unit from a display in a furniture showroom. There is no obvious trace of a personality, no individual signature I can find. I ask if she has changed anything.

She has, indeed, made certain alterations, not so much reclaiming the room in which her sister lived for the last few months of her life as erasing the traces. This is upsetting. I am distressed that I am distressed—but there it is. It is all I can do to suppress my annoyance with her for having done what she had a perfect right to do. It is her room in her house. I keep thinking of the phrase the police have, "tampering with the evidence," but their assumption is of a crime that has been committed. As far as I am concerned, this is, in itself, a crime. After all, these objects have so faint a voice, they need every advantage we can give them. Part of their message comes from the way in which they are arranged, their disposition in a room. Jumbled together, they are little more than their own corpses.

But there is no Society for the Prevention of Cruelty to Things, and I have not gone that far around the bend. From what I have gathered, Laura's behavior might or might not have been criminal. Certainly it was offensive. One can hardly blame Felicity, therefore, for having gone in there to empty out the dresser drawers and the closet. All her sister's stuff is now in cardboard cartons from the supermarket and suitcases from Vuitton, stacked up on a storage shelf in the closet.

"You'll have to pull those things down to look at them, and you might as well leave them down. The boxes, anyway. I was going to get them over to Goodwill, but I just never got around to it. So I stuck them up there. Dumb, isn't it?"

"The suitcases too?" I ask.

"You can put those back, I guess. If you would."

I promise to do that. I look around the room and ask, "Is this how the furniture was, before she moved in with you? Was it all yours or did she pick any of it out, or bring anything with her?"

"She didn't bring anything but the luggage. She bought that little TV but the rest was mine."

I nod and start pulling down the cardboard boxes, which she takes as her cue to leave.

I open the boxes, which are full of clothing—a lot of designer jeans, and bathing suits and tennis outfits, and underwear, and blouses. She liked silk blouses, evidently. The third box is mostly shoes, expensive shoes by Ferragamo and Bruno Magli and such. So her husband had been doing well. I grab one of the suitcases and open it. More clothing—sweater sets mostly, and dinner dresses . . .

And in one of the pockets of the divider, there is an envelope. Unsealed, so I look inside. And find the photographs—a little blurry, the way long-lens photos can be if they aren't focused just right. These are of a man and a woman. Dirty pictures. Or, more accurately, peeping pictures. Not at all posed. Laura's husband, then? And the bimbo. They were taken presumably by the private detective she hired, or by some friend she had commissioned. Or maybe she took them herself? Anything is possible. These pictures seem to have been taken from high ground, maybe even from up in a tree, looking down into a walled-in patio where the unsuspecting couple were enjoying themselves in what one may describe as unbuttoned confidence.

It is distressing to imagine the woman doing her own spying, up there clinging to that lofty branch, the camera with its long lens heavy in her hands, her stomach knotted, her breath shallow, her skin clammy. *Mal de branche,* one could say.

If she hadn't taken these photographs, or had them taken, she might have been able to get through her husband's adventure somehow, denying it or at least ignoring it. But these incontrovertible and unyielding photographs must have made that impossible. They might have been more the cause of her leaving than the events they recorded.

I go out to the living room to ask Felicity if she knew about the envelope or had seen the pictures.

"Oh, those," she says, remembering them. "She showed them to me once. I was shocked at the time. But later on, I began to wonder whether she hadn't had those pictures taken for my sake. To get me to feel sorry for her. So I'd take her in."

"Really?"

"Who knows? Well, it's not impossible," she says. "It wouldn't have been out of character. It wasn't beyond her. Nothing was beyond her. I really do think that she used them that way, for their effect—with the lawyers and then with me."

"You don't think she was using them to prove something to herself?"

"Oh, at first. But very soon, they became a weapon, something to hold in her hand and show people who might not believe her. She could prove she wasn't overreacting. As, of course, she was. But with those pictures, she could shock you into silence, at least for a while."

"After a while, that wears off, though," I say, following her suggestion.

"With me, sure. But she had her kids to think about. And with those pictures locked away in her suitcase, she could more or less blackmail Gary into doing anything she wanted him to do. Otherwise, the kids would see the pictures."

"Divorces often bring out the worst in people," I say, sounding sympathetic but knowing what I'm doing. I am hoping for more dirt. I am thinking of how much Lansberg will love this. And I am also thinking of whether Lansberg will make an offer for the pictures. And how the kids will feel, seeing their father's image, fuzzy and hairy, in the pages of our paper.

And then I realize how little differences it makes—for they will surely read what I write, and they will be able to imagine the photographs for themselves, will imagine worse, clearer, more detailed shots than any of these.

"Tell me about the kids," I ask her, because they have nothing to do with my story.

"Ricky—Richard, now, I guess. And Abby," she says. "Both in college now. Nice enough kids, really. They took it hard."

"The divorce? Or their mother's death."

"Both," she says, shaking her head.

It was a dumb question and I shut up for a moment or two. Then, to change the subject, I ask her what happened between her and her sister.

"She stole twenty-eight thousand dollars from me. Took it out of the business. And gambled it away in Nassau in the casinos."

"Terrible," I tell her.

"And the worst part of it is that I understand it," she says. "Gary had money and used to buy her presents all the time. Those suitcases, those shoes . . . And there was jewelry, lots of it, that he'd given her. She sold the jewelry. And she gambled that money away. Which was like flushing it down the toilet. Which was exactly what she wanted to do with it—and with him. And then she started playing with her own money, which was money she'd gotten from him, and she flushed that down the same toilet. But when that was all gone, she kept on playing. Because she needed to prove to herself that she was worth something, that she had some value. . . ."

"An expensive way to do it," I say.

"It had to be. That's what she was trying to prove. If you're using money as a substitute for love, it has to be a lot of money.

A lot of somebody else's money. And I was the only one around she could take from."

"I'd thought it was envy, maybe. You had a business and you'd made a life for yourself. It must have looked very attractive to her."

"Maybe. Who knows? It doesn't matter anymore, anyway. That nut just erased it all, the way a kid will erase a picture on a Magic Slate. It's all gone."

"Did you find out she'd been stealing from you before or after she was killed?"

"After. I'd wondered about it, I guess. But I'd assumed there were just mistakes. That she'd just screwed up a little and that it would turn up somehow. She wasn't very good at detail, which is what this business is all about. I remember, she once got up a set of tickets for a client of ours who wanted to go skiing in Jackson, Wyoming, and Laura sent her tickets to Jackson, Mississippi—which isn't one of your great ski resorts." She shakes her head, remembering it as if it is one of the pleasant memories of one of the good times, and I smile too, because it is less terrible than the rest of what we've been talking about. "But Babs Theodore didn't think it was so funny," Felicity Bowers says.

"The bobby pin heiress?" I ask.

Felicity Bowers looks stricken, unhappy that she gave out the name of a client and that I happened to recognize it. "You know her?"

"We have a mutual acquaintance," I tell her. "It's just a coincidence. She won't be in the story, I promise."

"I'd appreciate that."

"It has nothing to do with this," I assure her. But I am also assuring myself. That Ron Hapgood's playmate's travel agent's sister was killed in the fusillade that also killed his wife, Amanda, is a coincidence. It can't be anything else. There can't be a meaning in it, some peculiar message—because Hapgood isn't even aware of it.

And it wouldn't mean anything if he were.

9

NOTHING of what Laura Bowers left behind spoke to me particularly, but that was probably my own fault or at least it was the result of my having known from other sources about her dishonesty and unhappiness and her abrupt death. It wasn't as though I had just come across these things in some rummage shop and suddenly my hand hesitated and accurate images flashed on the screen of my mind.

On the other hand, I have been trying to think of relics of wickedness and there aren't very many of them. In part, this may be because the world's religions tend to favor virtue over vice and are therefore likelier to give room in their sanctuaries to the trinkets of the good. But there are places to look besides churches.

There was some guy I read about, in Princeton, New Jersey, I think, who collected cars and paid a lot of money for Hitler's Mercedes. More, certainly, than he'd have paid if the car had belonged to some anonymous German whose claim of ignorance could not be officially disproved. So it happens. But most of those collectors of Nazi paraphernalia are really secret admirers, sadists who would join the party tomorrow if only there were an office to which they could send in their checks. Where sane people see loathsomeness, they see a kind of virtue. After all, what ordinary criminals leave behind, undistinguished muggers and rapists and even killers like Babcock, is of no interest to collectors. Nobody wants to hold on to whatever adheres or inheres . . .

I have a pair of undershorts I never wear anymore. They're perfectly good Brooks Brothers boxer shorts, white with lime green stripes, but I don't put them on. Neither do I throw them away. I remember that about a week before she was killed, Leah picked them up from the chair where I'd left them after I'd taken them off and she used them to dust some cobwebs from under the dresser. I got upset about it. My clothing! My underwear, which admittedly, I ought to have picked up and dropped in the hamper, as she was about to do. But she saw those cobwebs and figured that the shorts in her hand were going to the washing machine anyway, so why not use them?

It's stupid and it's trivial, but I remember the incident because I spoke sharply to her and I shouldn't have. And then she was killed and the incident froze like a bug in amber. Or maybe it was only that I never had the chance to apologize. But I have thought about the incident a lot.

For a long time, it made no sense to me. Why did I allow myself to get upset? What triggered that disproportionate reaction? I couldn't figure it out. And perhaps because it was such a mystery, I came back to it, thinking about it at night in those unstable moments between turning off the light and falling asleep. At first, all I could come up with was that the shorts were something I wore next to my body. This didn't make them holy or anything, but it was better than nothing at all. It seemed suggestive, if not important in itself. There was some intimacy that Leah had affronted, some piety she had violated. But I couldn't think what it was.

Then, one Saturday, when I was doing my laundry—or, actually, putting my clean clothes back, hanging up my shirts in the closet and folding my underwear and sticking it into the proper dresser drawers, I pulled the wrong drawer open, the pajama drawer, which was just below the underwear drawer. And that was the connection!

I had associated the undershorts with the pajamas I wore when I was a kid, pajamas that my mother used to iron for me.

Mothers did that kind of thing, back then. They didn't have Dacron, I guess, and with cotton the choice between ironed and non-ironed was fairly clear-cut. Good women ironed their husbands' underwear and pajamas, and bad women didn't.

Not that I thought Leah was a bad woman, but I missed my mother. I missed my childhood. I missed my stuffed duck. I missed the Eden we all remember or imagine. And I missed my ironed pajamas.

It isn't as if my mother's ironing of my pajamas, and my sheets for that matter, had ever been my idea. In Paradise, you don't have to ask. Good things just happen.

Madame Chiang, on the other hand, used to insist that her silk sheets be ironed every time she lay down for a ten-minute nap. Which she did at least once a day. I remember reading about that and being shocked by her extravagance. Not that the pilfering of huge sums of American money or the waste of hundreds of thousands of Chinese lives in a pointless war didn't matter. But those things didn't speak to me with the intimate authority of the ironing board.

What is it that we really look for in museums among those broken pottery shards and coins and buttons? The inherent value of the material or workmanship, or the testimony to a lost civilization, a vanished empire? And how much worse when it was an empire in which we were ourselves the nobility, or even the autocrats?

That figurine in the showcase is identified as either a doll or a sacred icon, but is there any difference?

Relics are all child's toys, which are holy things. Transitional objects, psychiatrists call them. They offer solace if not security and are reminders of a better time.

I will never wear those undershorts again, but neither will I throw them away. I shall just hold on to them for as long as I can, as if I were the curator of my own collection. To remember the pang of regret at my brief moment of unpleasantness— which I still feel, even though I have come to understand what may have prompted it—is in some small measure to have Leah still with me.

Stratton's poetry is not very good. It doesn't do much for me, anyway. It may be that I know too much, or that I'm coming at it asking the wrong questions. If I didn't know Stephanie, didn't have a sense that these fragile verses were supposed to bear the weight of both their hopes, somehow justifying and redeeming both their lives, I might come at them with a more receptive attitude. But knowing what I know, I keep wondering how people could delude themselves into thinking such piffle had any importance.

> The air smells like soft bananas, and the clouds
> are the empty bags we'll use for garbage. It's a heaven,
> only the raccoons can recognize . . .

I guess there's worse that gets published. On the other hand, I was halfway to hoping it would be unimpressive, in order to make Stephanie Stratton's investment of her life and her energy all the more impressive. Milton's daughter, sitting there and acting as his amanuensis, taking down *Paradise Lost* as he dictated it, was admirable, but the poem's obvious worth makes her effort and her sacrifice understandable. It would have been outrageous of her to have refused. Consider another less fortunate young woman, taking down altogether worthless drivel from some poetaster we've never heard of, maybe even knowing it was stupid and perhaps willfully blinding herself to that judgment, working just as hard as Miss Milton but for no other reasons than loyalty and love. She gets credit too, doesn't she? She ought to get more.

On the other hand, there are lines I can't help liking. Or anyway remembering, which may amount to almost the same thing. For several days, I've been thinking about the passage in which

> like spinsters, the apples in Heine's drawer
> gave up their essence, month by month, their dwindle
> happier because they believed the poet
> was writing of them, to them, love songs and odes.

Silly, of course, but that doesn't make it worthless. It is a habitual move of Stratton's to come at things from odd angles, to adopt points of view that may be weird but are at least original. The raccoons in that first passage or the apples in Heine's drawer in this one are tricky places for an intelligence to perch on, reminding me of certain shots in Hitchcock, but that doesn't mean they are mere tricks. Or cheap tricks. A trick that works is a good one.

It was not just to read Stratton's poems, though, that I borrowed the book. And not for the article, either. Hardly that.

It was so that I could return the book to Stephanie Stratton. So I could see her again.

Which is why I have not telephoned. I am doing what shy teenagers do, putting it off so as to leave the fantasy unmarred. But while the fantasies of young boys are usually very clear and direct, I cannot describe my own. It is not sexual, although there may be some of that in its genesis. The tone is one of comfort, of ease.

If I had told her more about Pam and Leah, if I had truly unburdened myself, for whatever reason or for no reason at all, I might not have to return, or at least I might not have it so much on my mind.

To exchange comfort of some kind, then? Or even just to find out whether such an exchange is in any way possible?

Something like that.

It is also true that for as long as I keep Stephanie Stratton as a member of my mental repertory company, she and Leah are equals. Almost friends.

Stephanie, however, is not a shade but, like me, a creature of the light.

Which I resent a little. For the first month or so after their deaths, I looked at people I passed in the street and asked myself why they should have been spared, what their special virtue might have been that had earned them a reprieve from what ought to have been general desolation and ruin. What I wanted was a landscape that looked like Hiroshima in those terrible photographs.

What I wanted was the end of the world.

And now? I am not so murderous in my fantasy life, but I haven't come all the way back. I have moments of what could pass for normal life, but then sharp pangs of guilt, as if I'd caught myself being disloyal to Leah.

As, of course, I will eventually be. Only those Hindu women who fling themselves onto their husbands' pyres can avoid it.

Felicity is not merely an abstraction, as I had supposed. I had expected her to be an embodied idea, like Faith and Hope and Charity.

They, too, though, were people, daughters of Wisdom (or Sophia) who suffered martyrdom during Hadrian's persecution of Christians. Faith was scourged and had boiling pitch poured on her, but somehow she didn't die. So they beheaded her. Hope and Charity were also beheaded when they emerged unscathed from a furnace. And Sophia, their mother, died three days later, of grief, praying at their graves. The names are of course suspicious, so that even the credulous hagiographers are alerted. I choose to believe that there were such sisters, that they were beheaded—although perhaps without the mannerist excesses of the old narratives—and that their mother actually died of grief. The names were supplied later, by some creative semioticist, but his embellishment doesn't erase their suffering or its message for those of us who are willing to pay attention to it, learning from it and grieving for it.

There are also at least two saints, both of them martyrs, named Felicity. The one I prefer is she whose feast day is the twenty-third of November, the mother of seven sons all of whom were also martyred in the reign of Antoninus Pius. Felix, Philip, Martial, Vitalis, Alexander, Silvanus, and Januarius were put to death on July 10 by four different Roman magistrates whose passing fancies that day may have differed technically but were identical in result. Alexander, Vitalis and Martial were beheaded; Januarius was scourged to death; Felix and Philip were dispatched with clubs; and Silvanus was drowned in the Tiber. Felicity herself was then beheaded.

There is some doubt about the story—not of the martyrdoms,

which were all real enough, but of the family connection among the victims, who may or may not have been related. That they were figurative brothers is clear, and this must have inevitably suggested to impassioned preachers the real brothers in II Maccabees, vii.

Also undermining our credence is the all but identical account of St. Symphorosa and her seven sons in another version of the same bloody story.

These disasters of whole families are popular, I guess.

Or the need for them is persistent. And it has become, if anything, more prevalent in these disastrous times.

But to those in need of such morose comfort, the point of both of the stories is clear enough. Felicity dies; Wisdom dies; and we envy them. We recognize that they are better off, that their pain, at last, is over. There can come a time when nothing is left but grief, a cavernous blackness of despair from which no escape is imaginable but that of death. And death then becomes a kind of felicity. Or even wisdom.

Release, at any rate.

In the morning, at the office, Mr. Harris brings me the fruit of his labors.

MOM STEALS

DAUGHTER'S

HUSBAND

I look at it, look at him, feel his gaze upon me. And bask in his worry, as Lansberg basks in mine. It is a dirty but irresistible pleasure. I take a blue pencil and use it as a pointer as I explain that "Daughter's" doesn't tell us anything new. If it weren't the daughter's husband, the woman would not have been identified as Mom.

"It ought to be more than a label. It ought to be the name of her closest relative. You want to pack the most emotion into the fewest words," I tell him. And I fiddle with it, showing him how to economize:

MOM STOLE

MY HUBBY

AWAY!

He isn't enthusiastic about the third line. Neither am I, for that matter. It's filler, mostly there to make the item into a three-liner. Still, the different use of "Mom" that I get by turning it into a first-person statement is effective. And "Hubby" works in its loathsome way to suggest the intimacy of the situation, its stifling domesticity. If we were staging it, the whole performance would be in flannel nightgowns and bathrobes, in a set dressed with unmade beds and full of laundry.

The shock of the piece is in its familiarity, its ordinariness.

"I see," he says, probably not seeing but smart enough to know what to say. He wants the job, after all. And if I give it to him, I may feel momentary twinges of regret whatever happens. If he makes good, it will be as a wreck of what he'd hoped to become. If he fails, that, too, will be a sad result.

I tell myself that, either way, it's none of my doing. This is his life and his destiny. I am the Malebranchian agent, obeying orders.

I should be more comfortable, though, if I were a little more certain about what the orders are.

"You are married?" I ask him. "You have children?"

"Married," he says, "and one child. A boy, four months old."

I tell myself that it makes no difference, even though I know it does. If there were just the two of them, the wife could work, supporting the clever husband's ambitions to be a writer. Maybe they did that for a while. But now, he is looking for work, any work. Even this.

"And what have you been working at until now? How have you been supporting yourselves?"

"I've been doing some freelance stuff," he tells me.

"Oh?"

He hesitates. I refuse to pump him. He'll either be forthcoming or not.

He senses that it's a game and understands that he can't win

96

it. "It's nothing much, but it pays. Direct-mail advertising. Those little flyers you get in the mailbox. A friend of my wife's folks does that, and she lets me have some of the smaller stuff to do when she gets swamped."

"You have any of it with you?" I ask.

He nods. He opens his portfolio and brings out a few brochures, which he hands me. One is for an invisible fence for pets. One is for inflatable guest beds that can be stored in the closet. One is for a metal detector with which you can turn your beach walks into treasure hunts and make money on weekends.

It isn't great literature, but neither is what we're offering him. I am reassured, professionally and morally, too. We are likely to get along. He will be able to stand it here as well as anyone else. As well as I do, for instance. "These are all right," I tell him. "I think we can work something out. Why don't you leave them with me. I'll show them to Mr. Lansberg. And you'll be hearing from him either way."

"That's terrific," he says. And it is, whichever way he means it.

"It's not a bed of roses," I warn him, knowing as I do how useless it is. Nothing I can say will be as loud as his little boy's needy squalling. Or his wife's silence. Or his parents' encouragement and his in-laws' restraint. Biology is destiny. Or destiny is destiny.

"Good luck," I tell him, thinking of Stratton's line about how the apples "gave up their essence, month by month . . ." He was writing of himself, of course.

"Thank you, sir," the young man says. Harris.

I guess I look old. Or maybe it's just Princeton. Or whatever prep school he went to and still goes back to in moments of excitement or stress. Where they called him Tweedy, no doubt.

"Nothing to thank me for," I tell him, but that small honesty doesn't relieve me any.

The fact that a line of Stratton's has stayed in my head and has resonated when the right note was sounded in the random jangling of the outside world doesn't guarantee that he was a good poet. But it does mean something, that on some modest level his poetry does what poetry is supposed to do. It's something.

And it is something I can report to Stephanie Stratton, something that will serve instead of a critical judgment.

Critical judgments are not what she wants anyway.

I can't imagine what she does want. Or what I want. Nevertheless, I watch my hand reach for the telephone.

10

THERE is a slip of paper on my desk, a note I made for myself and then tucked away and forgot about, with interesting information about the Cabalists' belief that each person has his own Torah. I think it was a line in some book review but I can't remember what the book was or who the reviewer was or even where the review appeared. So there is no way to go back to the source. There is simply this message that caught my eye and has managed to survive, detached from any context. I don't remember that it ever had much context, though. My recollection is that this was a piece of showboat erudition the reviewer had dragged in to dazzle his readers, or at least to try to keep them paying attention.

Or maybe it was meant for me, was put in there because it was irresistible, fated to happen just so that I could see it and cut it out.

The suggestion is tantalizing, though bizarre. It is lovely to suppose that Malebranche was not so original (or so deviant) a thinker. Or so lonely. He simply inclined toward faith and pietism—and found himself in the company of other believers, who apparently do not even have to be Christians. If every man has his own Torah, then every man has his own law, his own fate, and his own relationship with the Creator.

This is not a proposition easily susceptible of proof or dis-
proof. Rather, it is a fundamental assumption one is inclined
to make or laugh at. Or, under certain circumstances, it may
be a neurological condition, something like déjà vu, which is
not at all to deny its truth but only to suggest that peculiar
conditions may be required for us to notice its mechanisms.
Similarly, certain manifestations of the activity of the sun are
discernible only during eclipses, although presumably those
processes go on all the time.

I am thinking of my encounter with Stephanie Stratton. I
am considering not only what happened but how it seemed to
me—and to her, too, I rather think—that it was out of our
hands, that what we said to each other and even what we said
to ourselves was all but beside the point. There was a script
neither of us had written. Or, better, we were on a ride at Disney
World, with elephants charging and alligators surfacing and
monkeys gibbering from the treetops not because they felt like
doing those things but because our craft had passed a certain
point on the track and had triggered some impressive but simple mechanism, which was what caused the machinery to op-
erate. That is a part of the fun of those rides, the knowledge
that our glances, our mere presences, are bringing the dummies
to life.

We had that giddy feeling that each of us was the other's
machine.

When I made the call, it seemed to me impossible that Stephanie was unaware that I had borrowed her late husband's book
in the first place partly in order to be able to return it. I had
the sense that she was a knowing collaborator—as young girls
must be in those awkward passages in which they help stam-
mering boys get to the point and blurt out actual words of the
invitation to whatever hop or movie or party they both want
to go to together. But he has to mouth those words, and she
has to wait for him to do so, prompting him, encouraging him,
helping him in whatever way she can, but also knowing that,
eventually and however clumsily, it will happen. Because she

has determined what her answer will be, even before she has heard the question.

And as with the invitation, so, too, later on, with the gropings and clutchings in the darkness of the hallway.

Self-consciousness? Was it perhaps merely a reprise of that adolescent awkwardness? But supposing some tendency in that direction, some worry that I might have lost the knack after my years of domesticity, could it be that my heightened self-awareness was partly the source of my strange conviction that whatever was going to happen would happen, whether I helped it along or not? No matter what I said or failed to say, I couldn't bungle it. The events had a will of their own.

I told her I had photocopied the book and could drop it by.

"All right," she said, without much expression. I imagined her as wary. Or weary?

"I thought we might have dinner together," I said.

"All right," she said, in just the same way—dignifiedly submissive. Which I found rather attractive as a model for my own comportment.

I told her I'd appear around seven and she said she'd be there.

Christianity has a great many myths, marvelous to consider, about the condition of man before the Fall. I think it was St. Augustine who suggested that in the Garden of Eden erections were voluntary and that Adam could will his cock stiff. It is a lovely idea, revealing as it does the yearnings of an old rake either for potency or for purity and then conflating these categories. *Credo quia absurdum!*

Malebranche also brooded about the prelapsarian condition of mankind, and it was his suggestion that in the Garden human will was poised in a state of *equilibrio* between love for God and love of self and the will did not incline toward self any more than toward God. The Fall, Malebranche contends, actually consists of Adam's directing toward a lesser being a greater love than he had for God. God then contrived a means of overcoming this woeful imbalance by the sacrifice of his son. The Crucifixion in its awesomeness counterposes itself to the pleasures of the flesh, "preventing delectation," outweighing our concupiscence, and restoring to us in some measure the prelapsarian integrity of our love of God and love of self.

It is not perfect, or at least not by Augustine's hard test. But neither is it altogether nonsense. Any death, any awe, will act as a counterbalance to lust.

Indeed, the connection between sex and death as parts of the same process of renewal of the species ought to be reflected in these elaborate systems, which are, after all, the productions of deep thought and delicate intuitions.

"Physical pleasure is the Weight of the Soul," he writes. He has Pleasure weighing it down even as Grace buoys it up.

It is not nuts. Backward, maybe. I'd be inclined to say that the burden of our losses weighs us down while the prospect of physical pleasure raises us up. But what do I know?

The result, though, is much the same. Malebranche's description of the human condition and my own both take note of the wavering we feel, our alternations between euphoria and melancholy, and the exquisite contrariety of our impulses.

And never mind our reason and our will: what we do seems to come from somewhere beyond these impulses.

At Stephanie's house, I hand her the book. She takes it, holds it for a moment, and then puts it down on the nearest table.

"They stick in the mind," I say. It is what I had settled on and the best I can do as long as I am unwilling to depart from the truth.

She shrugs. "I can't look at them now," she announces. "Maybe someday, but not now."

"That's reasonable."

"It isn't that they're too familiar or that they bring him back. It's the opposite—that so many of them are strange to me. I should have paid more attention." She adjusts her weight, leaning on one hip and crossing her left foot behind the right. "Or less," she says, and flashes a rueful smile.

She can still make jokes. I admire that. It was probably one of the things Stratton liked about her.

"The piece will run next week," I tell her. "It mentions the book."

She nods. "You want a drink?" she asks. "I've got gin and vodka. But I don't know about the tonic. It's probably flat. The bottle has been there for a long time. There may be some scotch."

"Gin and ice would be fine," I tell her.

She nods and goes to a glass-topped cart where the bottles and glasses are arrayed. I am convinced by the way she looks at the labels that these were Stratton's fetish and not hers. She pours a little gin into a glass and takes it into the kitchen to get some ice cubes. Stratton would have had the ice in the bucket. Or would have insisted that she have it ready for him.

It is possible that I am quite wrong in these guesses, but I can't ask because I don't want to know if I'm right. It's too oppressively intimate. Meanwhile, she is registering the information about my preference in booze, has already saved it to disc. I am tempted to ask about this, too. What is the risk, after all? I have the weird idea that it would be interesting to be as clumsy and gauche as possible, just to find out if I can disturb the ponderous inevitability of our conjunction.

But there is no way to make the experiment without appearing ridiculous, and we are not yet intimate enough for me to feel comfortable about that. So I say nothing as I accept the drink she hands me. She is having a glass of white wine. We raise our glasses in a silent toast to each other and the occasion and we take the first sips.

She asks me about the other victims. "Have you learned anything interesting?"

I shrug. "Interesting to the world? Or the paper? Or me?"

"Either. Any of those."

I tell her about the difference between good and bad relics. Or at least the possibility that my experience with Felicity Bowers has suggested. "Of course, what we know and feel and the questions we bring to these things have got to influence the way they speak to us. But even allowing for that . . . "

"You could try it out, I imagine. You could go to the property clerk at the police station and see how you respond to the objects they've picked up from the victims and those they've taken from the criminals. I doubt that you'd be able to tell much difference."

"Maybe not. But there's something in it. Why else would people spend all that money on writers' manuscripts and composers' autograph scores? Even if all the words and all the notes are exactly what we've got in the printed editions, there's something spooky about the piece of paper the man held in his hand and sweated over. Is that just nonsense?"

She smiles. "Maybe. A lot of what serious people do is nonsense, isn't it? Large sums of money don't make it any the less nonsensical." She rubs the side of her nose with the side of her index finger. It is something she has done for years, since she was a girl. I notice it because I had seen those crow's feet around her eyes when she smiled—and felt disloyal for having done so. It is something of a relief, then, to seize upon this unconscious gesture that remains, unlined and undiminished, from her careless youth.

"Anyway," I say, "the sister had embezzled money from the business, and all she left that was in any way interesting was a set of photographs she had kept of her husband and some other woman. Maybe it wasn't complicated enough for me. Maybe it was just too clear and too loud for me to pick up anything else that might have been there."

"Or it could have been that that's what her life really was," Stephanie says. "You were unhappy because it was trite, but people do trite things and live trite lives, most of the time."

"You mean doing daily things? Having dinner?" I ask, flirting with the idea of expressing the weird ideas that have been flittering about in my head. "Is dinner trite? Is this?"

"Predictable," she says, cocking her head to one side.

It is true, then. Or, at the least, if I'm crazy, I have company. She senses it too.

So that, true or not, reasonable or not, the mood is likely to affect the outcome. As any market strategist will be all too happy to explain to you.

"How about a nice predictable steak, then?" I ask.

"Sure," she says.

We go to dinner. We have a bottle of wine along with our steak—a Chateaubriand we can share, each of us relieved to discover that the other likes rare beef. (And this, and this? And do you like this? And how is that?)

Necessarily. Inevitably. And no dessert but a brandy with coffee. And then back to her place for what she calls "another brandy" although both of us now are perfectly well aware that those glasses will never be drained. We can already see them, the amber unnaturally bright in a sunlight that is, for them, unreal, waiting where we left them on the coffee table in the living room for her to find them tomorrow morning, when she will emerge from the bedroom. . . .

Each of us realizes that there is a farewell we are enacting here as much as a greeting. And neither of us wants to intrude too much on the other's emotions. The sensations are pleasant and reliable, but they are the ground for other melodies, as elaborate as they are private.

Indeed, there comes a certain point when I must decide whether to allow myself to drift off to sleep or else get up, get dressed, and get back into my car to drive home. Which is what I decide to do.

To let her sort things out. To do a little sorting, myself.

In pornography, there is a conjunction of the parts which takes over, so that character is overcome by the rhythms of sexuality and is reduced to, and even temporarily replaced by, the escutcheons of gender. A violation of good taste and of the highminded principles of art? Yes, probably. But that doesn't mean it is any the less true. Indeed, the insistent autonomy of sex is something that embarrasses us long after we have become accustomed to the other awkwardnesses of the act. That our individualities should be obliterated, that we should turn into less and less recognizable caricatures of ourselves, more and more resembling the figures on Pompeian brothel walls or Hindu temple bas reliefs, is an affront to our notions of the importance of our uniqueness.

It is the banality, the inevitability, of the routine that weighs upon us. Malebranche and his distant relative, the Marquis de Sade, shame us with our psychic nakedness. That all is fore-ordained should make us humble, as Malebranche intends. Or, on the verso of the same coin, contemptible, as Sade believes. Our pretensions, our airs, all the notions we have of civility are false, hypocritical, and foolish. At table, the fancy crystal and silver and china cannot disguise our wolfishness. And similarly in the bedroom—or on the living-room floor or on the billiard table or on the bouncing seat of Madame Bovary's coach or out in the straw of the cow barn—the mother-of-pearl buttons and the velvets and linens and silks only underscore the crudity of our ruttings.

The worshipers of Aphrodite understood this. Respectable men and women put aside their illusions with their togas to couple in the courtyard of the temple, not merely satyrs and whores but enthusiasts. Votaries. Transported beyond them-selves, they aspired at least temporarily to a different plane of reality—whether higher or lower is beside the point—and ap-proximated a condition some Christians might call saintly.

Perfectly ordinary people, but they could be touched by these extraordinary moments they took to be evidence of some sort of divine intercession.

Absurd perhaps, but as I drove south on the skyway, gliding under the stars of a subtropical sky, it seemed plausible enough.

11

LANSBERG hated the Bowers piece.

It wouldn't have been so bad if he'd simply killed it. Or killed the series. Either of those would have been fine with me. But the series continues. He has taken it away from me and turned it over to Tweedy Harris. At least in part in order to humiliate me. And maybe to make Harris feel uncomfortable, to demonstrate to the newcomer right away that his loyalty should be not to me but to him.

Or, more accurately, that loyalty has nothing to do with one's work here. Cosgrove could fire Lansberg, after all. He could replace Lansberg with a baboon or an orangutan, put a green eyeshade on it, stick a pencil behind its ear, and let it run the paper.

And Harris would have to be loyal to that, too. Either that or go back to his direct-mail "freelancing."

But never mind Harris. What would I do? I don't have a lot of other options, myself. And even if there were other choices, I wouldn't have the nerve to pursue them. I'm afraid I'd salute Cosgrove's monkey, say, "Yes, sir," and even sing a chorus or two of "Abba-dabba-dabba." If I made muster, I'd carry on with business as usual, performing such literary exercises as

David Slavitt

SPACE ALIEN

BODIES FOUND

ON MT. EVEREST

It is natural that they should be on Everest, isn't it? The highest mountain? The place they're likeliest to land on in their starships? Never on K2, even though that was for a while thought to be a few feet higher than Everest.

It must be crowded as hell up there on Everest's peak. It is, if one believes our reports. The spirit rebels against gravity's drag and our imaginations soar to higher and higher ground, rarer and rarer air. That the range of what we imagine up there is so restricted and banal is not surprising but only sad.

I can already imagine how in the next week's issue, I'd be doing an update:

LITTLE GREEN

CORPSES MANGLED

BY BIGFOOT

It is tempting to put the expression of such a concern into the mouth of some plausible malcontent, an envious neighbor from Bhutan, perhaps. Why should the Tibetans have a higher mountain than Bhutan or Sikkim? Some unnamed Bhutanese trade representative, perhaps. Why not? If there are rumors, someone must be spreading them. Our more respectable brethren in journalism have taught us that lesson from their safaris on the campaign trail.

It would certainly be difficult to prove that no trade representative from that desperately poor Himalayan country has ever betrayed this particular apprehension. The majesty of the majuscules need not blind us. Our witness could also be described as a simple salesman of whatever products the Bhutanese economy is attempting to promote around the world—ghee, perhaps. Or cardamon, or lac.

Or those odd brown conical hats they wear in Thimphu, the capital city.

Having wasted much of the morning with such woolgathering, I bat out the piece on the space aliens on Everest, which is, alas, real. The piece is, I mean. I'm somewhat less confident about the aliens. And I invite Harris to lunch, to let him know I bear him no ill will. Or at least to keep him wondering. I am not delighted by his taking over the series on relics. And that is worrisome. Lansberg may be right about my having become too much involved with it. If I am starting to take these pieces seriously, it may be proper and right for me to return to pure foolishness. Which I can do. It isn't much of an accomplishment, but it isn't absolutely negligible, either.

You believed me about the hats, didn't you?

Lunch was a mistake. It isn't that Harris is such a terrible guy. Quite the reverse! I rather like him and feel some degree of empathy. The poor bastard!

But why should I feel sorrier about his having to work here than I do about myself? He is younger, but that shouldn't matter. Young people have to do disagreeable things. I hired him, but that shouldn't matter either—I didn't go out with a net and catch him. He volunteered. He wanted it, was eager for it! He is responsible for his own life!

I am not. And yet, I feel odd twinges. As, perhaps, Lansberg feels for us all—assuming that there are any feelings left in that wreck, that former person. In a reasonable universe, he'd be condemned as dangerous, no longer fit for human habitation, and would be demolished, like an out-of-fashion hotel that declines to a repository for retired people, then to a welfare hotel, then to an abandoned building where derelicts go and and where Cubans and Colombians trip over them in drug deals. So the drug dealers do the efficient and humane thing and set the derelicts on fire. And society reacts reasonably and humanely, by knocking down the building.

Architectural bleeding hearts show up to take photographs and to protest about the destruction of an art nouveau treasure.

And I make fun of them.

I used to make fun of Leah for believing in them, agreeing and even on occasion marching with them.

I could get a placard that says

SAVE LANSBERG:

AN ART NOUVEAU TREASURE

but he might not appreciate being so well understood and I'd be out on my ear.

And would Harris be troubled by my departure? I rather doubt it. A pang, maybe, but he'd ride it through. As I plan to ride through my little pang on his behalf.

At lunch, I ask him, as a favor, to do Kezemi next, instead of going back to talk to Felicity Bowers. Eventually, he may have to do that, but, as he can perfectly well understand, it is a bit embarrassing for me. For him to go and tell her that he needs to look at her sister's things because what I did was incompetent is a bit awkward for both of us, really. He can see that, can't he?

He sees, and after lunch I give him the file I have assembled to prepare myself for the Kezemi segment.

I had not intended to do this. It is not really in my interest. We are not friends, as I keep reminding myself. I can't even decide what I think of him, whether I like him or feel contempt or pity. As if it made any difference. My mind wanders from the subject of our conversation to his shirt, to which I am rather attracted. It speaks to me, not because it is such a great shirt but because it isn't. There is a place at the tip of the collar where the threads are beginning to fray. And I can see that one of the buttons at the cuff has been replaced amateurishly. His wife is a klutz? Or a woman of principle who insists that he should take care of his own clothing? Or perhaps she was quite willing to do it but exhausted, having been up all night with a colicky infant. So Tweedy tried it himself—hell, how difficult is it to sew on a button?—but he didn't do much of a job. The threads do not follow any particular pattern as they go from one hole to another. I find myself supposing that the shirt is evidence of how long poor Harris has been out of work, how thin the family reserves have become. For far too long, he hasn't been able to buy himself new shirts. How can I be less than helpful to anyone wearing such a garment?

It is not a reason, say, but an impulse that is irrational but nonetheless irresistible. Perhaps all I am saying is that it is somehow my destiny to behave this way. Or at least to co-operate with whatever is going on in Lansberg's mind and perhaps in God's, as well. I am also curious to see what Harris will make of this peculiar material.

What I give him is a slender sheaf of pages I have photocopied at the university library, pages I have found that he may or may not find helpful and that may only raise doubts in his mind about my mental condition. The subject of my research is the Sufi doctrine of *erfan*, which is "mystical knowledge of the true world" and is attainable through a number of curious routes. The one I like best is the constant repetition of prayers, all night long, which probably works, if only because of sleep deprivation.

Just before you pass out or go mad, you get a glimpse of something that looks to be real. Or you lose the ability to tell the difference between reality and neurological static.

The passages I have highlighted—for myself, I had thought—resemble or even confirm, if you will, the findings of other mystics and pietists: "There is no might and no power except in God."

Malebranche would have nodded and said, *"Bien sûr!"*

Or: "The basis of *erfan* is that you should see every person as a sign of God." Which is Malebranchian but also Kantian.

In this event, it is perhaps not quite so crazy as Harris may think to consider the mullah's recommendations: "Perform the nighttime prayers. Every time you prostrate yourself, remain prostrate until you have asked God for the spiritual qualities you want. Don't sleep after midnight on Thursday nights. For forty days, say to yourself continually, 'O He, O he who is He, O he who is naught but He!' "

Forty days of that, and you're ready for the funny farm, right?
The world is a funny farm.
"Watch, watch," say the Sufis. "You will see the light."

I have been watching Harris read this material. Even from across the room, I can tell that he is clearly worried. He cannot decide whether I am pulling his leg or am insane. What would any of this have to do with the Kezemi piece? Nowhere is it established that Hafiz Kezemi was a Sufi, or even a particularly devout Moslem. After all, he fled Teheran, didn't he? He was no ordinary towel-head, marching in the streets, chanting, clenching his fist, obeying the Ayatollah, and eager to die for Islam. He came here to be safe from all that craziness, to get an education, to better himself and to learn how to do useful things for his country if any reasonable state of order and calm is ever achieved there.

Still, the likelihood is that he was at least knowledgeable about these practices. They float in the air in Teheran. They are the air.

Harris may also be worried that I am trying to sabotage his work. He is perhaps convinced that I am trying to get him to turn in a learned essay about Kezemi's religious beliefs, as the only appropriate context for the irony of his fate—the flight from Teheran's madness was not to safety but only to a different kind of lunacy, after all.

Well, I suppose I am saying that. I am saying at least that he should have such an essay in his mind when he comes to write the simpler ABC prose of our version. The other knowledge will illuminate, will somehow suffuse his piece.

Do I seriously believe this? No, not really.

But I want to.

Evidently, such repetitions are practiced not just by Sufis or Shiites but by all Moslems. The great-grandson of the Prophet, the fourth Imam, is said to have taken time in his prayers to cry "Forgiveness" three hundred times.

In just such a way, Catholics perform novenas and say their rosaries. As penance.

Still crazy, but at least Western, right?

The idea, either way, is the same—that with each repetition, the words become more meaningful, as if their external coating were being worn away, as if the teeth and the tongue were polishing them from unimpressive pebbles to glittering jewels. The same word or the same phrase, over and over, takes on a shimmer, seems more and more true, seems, at last, the only truth.

O He, O he who is He, O he who is naught but He!

Try that for ten minutes.

I have.

Better yet, Harris is convinced that I am a nut case. And his worried look is one of concern not only for me but for himself, too. He worries lest this new chapter in his life's story turn out to be even grimmer than the previous one. His descriptions of fake mantel clocks (the pendulum is driven by a battery and is purely decorative) or commemorative plates of great episodes of *The Honeymooners* weren't so bad after all. At least they were short. And there was the fun of writing to space, which requires a certain dexterity and offers a physical satisfaction.

Before, all he had to fret about were greed and vulgarity. Here, he is looking more directly into the heart of the beast, its credulities, its stupidities.

To do that for any length of time is to put one's own sanity at risk.

He looks across the room and sees that I am looking at him. He manufactures a grin and waves. As one might wave to a mental patient.

Maliciously, conspiratorially, I grin and wave back.

Why am I playing with him this way? Perhaps for his own good. Perhaps for my own amusement. Or both.

What's really amusing is that there has to be a way to make the readers care for Kezemi, that to counter a predictable anti-Iranian bias, there will have to be some kind of razzle-dazzle, and that Sufi mysticism is as likely a way to accomplish this as anything else. It's all I've been able to come up with, at any rate.

Mentally, I send him a message: *Watch, watch! You will see the light.* And I wave again, to worry him a little more.

At home that same evening, I realize how absurd I've been. Harris is not the problem. I am the problem.

I have to ask myself what I'm doing there in that hateful office, why I continue to put up with Lansberg and Cosgrove and the wretched public that may or may not be mere figments of their imaginations. I used to be able to tell myself that I was doing it for Leah and for Pam. I used to perform a less interesting and less profitable version of Lansberg's own trick, turning to my family to justify my actions.

Now my excuses are gone. I have to earn a living, of course, but that isn't difficult. I could certainly find something less distasteful to do. I am reasonably fit in mind and body, could find some innocuous and rather boring task to perform. Perhaps Harris's old job, writing the envelope stuffers for direct-mail advertisers?

I could give up the apartment, take a position as a tour guide, and escort blue-haired ladies through Europe, making sure their baggage was all accounted for and that they were all on the bus. I saw an ad for such a job in the paper last Sunday. It is a dreadful job, rather menial and requiring a lot more patience and charm than I can offer, but there are pleasant aspects of it. To live nowhere, to carry only a few necessaries in a suitcase, and to float aimlessly at the whim of others.

Malebranche says that whether we know it or not, this is the human condition.

Hoo hee! O hee who is haw!

It has crossed my mind to call Stephanie, but it also crosses my mind that that may not be so great an idea. Neither of us is ready, neither of us is balanced enough for this kind of thing.

Each of us is too easy a mark, too vulnerable.

So I don't call. I do a crossword puzzle instead. But I am aware that I imagine her watching me do it, praising me as I fill in the blanks of what is not so easy a puzzle.

I used to imagine Leah watching me do puzzles. In the real world, it never happened.

12

HARRIS is clutching while I am letting go. That, I think, is the main difference between us. But from that first distinction, others arise. I am easily distracted while Harris keeps his eye on the task before him. His dedication would be, in most jobs, advantageous, just the thing to guarantee success—or at least the favorable notice of his superiors. But here, one can miss the point by trying too assiduously to stick to it.

His first effort on the Kezemi piece reads like a bill of lading a moving van company might have prepared, or a laundry list. It enumerates the books and articles of clothing left by the deceased. The titles are not illuminating. Most of them are predictable engineering texts and related schoolbooks, including *The Random House Handbook*. (Is it possible that Kezemi was in one of Stratton's composition classes?) There is a Koran, but that's hardly surprising.

And the clothing?

- Socks, black, twelve pairs.
- Shirts, white dress, twelve.
- Undershorts, boxer, fourteen.
- Pants, khaki, three pair.
- Sport jackets, two.
- Sneakers, one pair.

· Shoes, one pair.
· Neckties, two.

What are we to make of all this? I see only the rhythm of
his visits to the laundry and the dry cleaner. A repetition that
seems sad now that it has been so arbitrarily interrupted. Perhaps a bit finical and fussy? One might see it that way too.

But Harris does not see it any way at all, he does not close
his eyes in order to see better, will not allow these mute objects
to talk to him. He is trying too hard. And I can't correct him
because he doesn't trust me.

Woolgathering is sometimes the path to virtue.

Sufi actually means "wearer of wool," because of the hair-
shirt asceticism of some of the founders of that movement.

One must gather the wool before one can put it on.

I wonder, for instance, how exhaustive the list may be. Is
this all there was? If that is the case, then there is another kind
of pathos, isn't there? Whichever way we imagine his background, as a son of one of the fat-cat families that prospered
under the Shah, or as a member of the more modest middle
class, he was still living a Spartan existence. He worked, on
weekends, as a counterman at a fast-food restaurant. It was not
a life of excess or ease.

"What do you think?" Harris asks me.

"Fine," I tell him. "Just fine."

What else can I say—that I like his dingbats, or whatever
you call those dots before the items? They do look official.

"How are you going to do it?" I ask him. "What's your angle?"

"I don't know."

"Well, there's a Koran. You could use that stuff I gave you."

"I don't know," he says.

"All right, then think of something better. Or something else
that's as good."

He shrugs and walks back to his desk.

It is terrible to look across the room and watch him think.
He does not see it. He sees it only as a problem in journalism,
in pleasing Lansberg. Those are perfectly reasonable considerations, but they ought not blind him to the sadness of the

story, its outrageousness, its truth—that the poor son of a bitch fled to safety here. That he lived modestly and worked hard, and that one of the bullets John Babcock sprayed out over the parking lot happened to find him. St. Maruthas, who is patron of Persia, did not protect him. Nor did Anthony of Padua, or Christopher, or Gertrude of Nivelles, or Julian the Hospitaler, or Nicholas of Myra, or Raphael, or Caspar, or Melchior, or Balthasar, all of whom watch over travelers. Nor did Catherine of Alexandria and Thomas Aquinas, who look after students.

Not even Lawrence and Martha, who pay special attention to cooks, which is what he was on the weekend.

Perhaps they weep for him, plead for him, offer their intercessions only now.

Still, it seems to me all the harder to bear, knowing how many could have helped, had he only known how to ask.

Late at night, I drive again, but not on my usual route. I am reluctant—or too eager—to pass so close to where Stephanie lives. I am afraid I will not be able to resist the impulse I can already feel to turn off the expressway, a physical tug as if the wheels were out of alignment. So I go, instead, to the beach where I can walk along the water's edge. There is a somewhat sinister beauty as the moonlight shimmers on the water and I worry about drug dealers and the other less professional criminals, not to mention the vagrants and bums, any of whom could materialize from the bluish velvet shadows to assault or even kill me.

The silvery light on the black water is all the more fascinating because of the element of danger—poison floating on poison. I am more alert, certainly, and my senses are keener. So I take it in. It takes me in.

"Watch, watch. You will see the light." And there it is, a swath of inviting glitter, an almost garish niello that is only waiting for a postcard photographer to come along and take a picture of it. The clarity is such that I can imagine myself getting undressed and wading out there. I can see myself, weightless, walking on that crust of light and not submerging, not drowning. I can feel the oiliness of the light on the water's surface.

At length, I get back to my car and drive away. I feel again that tug of the wheel, even though it is too late now to stop off at Stephanie's. But to pass by?

Silly. I resist. But the impulse was there, whether I acted upon it or not. Either way, it's a little scary.

What Harris and I agree to is mutually comfortable. We will assume for the moment that neither his competence nor my own is in question. We will at least temporarily suppose that it was Kezemi's fault, that his life was somehow intractable, too melodramatic and absurd even for the expectations of Lansberg and our readers. The difficulties we have both experienced with that segment of a presumably successful series are most conveniently explained if we make this attribution. And we will make amends to each other by joining to attempt to deal with the story of Ambrosio Martínez.

What neither of us says aloud—it doesn't need to be stated explicitly—is that we have each other's company should this attempt also prove to be a failure. In union there is strength. Or, less heroically, small fish swim in schools—to confuse predators.

Let Lansberg wonder whether the series ought to be discontinued. Let him terminate it rather than one of us. Or both of us together.

Do I care that much? No, but out of habit, I come to work every day, not so much afraid of losing the job as I am of what would become of me without it. I'd lie there in the bedroom and watch the dust puppies grow into dust ponies, dust oxen, dust hippos.

Dust tyrannosaurs.

Meanwhile, in a spirit of uselessness and subversive irrelevance, I have looked up St. Ambrose to see what sort of fellow he was.

An *homme d'affaires*. A man of thought and action who, as

bishop of Milan, exercised a very considerable degree of influence over Theodosius, fighting for the church against secular authority of the emperor, against paganism, against Arianism. And against Jews, too.

When Theodosius ordered the bishop of Kallinikum, in Mesopotamia, to rebuild a synagogue that the Christians there had destroyed, Ambrose denounced the order, preaching against it from his pulpit, and Theodosius backed down, rescinding it.

I wouldn't have liked him.

He wouldn't have liked me.

The four great Latin doctors of the church are Ambrose, Augustine, Jerome, and Gregory the Great. Stick busts of them up on the walls of your room. Put them in the centers, with Catherine, Margaret, Agnes, and Barbara at the corners.

And let them all glower down in the power of their pain and anger.

We drive by. It isn't shrewdness or even caution. We are trying to confirm the address the newspapers gave. Martínez isn't listed in the telephone directory. But then people like him aren't usually listed. The probability is that he was either a revolutionary or—more likely—a counterrevolutionary. Or a drug dealer. But either way, the only people he wanted to hear from were those to whom he had given his number.

The house looks right. We can see very little of it—mostly a wall, with bits of broken glass set along the top. And television cameras mounted on large creosoted poles. There are, presumably, other security devices, alarms, man-traps, claymore mines, and only the devil knows what else. He seems to have been involved in something more menacing than bananas or coffee beans.

Tweedy is impressed. His name is William, but I have rejected that. It tries too hard, as vests would, or sideburns, and doesn't quite fit. I prefer Tweedy, which I can't use. As an unsatisfactory compromise, I just fall back on "Harris" as a vocative of direct address—which is also rather preppy.

I am impressed too, for the implication of such defenses is

of some equivalent menace. But there was no way to defend against a Babcock whose free-floating threat was altogether unpredictable and irrational. And who may, in this particular instance, have performed a public service.

Security analysts down here in Glade County are not necessarily employees of brokerage houses. Instead of those conservatively dressed fellows with slender attaché cases, they can be gruffer sorts in fatigues who come in to look at defensive perimeters and gauge fields of fire. But they too deal in probabilities and like most of the rest of the world rely on cause and effect. Their walls and television cameras and electronic sensors and alarms were of no use in protecting Martínez or in predicting what only a Malebranche could have allowed for.

There was no earthly reason to worry about a John Babcock. Because there are no earthly reasons.

I park the car. I grab a copy of the paper.

"What are you going to do?" Harris asks.

"I am going to try to sell them a subscription to our paper."

"That's crazy."

"Can you think of anything better?" I ask.

He shakes his head. "But you don't look right. Kids do that stuff."

"Who can say what madness awaits in Lansberg's brain? Or Cosgrove's? Who can be certain that they are not even now discussing how the writers should stay in closer touch with readers? By the time we get back to the office, there may be memos waiting for us that will instruct us to do exactly this humiliating task, for the purification of our souls or at least the deflation of our egos. It is only too plausible. The people in that house don't even know Lansberg, do they? All they have to go by is my conviction that it's the truth. And, as you see, I'm well enough convinced."

"What do I do? Just sit here?"

"If you please. If this doesn't work, you are our only other shot. Besides, you can sit behind the wheel and keep the engine running—in case we need to make a departure of unseemly abruptness. You do drive, don't you?"

"Oh, yes."

"Good. Very good."

I get out of the car and approach the front gate. There is a speaker affixed to the concrete gate post. And, from inside the compound—one can call it nothing less—a television camera focused on the gateway. I am not hopeful as I press the button that sounds some bell or buzzer or flashes a light on a panel somewhere.

A "Yah?" comes squawking from the speaker. It is impossible to determine the sex of my interlocutor. From the timbre of the voice I hear, the individual can't be more than two feet high and may be made of metal.

"Is the lady of the house at home?"

"Who're you?" The metal is tinny and dull.

"I have a free sample issue of a newpaper for you," I say. "We're having a circulation drive. Absolutely no obligation."

"Stick it though the gate." It strikes me that there is a distortion device built into the system. It isn't low quality at all but a deliberately contrived effect.

"I have to hand it to you. It's a rule they have."

"Too bad."

"If you could just come to the gate . . ."

"Get lost, or I'll call the cops."

"Excuse me?"

"Or would you like me to blow your fucking head off?"

That seems clear enough.

I go back to the car and tell Harris to drive on up to the next house. For one thing, that's what a canvasser would do. For another, they may be able to tell us something.

The security arrangements here are not so formidable. There is no television camera, at any rate. And one can see through the hurricane fence. A rainbird twirls, scattering diamonds in the sunlight—watering the lawn, of course, but also discouraging casual intruders who would rather not get themselves soaked.

I try the gate and it opens. I call out a "Hello?" to see whether large dogs will come bounding across the lawn, but nothing happens. I pick a route that will subject me to the least possible sprinkling and get to an inner barricade, a construction of redwood slats heavy enough to keep out unwelcome visitors. There is a speaker arrangement on this inner doorway. I press the button and go through the same routine as before. This time I manage to strike up a conversation with a woman who is almost certainly the maid and eventually I succeed in persuading her to come out to let me give her my free gift issue of our paper.

She is a coffee-colored Caribbean woman with one of those lovely British accents, and she is worried about taking advantage of me because she isn't planning to subscribe to our paper. I reassure her and tell her how much less trouble this is than I had next door, where they threatened me. I ask her about those people. She tells me what I am eager to know—that they are very private, very much keeping to themselves. And they have gamecocks. The police are watching them and the SPCA. Big cockfights out in the glades. Who knows what goes on. But those roosters crow all the night long, which is a nuisance. One can understand it. The glow of the city, you see. It always seems to them to be daybreak. This doesn't make it any the easier to sleep.

I ask if there are other illegal activities they might be involved with.

"Only the Lord knows," she says, "or the devil!"

I thank her for her time and I tell her, quite honestly, that it has been a pleasure. Her accent is so pleasant and musical. She thanks me. She is from Tortola, she says, and she misses it. She hasn't been home now for seven months.

Back in the car, I report to Harris that we now have as good a warrant as we're likely to get to write whatever we please. Señor Martínez was engaged in cockfighting, all manner of illegal activities, drugs, munitions, and the devil knows what else. Maybe even devil worship. (Why in hell not?)

What I don't tell Harris is that it's thanks to our old pal Jack Babcock that Martínez is no longer around to trouble decent citizens and profit from the weaknesses and failings of the rest.

Do I believe that? Do I believe anything?
Not enough to help.

We agree that he will take the first stab at the Martínez installment, give it to me, and let me fiddle with it before we try it on Lansberg.

13

THE series is dead. (Shall we go together, Harris and I, to inspect its relics and do a piece about what they suggest to us?)

Harris and I have shares in the failure, which was a part of my scheme. I figure that it was a third his, a third mine, and a third Lansberg's—for, after all, I'd been trying to get out of it and was only persisting at his insistence. I am working on another piece, part of an ongoing series that has not been identified as such but that is nonetheless connected with pieces we've done before and will, no doubt, do again.

SEVEN-YEAR-OLD

IMPREGNATES FOUR

BABY-SITTERS

Or so it is alleged. My suspicion always is that the baby-sitter's other playmate was the father, who, on the way home, took advantage. But that makes for much less spectacular copy. If the seven-year-old was the actual impregnator, then we have a prodigy, as in chess or violin playing, but in an arena (or art form?) that is better established in the public imagination. A freak of nature—which is an expression of divine will. Is Don Giovanni reborn in the person of a Roslyn, Long Island, adolescent? Has Giacomo Casanova come back as a Terre Haute, Indiana, third-grader? How else could the cunning little dickens have persuaded all four of his sixteen-year-old sitters to be so obliging?

One baby-sitter is, conceivably, a slut. But all four of them? The odds are very long against it. So there had to be some knack, some gift of gab or physical charm the kid must have exercised. He is the seducer every one of us fears (or hopes for), incarnate in the most unlikely envelope of barely adequate flesh.

Or maybe we just like to root for the underdog?

Even as he, the overdog, ruts.

Harris is very cold. I think he thinks I've sabotaged him somehow. It would not have been so terrible an idea, but it didn't occur to me. It was not in my mind to do anything of that kind. And therefore I resent the imputation.

But let him think whatever he likes. We shall not be working together again very often. He will sink or swim on his own. Conforming to his destiny.

That's one of the best parts of Malebranche: he may not be an antidote to melancholy but he gets rid of a lot of paranoia. It may be the case that I have enemies, that Harris hates me, that Lansberg is out to get me—but it doesn't matter. If it weren't they, it would be another bunch, just as irksome, just as unattractive. It's my destiny that I'm worrying about, not theirs. They are mere agents, the bit players in my biography. They aren't worth hating.

It is a serene philosophy. It enables me to smile benignly— and to make them even more nervous and suspicious.

The Springers will remain a mystery. I have no business with them now. I have only my own curiosity, which is hardly an excuse for intruding into their shattered lives.

But then, why is Lansberg's curiosity any more an excuse than my own? Or Cosgrove's? Or that of all of our readers put together?

We are not exposing political corruption or doing whatever

it is that a free press was supposed to do in a democracy to ensure the liberty of the people. That was what the founding fathers supposed we would do, but they were wrong. We play instead to the worst superstitions and prejudices of our readers and try to arouse (on the cover) and satisfy (on the inside pages) their idle curiosity. We do in a calculated way what the seven-year-old kid discovered he had a knack for and was able to do spontaneously. But we're fucking with millions of people of all ages, sexes, and conditions, not just four baby-sitters.

Why is the press pass any kind of excuse to bother these poor people, who must still be in shock? We aren't used to losing children these days. It was expected, more or less, in earlier generations—when I was a young child but still, in my lifetime—before there were antibiotics and fancy feats of transplant surgery. Infant mortality used to be commonplace with diphtheria and whooping cough and such diseases carrying off children in large numbers. It was sad, of course, but not incomprehensible, not unimaginable certainly. People accepted it as a part of life, as fate.

And now? One still reads of the deaths of children in freak accidents in playgrounds or, as here, in parking lots where maniacs are spraying bullets all the hell over. But it's news now. It didn't used to be.

Which makes the Springers feel better or worse?

Which makes me feel better or worse?

The terrible thing I can just barely admit to myself is that I am tempted to go and talk to them anyway, to find out how they have managed to bear up. To learn whether they have anything to tell me.

It is as if their loss were a part of my story, or even as if that were the point of it!

(Which is, I realize, crazy and wrong. But it is a notion I have to fight off, admitting its temptation even as I do so.)

Little Edward Springer had just begun to manifest his individuality, his uniqueness—to which we give perhaps too much importance here in the West. I have the idea that in China and India, where societies are more traditional, they are not quite so fascinated by these quirks of individuation. Perhaps it is merely that there, with those teeming hordes, they can't really afford to pay much attention to minor variations on what are, after all, only a very few common themes.

We are sentimentalists, then? Perhaps so. But the preference a little boy shows for blue over red, for string beans over cauliflower, for ruffled potato chips over smooth . . . Where do such things come from? Are these what the gods had planned for him? Are they clues on the opening pages in what should have been a full-length novel? Are there such books of life?

Isn't that what Malebranche believed?

I spend the weekend assaulting the objects that I have been ignoring for so long. Not the relics that Pam and Leah left behind but my own mess. My own garbage has surrounded me, diminishing the useful part of the house to small areas in a couple of rooms. But I force myself to reclaim, square foot by square foot, the kitchen, the bathroom, the bedroom, and the study. I am inefficient, getting bogged down at any random item that carries some emotional charge—a pot I used to warm up nursing bottles, for instance. But I stick it in the cabinet next to the oven. Another uninteresting aluminum pot. Not good for cooking things with tomatoes in them—although I've never actually noticed any bad effect, myself. Still, that's what we're supposed to do. We learn these things.

Always buy gasoline in the cool of the morning, before the heat of the day has caused it to expand.

Never wear a brown hat with a blue suit.

You can tell whether a cantaloupe is ripe by looking at the webbing. You can tell about pineapples by pulling a leaf out of the crown.

You peel an orange by taking off the north and south poles and scoring longitudes, which then come off easily.

Stupid, humble, valuable stuff like that, things your father and mother told you. Things I will never to able to pass on to Pam.

These are as close as I am likely to get to what the Chinese and Indians feel in their versions of the loss, the sense of waste, their experience of the goodness of life being ripped away not only from those who die but also from those who are left behind to grieve. They have different starting points for grief but the end is the same, an undifferentiated leaden ache.

Compared to that ache, nothing else seems worth bothering about. I am watching this small and sordid bit of political maneuvering at the office as if I were not personally involved, as if it were some late-night movie that buzzed on while my attention wandered and my eyelids drooped, its sequences ending abruptly or stretching out to unintended comical effects. Are they still worrying about *that*? How very droll!

In the back of my mind somewhere is the conviction—or only the superstition?—that I'd better try to hang on to the job. I am aware that if I don't have to get up in the morning and go somewhere, I could easily turn into a recluse, just give up and let the garbage win, expropriating ever larger pieces of the house and eventually leaving nothing but the bed, a narrow track to the bathroom, another narrow track to the refrigerator (with food in the bottom and vodka in the freezer above). What more does a fellow truly need?

Or better ask, what more can he bear?

Another possibility ought by no means to be excluded. I am interested to see that my piece about the infantine Lothario has gone through. "Nice job," Lansberg says, or, even more persuasively, scrawls on a page of his memo pad. To keep me from worrying too much about the termination of the relic series? To encourage me? Or, in what would be the best possible way, without any reflection or motive of any kind? It could be a simple ebullition of praise for the job I did with the material I'd been given.

That is what raises this other actually amusing spectre—that I could continue, zombielike, to knock out these little stories, doing all the better because I don't care, because I don't let my own taste and education get in the way. I just do what I'm supposed to do with these dreadful little snippets, turning them into the sideshow marvels for the ABC weekly carnival of fun.

DEAD HUBBY'S
FALSE TEETH
STILL TALK TO HER

is the tentative headline for the new exercise. It is grotesque, but what's new about that? I wonder whether the teeth are still in the glass where the old guy left them. It's possible. She is just too grief-stricken to touch them. And they sit there, floating in water or cleanser. And she imagines them trying to speak to her. Or are they out there on a table, clacking away like the joke-shop choppers you can buy along with the plastic vomit and the doggie-doo, if you have a taste for such things?

If you had the taste for it, you could make a connection to the now defunct relic series. If you were paying attention, that is. But attention only gets in the way. Inattentive, barely functioning, I could, in my distraction and diminution, sail splendidly on, even get promoted and take Lansberg's place one day . . .

What a dismal notion! Would I have the character to refuse? Or the taste, at least?

He didn't, poor man.

It is a catastrophe, whatever happens. To get fired, to get promoted, or to stay where I am—they are all exquisite variations of the same disaster.

Fortunately, I have developed a taste for catastrophe, as well as the knack for it.

I call Stephanie Stratton. I get a busy signal. I take it as a signal of another kind and call the number on the scratch pad before me.

It is Jeremy Springer's number. I am drawn to it. But even as I dial the digits, I am aware that I allowed the fates a chance to divert me from my purpose.

A woman's "Hello?"

"Mrs. Springer?"

"Yes." Not interrogative. Not even particularly guarded. I

wonder if these are the right Springers but can't quite come out and ask.

I identify myself, giving my name and that of ABC Publications. And I ask her whether it might be possible for me to come and talk to her and her husband.

A sigh. "I'm afraid that won't be possible," she says. "My husband and I have separated."

These are the ones.

14

WHAT visitors from the North often find unsettling is the impression they get here of insubstantiality. They are used to cities with some history, with evidence of a nineteenth-century or maybe even an eighteenth. But all the buildings down here were thrown up at once. Even the oldest of them, downtown, are relatively recent. The railroads came through, the swamps were drained, and the mosquitoes were killed off—in whatever order. And architects swarmed down here to fill the void with their wildest fancies. Down in those years, but more recently up, from South American cities where they have learned how to throw off the yoke of European restraint and give free rein to extravagance and caprice. We have, now, lots of pastel buildings, free-form structures in concrete, glass, and shiny metals, with aggressive ornamentation—even holes in the buildings in which large green trees have been placed to startle and arrest the restless eye.

And the patterns of growth have been similarly abrupt and arbitrary. Modest blue-collar neighborhoods hide enclaves of redeveloped splendor. You cross a little bridge over a canal, or simply turn a corner, and suddenly there is a walled-off subdivision with a gatehouse in which a smartly uniformed security guard presides over an intimidating television screen console with simultaneous views of the parking area, the tennis

courts, the putting green, and the pool patio. These develop-
ments look as if they were completed not more than twenty
minutes ago, so that one imagines they could be torn down
twenty minutes from now.

Which wouldn't be such a bad idea!

My worry—that the Springers will turn out to have been
residents in such a development—turns out to be baseless. The
wall makes a ninety-degree turn, but the street continues for
a while and, before it ends in palmetto scrub or swamp, has
more to offer. A supermarket and small shopping center, and
then an area of older, larger houses that may have been built
perhaps thirty years ago when all this would have been way
out in deep country. The architecture is not distinctive but the
trees have grown to mammoth proportions—various kinds of
ficus, bottle brush, avocado, mother-in-law's tongue, the inevitable clumps of banana trees, and a lot more that I don't
recognize.

Because of the settled quality of these houses, there is a sense
of something other than raw money. I don't suppose that many
of these places are still owned by the people who moved in
here a generation ago, but I can at least imagine that there has
been some kind of calculation of how much one can buy with
a limited sum, which is a precondition for taste if not its equivalent. These are quite conceivably young families wanting a
place where they could live and bring up a child.

I am projecting too much. I am adding what I see to what I
already know and leaping to conclusions. I am conflating my
own sad story with theirs, which is not necessary. Either story
is perfectly well able to stand alone.

Either is sufficiently devastating.

I park the car but don't get out. I just sit there, holding on
to the steering wheel, staring at the house and trying to decide
whether to go ahead with this. Should I bother them? Or her,
if they're separated? If I were in there, would I want to talk to
some nosy stranger?

There are people who get off on disaster, who became ad-
dicted to it. These people are only slightly more bizarre than

our readership, with which they share their morbid passion. They flock to fires, to those monstrous sinkholes that occasionally open up down here to swallow automobiles, trailers, and even houses, and to such other scenes of mayhem as the Piggly Wiggly parking lot . . .

That Piggly Wiggly's business was up 15 percent in the month following the shootings. And by 28 percent for that week.

But I am different from those casual gawkers. I am here to learn. I cannot come right out with my questions, cannot directly ask *How does one live? What is the meaning of suffering? How are we to bear it?* But I can hope for some hint, some sign of which Mrs. Springer may, herself, be quite unaware.

Mr. and Mrs. E. J. Springer. The E stands for Eustace, which is perhaps why he doesn't list it in the telephone book. But on the city tax rolls, one can find out his little secret.

Out of curiosity and habit, I looked up St. Eustace—a theological or at any rate a hagiographical disaster. A Roman general under Emperor Trajan, Eustace was converted to Christianity in the same curious way as St. Hubert: while he was out hunting, he saw another one of those stags with the figure of a cross between its antlers. Astonished, he converted, whereupon one might expect that his luck would improve. But it didn't. On the contrary, it deserted him entirely so that he lost his entire fortune and also his wife and two sons, who left him. He was a kind of minor-league Job. And like Job, he was retrieved, or at least recalled to the army, where he was needed again. He won a great victory, which sounds good, but in stories of this kind one must be cautious. Catastrophe lurks everywhere in this vale of tears. Eustace was called upon to offer sacrifices to the gods during the victory celebration, but of course, being a Christian now, he refused. Defiant in the tradition of Shadrach, Meshach, and Abednego, he refused to bow down or to do whatever it is that one does. He'd seen that stag.

And was he delivered, like them, from the fiery furnace? No, not at all. Poor Eustace was roasted to death! And to make it worse, they threw his wife and two sons—with whom he had just been reunited for the festive occasion—in with him.

The name means "Happy in harvest."

There is no evidence that Eustachius ever actually existed, but that is only temporarily consoling. If this is a fiction, a mere "pious tale," what could its point possibly be? What kind of doubt could find reassurance in such a story? What kind of grief could be soothed by so savage and unreasonable a series of reversals?

I cannot imagine. Meanwhile, Eustace Jeremy Springer has fled. Or has been thrown out. He and his wife could no longer live together, each of them being a reminder now of the unbearable loss they share, of that little boy so unhappily harvested. Each of them is like an idol in some Indian temple that was once beautiful and full of meaning but from which the great jewel has been plucked, so that now it stands as an emblem only of ruin and ugliness. For those things, too, I suppose, there must also be gods.

How can I bother the woman?

She lets me in. Her name is Lucy. Did her parents read Wordsworth? Or watch television reruns? Or maybe just read the funnies? I don't want to know. I tell her that I am not here for any legitimate professional reason. The series I was working on has been . . . I hesitate, avoid the word "killed," and instead bail out with "discontinued."

"I don't understand," she says. She is a young woman, pale, blond, slender, and fading—not only to age and sadness but in the way ghosts and spirits can fade away in movies that depend on special effects. She seems to be already in the process of dissolving into an ectoplasmic wraith.

Because there is no series anymore, I don't have any ethical problem about using my own disaster as a token with which to trade for the details of hers. Now that Lansberg and Cosgrove have nothing to do with our conversation, we are just two human beings confronting each other, and not to speak would be unspeakable. I tell her about my loss. And I go on to say that I am here to ask her, in a dumb way, how she has been getting on, how she manages. "Especially, now that you and your husband have separated," I prompt. I am interested to see that, on my own, I can be as shameless and pushy as any Lansberg could ever want.

She tells me what happened. Or what she thinks happened.

It is possible that Jeremy would have some other version, altogether different, that would put him in a better light. But he is not here. I listen to her and nod at intervals to show that I comprehend as she tells me, rather dully, how "It just happened. He left. I kind of knew he might, and he did. The way you know sometimes that the phone is going to ring, and then it does? I mean, there are reasons. The phone rings because somebody is calling. And he left because he couldn't stand it. But I couldn't stand it either. We'd kept together for Eddie's sake. Not that either one of us ever said so, but that's what I'd thought. And I think Jerry must have thought it, too. Without Eddie, there just wasn't . . . any point anymore."

"To this marriage or to any?" I ask, because there seems to be a generalizing tendency to her remarks.

"I don't know. I can't speak for all marriages. This is the only one I've been in. But I don't understand how people have anything left to talk about after six months. After six weeks, for that matter! There's a kind of mystery, at first. In the beginning, you find out the answers to all kinds of things. How does he take his coffee? Does he like rye or whole wheat? Does he like his shirts with starch or without? Does he like ketchup or mustard on his hamburgers? Does he love anchovies on his pizza or hate them? You learn all that stuff. There's also politics, religion, movies, sports, books. . . . But it's all about the same, isn't it? Once you've found out what all the answers are, the questions all turn into the single question—can you stand someone like that? And he's asking himself whether he can stand you! Anyway, that's what it was like with us. That's what I think it's like for most people, whether they admit it to themselves or not."

She looks at me, defiantly, waiting for me to contradict her. Why? It takes me a moment before I understand that, in her eyes, I am lucky. If I have suffered, at least my pain is all of a piece. It doesn't contradict itself the way hers does. Pam and Leah are gone, but at the same time and in the same way. Hers is a terrible composite of bereavement and betrayal. And guilt, too, perhaps.

"You were there?" I ask.

She nods. "I was there. I was carrying him. He was in my arms when he was hit. . . . It wouldn't have been much more than the smallest fraction of an inch of difference and I'd have been killed. Or both of us. But just him." She adjusts her hair. There is a piece of it that keeps falling down over one eye and she sweeps it away with her hand only to have it fall again. Or, between sweeps, she just shakes it out of the way. The curious effect of this is that as she is speaking to me, there are random gestures of vigorous denial, intervals of head-shaking that seem to mean, *No, no!*

"And you blame yourself?" I ask. "You shouldn't."

"Easy to say. But if I'd gone ten minutes later or ten minutes earlier. Or if I hadn't gone at all. There are closer supermarkets, for God's sake, but there's a bakery up there in the same mall, and they make cookies that Jerry likes. Liked. Which makes it his fault, doesn't it? Or if I'd just parked somewhere else . . ."

She shakes her head again, this time not for her hair. "None of it was predictable," she says, "but any of it could have been changed, and then everything would have been different. I keep thinking the same things, over and over, going round and round, like some kind of dumb wind-up toy." Her head shakes once again.

I wonder whether she is thinking of one of her little boy's wind-up toys or one she remembers from her own childhood. Which is the sadder? But that is hardly a useful question. I owe her more respectful attention and whatever comfort I can offer. I tell her about Malebranche and his idea of destiny, that I have been reading him and that he would have maintained that it had been fated all along for her son to die this way.

"That's a load of crap," she says, but not angrily. It doesn't bother her if I find this kind of thinking helpful. It just isn't any good for her. She might have tried it on, looked at herself in the mirror, decided it just wasn't her, and rejected it.

I shrug. "I didn't mean to be crazy. It's just an idea I've been playing with. You think all kinds of odd things. I do, anyway."

"None of them helps," she says. "I don't know what the hell you think you're doing. What you expect to accomplish here."

"I don't know, myself," I say. "I never wanted this assignment. And I was glad when the series was abandoned. But now that I'm free of it, I can't let it alone."

She accepts that. I ask her if I may see her son's room.

"There's nothing there. I gave it all away. I called Goodwill and they sent a truck. Everything. The bed, the dresser, the toys, the clothes. It's all gone. It killed me to look at it."

I nod. "Still, that confirms in a way what I was doing. That there's a power in those objects."

"Oh, yes."

"And even in their absence, too, maybe. I mean, think of those craters they've still got in London from the buzz bombs. Just holes in the ground, but important."

"You want to see an empty room? Go ahead. Down the hall, on the left, before the bathroom."

"Just for a moment," I tell her.

"I think it's ghoulish," she calls after me. "I think it's nuts, if you want to know. But that doesn't mean much. One of us is crazy, or we both are."

I go back to the living room so I don't have to shout. "We'd be crazy if we weren't affected some by what's happened."

"Go on. Get it over with," she says.

I go back down the hall. The room is empty. It looks as it must have looked on the day the builder finished the house. Or the day the painter finished. In fact, I realize I can still smell the paint. She has had it painted. To change the color? To cover finger marks he might have left? There is nothing but an empty cube. A casement window looks out onto the side yard; a sliding door opens to reveal a double closet with not a single piece of clothing, not even a wire hanger. Bare. It doesn't tell me a thing except that there is nothing left.

I lie down on the floor where the bed might have been. Expecting? Who knows what? I look up at the ceiling he must have looked up at. That is the same. Or out the window, where the Bermuda grass and the gardenia bush are presumably the same.

Nothing.

But there is a glint of green I notice inside the metal grate over the vent in the wall for the air conditioning and perhaps for the heat, too, if they have one of those reversible units. I have a screwdriver gizmo on my key chain, and I unscrew the grate. Inside, there is a small wooden piece from some elementary board game. Bright green with a little face on it. A token. A man.

She missed that. She hadn't thought to look for it. Only a little boy, down for his nap but unable to get to sleep, bored, left to his own devices, might have poked one of these pieces into the grating. Just to see if it would fit through the metal louvers.

It did. And I get it out.

I screw the grate back on. I put the little green man in my pocket.

Lucy Springer didn't want it. That's clear enough.

Should I take it? Does my good will qualify as well as another's?

"Was it interesting?" she asks. "Are you satisfied?"

"It was interesting. Thank you."

"I shouldn't have let you do it," she tells me. "It's ghoulish. You're a voyeur. Except that voyeurs are usually interested in sex, which is more attractive than what you like to stare at."

"I'm sorry you think that," I reply. "I'm not sure whether it's true or not. But who gets to choose?"

"That's crap too," she says.

"I wish I could make it up to you somehow, offer some comfort or distraction, be of some help. Would you like to have dinner with me?"

"I don't think so."

"If there's anything I can ever do . . ."

"I don't think so," she says again, cutting me off.

"Are you going to stay on here?" I ask, because I have the sense that she is about to throw me out and I'm curious to know what her plans are. If I have any questions, I'd better ask them immediately.

"I've been thinking about it. I don't know. I don't much notice where I am. It doesn't make a lot of difference to me, now that that room is cleaned out. Nothing matters much, one way or another. Why do you care?"

"I'm trying to decide what I'm going to do. It's painful to stay, but painful to think about moving."

"You think about it too much," she says. "That's what's the matter with you. You spend all this time and energy thinking about things. What difference does it make what you think or what you do? You can't change anything. You can't bring them back. You're just making it harder on yourself. And on other people too, for that matter. People like me."

"I'm sorry," I tell her. "I agree with you. Thinking doesn't help. But I'm not sure I have much choice."

She shakes her head. Disagreeing with me? Fighting with that unruly strand of hair? Wanting me to leave? I have no doubt but that she wants me to leave, whatever the gesture may signify. And if I can do nothing else for her, at the very least, I can do that.

"I'm very grateful," I tell her. "I won't bother you any further."

She nods. I leave. In the car, I look back at the house, a perfectly ordinary place, as unremarkable as a space on a game board. And as I buckle my seat belt, I can feel the game token in my pocket. I switch on the engine and drive away. The sky is a gorgeous red—the pollution does that, the particulates in the air. Our sunsets have been spectacular in these recent years. I get on the skyway and drive for the soothing mechanical absorption of the activity, the familiarity, the lovely aimlessness. I am mindful of the sunset but not particularly impressed.

Or, no, not aimless. I am going toward Stephanie's house. I am going to drive by, not stopping, not risking that she will reject me as Lucy Springer did.

Am I a voyeur, as she charged? There are probably worse things to be. Voyeurs are mostly harmless, and they do have a kind of love for the subjects of their scrutiny even if they are too messed up to be able to express it.

What is difficult to bear is the great pity I had for her. I was unable to tell her anything of it, but it was there. Pity and the impulse to try to make it up to her in some way, to make good on what she had lost.

An impossible enterprise. Unimaginable.

And then, it crossed my mind that with Stephanie Stratton it was not unimaginable.

15

ON my desk, Edward Springer's little green man stands like a holy icon, with its cartoon eyes, its conventional umlaut for nostrils, and a simple arc representing a grin. Crude, but efficient, it serves as a vehicle, a vessel. The player of the game invests himself in this bit of painted wood, endows the inert object with a shred of self, and watches its progress around a pasteboard maze, rejoicing in its successes and groaning at its setbacks. And if the board is gone and the rules are lost? Then the green man can stand wherever chance disposes, hardly even noticing that the spinner or the dice have been supplanted by another more cumbersome aleatory mechanism, but still content to be governed by whatever forces pick it up, move it, and set it down. And in the presence of such serenity and obedience, how can I withhold that connection, that shred of self for which the manufacturer's crude design made provision? What that face represents is both Eddie Springer's diminutive visage and my own.

Lucy Springer missed it. And it is difficult for me to resist the thought that there was some inevitability involved in my coming into that room—despite her reluctance, despite the fact that Lansberg had killed the series so that I had no business in the house at all—and in my noticing its green glint behind the louvers of that grate. It claimed me as much as the other way around.

That Lucy didn't see it is interesting. Lucy, after all, is the Syracusan martyr who was denounced as a Christian in Diocletian's time by a rejected suitor. The Romans put her into a brothel. A series of miracles are alleged by which she was preserved there unmolested. She was similarly saved from death by fire. Finally, she was killed by a sword thrust down her throat. But she is patron saint of eyes, and is often represented holding two eyeballs in a dish—like a couple of eggs, sunny side up. According to one tradition, this gory symbol refers to her judge's having torn her eyes out. In another version of her story, she tore her own eyes out to deter that unwelcome suitor. But in both, the conclusion is the same—that her eyes were miraculously restored. To her, therefore, people with ophthalmological problems direct their prayers. Either to her or to St. Hervé, a sixth-century Breton who worked as a farmhand and, later on, a teacher at his uncle's monastic school at Plouvien. Having been born blind, he, too, is a patron of eyes. Among the miracles ascribed to him is a droll story of a wolf who ate the donkey that was pulling his plow. In answer to Hervé's prayer, the wolf put himself into the donkey's harness and completed the plowing.

My question, reading this curious story, is whether the blind Hervé knew what was going on. Did he notice that anything at all untoward had taken place? Wasn't the miracle all the more miraculous—to those in the next field or in the monastery, who looked on in amazement—for the way Hervé just kept on plowing the field with no idea in the world that a gorged wolf was tugging at the plowlines in front of him?

The legend is stupid but it resonates. I like the idea of this semimoronic guy, absolutely oblivious to what is going on around him, just holding on and going about his business. As Harris has been doing at the office. The news is that he has had a great success, has even managed to attract Cosgrove's wavering attention. And how has he contrived this nearly impossible feat? By the cogency of his prose? The precision of his perceptions? His insight and keen analytical powers? His rich philosophical and cultural background? None of the above had anything to do with it. It can be characterized only as extravagant and improbable luck. Or Malebranchian destiny. According to Lansberg, this is the likeliest reconstruction:

- Cosgrove discovers that his stapler is empty.
- The stapler on his secretary's desk uses Swingline staples. His requires Bostich. So his secretary's staples don't fit his stapler.
- Cosgrove makes a rare foray into the editorial offices of his paper, not to supervise or interfere but only to search for compatible staples. Someone else must have a Bostich stapler, or so he imagines. He sets out to find one, and to rummage through the drawers of that employee in hopes of finding a box of staples.
- Tweedy Harris is the lucky fellow, having inherited the stapler with the desk. And because his desk is near the door, it is his Bostich stapler that Cosgrove first spies.
- Cosgrove searches the drawers of Harris's desk to find the staples and comes across a copy of the piece we did on Kezemi with that laundry list Harris produced of the dead Iranian's effects. What strikes Cosgrove is the dingbats, those vulgar little dots Harris used that act as punctuational fanfares for each of the items.
- Cosgrove decides that that's what the paper needs: more graphic lapel grabbing. And the dingbats are like buttonhole rosettes.
- Harris, he decides, is a genius. Just the sort of fellow who should be advanced and promoted here at ABC. Because of our story that was, in any event, killed. As dead as Kezemi.

Good for Harris! One can't argue with that kind of insane luck. One can't even be envious of it. Craziness. It is difficult to describe, let alone try to analyze it. I see that I have made rudimentary gestures of rationality in the foregoing account that are unfaithful to the spirit of the events. I said, "And because his desk is near the door, it is his Bostich stapler that Cosgrove first spies,'' as if that were an explanation, as if in an altogether irrational process the one logical connection that it's possible to make could hold the general arbitrariness at bay. It is quite the opposite. With a maniac like Cosgrove, that arrogant, stupid, clownish boor for whom we labor, one might as well stop making such connections entirely. Had Harris's desk been the farthest from the door, had it been tucked away in some all but inaccessible cubbyhole, I have no doubt but that some neural irregularity in Cosgrove's constricted brain pan would have led him there, as surely as the tiny migrating birds are led from Canada to Mexico or from central Africa to Norway and back. They have some mechanism that makes them do what they do, but they don't understand it or think about it at all. Nor does Cosgrove. He is God's little green man, and he moves about the board in ways that may seem purposive to him but really have nothing to do with his intentions. He was looking for a stapler. He found an assistant managing editor. What sense does that make?

Except in the mind of God!

And couldn't one therefore maintain that Cosgrove, being dopier than anyone I know, is closer to God, more comfortable an instrument of God's intentions than, say, Sid Lansberg or even myself? We spin our wheels, contemplate and cogitate, resist, and try, however vainly, to conduct ourselves in a rational way. This is nothing but pretension. Cosgrove, a simpler mechanism, is the more efficient, the better designed.

Which would be why he is the publisher and we aren't—if there were such a thing as a why.

I have the word from Lansberg himself, who uncharacteristically invited me to dinner. I worried that it was his gentle way of letting me know that there was no longer a place for me at ABC and I was half tempted to refuse, to make him fire me there in the office. But something in his demeanor gave me other kinds of signals. I supposed that, if I wanted to make a scene, I could do that as easily in a restaurant as in the office.

In fact, it could be worse, more humiliating to him in a public place.

So I accepted, albeit with reservations. Or, no, he made the reservations—at a quite good place some Frenchman has opened up here. He came down from New York, where he had a three-star restaurant. He wanted to retire. He was bored. He opened a place down here to have something to do. He was open, at first, just on Fridays and Saturdays. And then Thursday through Sunday, just for dinner. Now it's six days a week, for lunch and dinner. And he's doing more business than he did in New York, and is making more money because his rent is lower. Or maybe he owns his own building down here.

Anyway, that pricey oasis in our gustatory Sahara was what Lansberg proposed. I had another set of contradictory impulses. Surely, a meal as expensive as that had to be part of my involuntary departure. On the other hand, that was the last place in Glade County where Lansberg would want to be yelled at, cried to, or cursed by an out-of-control employee.

"Fine, wonderful," I said. "I've only been there once before. It was very good."

It was for our fifth anniversary. Leah and I splurged. I had the sweetbreads with chestnut sauce. And she had the lobster in snail butter. I am distressed to say that I forget what wines we had.

"Yes, it is," Lansberg agreed. I couldn't read his expression. Defiant? Slightly crazed? Or was that just my own condition that I was projecting?

We meet at the restaurant. Lansberg is waiting in the bar. He has a martini in front of him in a glass only a couple of sizes smaller than the ones they used to use in production numbers in musicals, in which showgirls swam like goldfish. "Join me?" he asks.

"That's what I'm here for."

"One of these for my friend."

Friend? I cannot remember any such reference in the history of our relationship. And I am not much reassured. It would be friendlier for him simply to give me the unembellished news—

that I am fired—and let me go and lick my own wounds in my own way.

The bartender puts down before me what must be a triple martini. Lansberg raises his glass and says, "As the old ram said, raising his glass, 'Here's looking at ewe, kid.' "

It is not at all his style. Is he drunk? Mad? Dangerous? (But even sane and sober he is dangerous.)

"*Salut!*" I reply, being unable to come up with anything like an appropriate response.

We have a few contemplative sips. It's very good. Or, at least, very dry. In fact, it may not be a martini at all but just iced gin with a twist of lemon peel. But good gin. I am still considering this question when the maître informs us that our table is ready. We follow him into the dining room, are seated, and are handed menus.

"Don't stint youself," Lansberg says. "It's on the company."

I can no longer restrain myself. "What is it, Sidney? Am I fired?"

"Not that I know of, no. Enjoy yourself. Relax. I . . . It's something I should have done months ago."

Does he mean that he should have been friendlier or more supportive after Pam and Leah were killed? Or that he should have been a different kind of employer and should have recognized my dedication and the high quality of my work? Has he read *A Christmas Carol* out of season and resolved upon a new life? None of these is likely.

I decide on the stone crab and then, because I had them here before, the sweetbreads. Lansberg has the steak au poivre and he picks out a Grands Echézeaux that ought to go nicely with both our entrées. At $80.00, I should hope so. But I am only more deeply puzzled.

And the table talk is similarly mysterious. I am expecting it to have some vague connection with work. But Lansberg is asking me what movies I've liked, what books I've read, what I do for diversion. . . .

I don't feel like telling him about Malebranche, which is too close to admitting to a low-grade form of madness. And I have few movies or novels to talk about. I don't go to the dog track or play golf or tennis or sail or do any of those hearty, outdoorsy things.

"You write, then?" he asks.

I have been writing, but nothing that I want to talk about. Or not with him.

"No," I tell him, rather proud of myself for my restraint.

"You don't? I thought you all did. I did. I used to. That's how people get into this business, I thought. We're all failed poets or novelists or playwrights. Which is why it's easy for Cosgrove to exploit us. We feel guilty to begin with, and we welcome his humiliations as being exactly what we deserve. We conspire with him. We become our own torturers. It's what they do in those re-education camps in Red China, but here it's in the name of capitalism and democracy. It's the same strategy, though, isn't it?"

A rhetorical question? Or a trap of some kind? Or is this what Lansberg has been thinking all along, managing only by a kind of maturity and artfulness I can't even imagine to keep the rest of us from guessing at?

"That's rather a romantic view, isn't it?" I'm not admitting anything but neither am I positively declining to discuss the subject. Still, with all my caginess, I'm worried—both about myself and about him.

"You think so?" he asks. "Or do you just mean that it isn't what you expected from me? I'm not such a bad fellow, deep down. Of course, that could have been Goering's epitaph too, I guess. But I used to be a real journalist. And some of the worst things I've done have been from perfectly good motives."

"Oh?" I wonder whether I shouldn't be recording this. To use later on, when the necessity arises. Or just for archival purposes—to prove to myself that this actually happened.

"I should never have sent you on that relic series, for instance. That was outrageous. But I really persuaded myself that it would make livelier copy, would make for a better series—whatever the hell that means. That's what I wanted to believe. It also occurred to me—it was a piece of wishful thinking, of course—that it might even do you good, might give you some perspective, might help you get over your own loss a little.

Take you out of yourself. We can talk ourselves into almost anything, can't we?"

"I don't know what to say." I'm still apprehensive that something dire is about to transpire, that he has some unpleasant piece of news for me, for which all this food and wine and soft-soap is just the prelude.

"You don't have to say anything," he says. "I'm apologizing. It isn't a game. You don't have to perform. I'm sorry. I shouldn't have put you through any of that. I shouldn't have added to your burdens with that assignment. I shouldn't have presumed . . . "

"I appreciate your saying these things," I say. What does he want? Forgiveness? Absolution? "It's hard to say what kind of burden it's been. Or what kind of help. I did get interested in it, as you know. And for me to be interested in anything is a step forward, I guess. I'm still interested. I found a little game-piece that used to belong to the Springer kid. And I thought it would be interesting to show it to Babcock and see what his reaction is, if he reacts at all. It's an encounter all victims dream about."

"You really want to do that?" Lansberg asks.

I nod. "It's not all that expensive, and if I get anything decent out of it, it will make up for the defects of some of the other pieces."

"There's nothing to make up. You don't owe me a thing."

"Even so, shall I go? I'm willing. Even interested."

"If that's what you want, sure. Go ahead. Of course."

The waiter brings our first courses, Lansberg's oysters Bienville and my stone crabs, and we turn our attention to the food. I'm still worried, but there's not a whole lot I can do about it— whatever it turns out to be. If Lansberg has something to tell me, he will do so in his own good time.

And, indeed, with the cognac, he does let me have some hint about what's on his mind. He tells me about Harris's promotion to assistant managing editor. And he tells me what the reason is—the dingbats that Cosgrove noticed when he was looking for the stapler.

Suddenly the evening makes sense. Lansberg is hunkering

down, getting ready for the battle, and mending his fences. He wants me to be his ally. Despite whatever may have happened in the past, he wants me to be friendly. Or at least neutral. Which is enough to explain the dinner and the approval of my trip up to the state prison.

I wonder if I should ask for a raise. And then I decide that if Lansberg is feeling weak and vulnerable, this is not the time. When he is celebrating his victory over Harris, I'll ask for it. Or when Harris is celebrating, I'll address my request to him.

On the way home, I turn off the skyway and pass Stephanie's house. Or, actually, I even stop. But I don't get out of the car. As I sit there, I try to imagine myself telling her about the evening, and there's no way to tell her about my satisfaction in having wangled the money to go and visit John Babcock in prison. I can't explain this to myself, for that matter. But to her, it will seem ghoulish and obscene.

Nevertheless, I cannot just drive away. I have been drawn here. I sit and feel the magnetic tug of her presence, of Stratton's desktop with those pencils still lined up, of the sad interrupted domesticity that Babcock obliterated.

It is like looking at the site of some natural wonder. Gibraltar, say, where the earthquake or volcanic eruption or whatever it was opened the fissure to let the Atlantic come into what had been, for a few hundred thousand years, a desert. And those unimaginable torrents of water came roaring in.

So, at any rate, geologists now suppose.

It must have been something to see!

People still come to look, even though there isn't anything to see, really. A crushing wall of water and the mass death of whatever had been living in that desert basin. Nature's power and heartlessness.

There is a part of me that can imagine how, when this trip is behind me, I shall be able to knock on the door and go in. To tell her about it or not, as it seems right to do. Depending on how it goes. As it now stands, I don't even know what to expect. Which is why I have to go.

It's too late, anyway, to knock on the door. It's almost midnight. The light is on in her bedroom, but she may have gone to bed. She may be reading, or watching television, waiting for her eyelids to droop with fatigue and the promise of at least a few hours of unconsciousness. I am tempted, of course. It is attractive to imagine the warmth of her bed, the softness of her belly, the mutual delights of sex. But I cannot assume that her previous assent gives me a license, entitles me to an assured welcome in the future. And there would be something peremptory in my appearance here at this late hour. It would be the exercise of a right only a husband can properly claim. And I'm not her husband.

Neither am I one of those freaks who sit outside women's houses, looking up at their lighted windows and thinking about them until they have an erection. . . .

I shift into drive and depart.

16

SETTING up a visit with Babcock turned out to be a fairly complicated piece of business. I shouldn't have objected if it were a matter of policy. I wouldn't have given much of a damn if they'd kept him in solitary and fed him on moldy bread and brackish water. But there isn't any policy, or no more than the system needs in order to allow for finagling and petty corruption. I made my application directly through the Department of Corrections and was referred to the warden's office—and one can't just call but must apply to the warden in writing. I did that and was rejected out of hand as not being a relative of the prisoner or his attorney, or a member of the staff of his attorney of record. So I got the not remarkably bright idea of calling upon his attorney—a poor soul named Carswell (no, he isn't even a relation of the rejected Supreme Court nominee, just some poor innocent who couldn't have been a druggist or a carpenter or a farmer but had to go to law school and now drags around for the rest of his life an absolutely irrelevant burden). So far as I am able to tell, the bulk of his practice is derived from hanging around courtrooms in the hope of picking up odd bits of business from those criminals who are not destitute enough to qualify for the Public Defender's Office and have been recommended to him by some bail bondsman to whom he doubtless pays small kickbacks. And on rare occasions, such plum assignments from the court as the defense of Babcock fall into his outstretched hands. The Public Defender doesn't handle murderers; they get counsel appointed for them even if they can't afford to pay.

So Babcock's killing spree turned out to be Carswell's lucky day!

And my appearance in his offices was another. Or actually, the plural is an honorific, because he doesn't even have a whole singular office. He's got a fraction, desk space in a large room, and a phone with a lock on it. All the other phones have locks on them too lest the office mates be tempted to make their long-distance calls on each other's phones. I guess he has a telephone answering service and a woman who does his typing for him somewhere. Somewhere else, that is.

I was encouraged by what I found, knowing at once where we stood. I told him who I was and that I worked for ABC Publications. And that I wanted to interview Mr. Babcock, who was his client.

"I'm afraid that's impossible," he said. "The rules are very clear. Only relatives and his attorney—and members of his attorney's staff, of course—are allowed to visit a maximum-security prisoner."

I was way ahead of him. I told him that I'd already been informed that this was the case and that it was my hope that we might work out an arrangement by which I could become, at least on a temporary basis, a member of his staff. My paper was of course prepared to compensate him for his trouble.

Not surprisingly, we were able to work out an arrangement. At the very least, he could get his laundry and dry cleaning out of hock.

The tie he was wearing, a maroon and cream stripe, was begrimed beyond any cleaner's art, but I was offering enough to allow him the indulgence of a new tie, or several of them if he was a careful shopper.

His request, almost an afterthought, that he be allowed to review the copy of anything I wrote and published—in order to ensure accuracy, of course—was a formal gesture, a reminder to himself as much as to me that he really was a lawyer.

I agreed, of course, because I knew it was extremely unlikely that I'd ever write anything about Babcock.

I was forced therefore to admit to myself that I was doing this for entirely personal reasons. Which, even then, I understood as making no very great sense. Babcock wasn't the killer I was really interested in. He was a loony, a tabloid horror.

On the other hand, he was all I could stand.

Which was and remains the point.

As Babcock explained to me, "Once you decide your life is over, nobody else's life matters either. Right? Right?"

He had a scrawny neck and a way of darting his eyes to the side so that he looked a little like a crazed chicken. Or a nervous lizard. One of those creatures between the reptiles and the birds. A midget pterodactyl, maybe. But certainly not human. As he had more or less concluded himself. He had given up on being human, had turned in his tattered membership card. And having done that, he found that there were no more distinctions that held any truth or power. Other people were mere figments. He was a mere figment, himself. He had no particular animus against the people he killed. He had only a general rage.

"I expected that someone would shoot me down. I was even disappointed, you know? I figured that that's what sensible people would do if a guy came with a rifle and started blasting into a crowd that way. I was a dead man. I'd written myself off. And I figured I might as well have some company. Those kids that had been bothering me? Sure, they'd have done. But they were only kids. Why not make it bigger? Why not take everyone in the damn world along with me—or as many of them as I could. Like the Egyptian pharaohs used to take their servants and their dogs and all? It'd be big! Right? Right! And I wanted something big. Because everything in my whole damn life had been small potatoes!"

"So you just didn't care whom you hit."

"No, I didn't give a shit. They weren't people, they were numbers. It was like . . . like stepping on ants. You ever do that as a kid? Step on ants? Or pour lighter fluid on them and set it alight? Kids do that a lot. To see if they feel anything.

And they don't, of course. It doesn't even feel good. Nothing at all. Well, it was like that." He smoothed his lank hair. Or hairs, one might say, because there were so few of them. I had the impression that he was somewhat surprised to find them there, as any flying lizard would be.

"And now that you're in here? You still don't care? You're not sorry?"

"Not a whole hell of a lot, no. I'm not so bad off in here. I'm too old and too ugly to have to worry about getting fucked. The worst they can do to me is kill me, and I'd already given up on life anyway. Right? Right?"

"But people change their minds. They have second thoughts. You never did?"

"What do you want me to say? That it wasn't such a good idea? I'll go along with that. But is that going to be enough? Is that going to do you any good? Or them? No sir! It's like those guys who worry about the poor kids in Hiroshima and Nagasaki. Up until they dropped the bomb, there was a war going on, and it looked like a good idea. And then when the Japs surrendered, there wasn't any war anymore. But that's what I really would have wanted. A fucking bomb! An atomic bomb that would have taken out the whole damned city! Leave a great big hole in the map. A big empty hole with smoke coming out of it."

"Why?" I asked.

"You want to know why? You want to know what's the point? There isn't any point. That's the point!" And he chuckled. Or cackled. A dry, coughlike, double exhalation: "Heh-heh."

I showed him the little green man. "This was the kid's. One of his toys that his mother missed. I found it."

He looked at it but did not reach out for it. He seemed to hesitate. Chagrin? Remorse? Indecision, at least?

"It's a piece of wood, a thing," he said. "But that's just it. They all were. I was too. And I still think that that's the way it is, if you really want to know. I'm in here not for what I did but for finding out the great secret—that we're all just things like that piece of tree you've got in your hand there. One thing

and another thing. And there's not such a big difference between any of them except that our kind of thing reproduces
itself. Our kind of thing is overrunning the world. We're weeds.
There are just too many people. All those starving babies in
Africa and South America . . . Something's got to be done. You
need your basic pest control. If I'd gone out and cut down a lot
of weeds, it would more or less have been the same thing. It
would have felt about the same, you see. But weeds wouldn't
have shot back—and I was counting on it that somebody would.
I figured that there'd be some cop, somebody with a gun. I
didn't think I'd live to empty the rifle. But I did. And I remember
how I was going to reload and shoot some more, but it just
didn't seem worth the effort. I was just tired of it. Like I'd been
working in a field all morning, clearing brush. So I stopped.
And they thought I'd run out of bullets, and they arrested me.
Isn't that a sketch? They didn't want to shoot an unarmed man.
I don't know why not. Heh-heh. I mean, if you're playing by
those rules, that's just what I'd done, isn't it? Right? Women,
kids. . . " He shrugged and then held out his hands palms up,
as if to demonstrate his honesty. Everything was on the up
and up.

I didn't know what else to ask or what there was I could say
to him. The worst of it was that I could understand what he
was saying. It wasn't how I looked at the world, but it was a
point of view. Eccentric but still a point of view.

Right?

More to the point, what John Babcock had done was what
I'd done myself. If the boys who were cutting across his lawn
were not suitable objects for the intensity and generality of his
rage, he would go to the mall to find substitutes. If I could not
face James Macrae—the drunk who killed Leah and Pam—I
could go and interview some other killer with whom I was not
so personally involved and whom I could bear to confront.

And, in some small way, torment?

Probably.

I am not proud of myself, but I assert in my defense that we
all do these kinds of things all the time. We get annoyed at A

and take it out on B. We are upset by X, which is too much to deal with, so we become obsessed with Y and Z. I have stood at the frozen food case, unable to decide between the chicken divan and the chicken Florentine, knowing perfectly well that they both taste the same and dissolving into tears at my inability to grab a box from one stack or the other. Or looking at the bright designs on the cereal boxes, I have felt my throat tighten and my eyes begin to water. This could happen to me so quickly that I didn't even have time to make the conscious connection, hadn't yet associated those boxes with breakfasts back in my other life. I'd just break down, and only later figure out why.

And I am not alone. Look at the vegetable aisle sometime, or glance to the left and right at the meat bins, or observe those customers whose wagons have come to a stop before the display of canned soups, and you will see, trickling down their cheeks, tears of grief and rage and chagrin at whatever abyss has opened at their feet as they try to perform the routines of life. I know. I'm not exaggerating.

The glare from the bright lights is merciless, the Muzak is grotesque, but suffering is impervious to these pranks of the set decorator and the director. These people are stricken, dazed, and do not much care where they are.

But what do these displacements and crossed connections mean to our presumptions of reason, the ordering principles we suppose to be governing our lives? At the very least, there is a different kind of logic, a psycho-logic, but even that breaks down. Everything breaks down.

Malebranche would say—with compassion and faith and real wisdom—that chaos is the true nature of everything and that only the imposition of the mind of God can maintain, from moment to moment, the semblance of order that we, God's children, take for granted and attribute not to Him but to the world around us. We are like the children of some rich and powerful parent, assuming that the world is full of expensive toys, that its natural aspect is combed and cleaned and polished and bedecked with silk and satin, damask and eiderdown, gold and silver. And the fond parent never even lets the child suspect what roughness and savagery lie everywhere in wait just outside the gates of the château.

Think of the spectrum of energy, a small band of which presents itself as visible light. Reality is like that, with a relatively small range of experience susceptible of some sort of logical interpretation and analysis. Smaller experiences, at the atomic level, for example, and much larger ones are not logical or rational at all. They are the frightening ends of the spectrum, where the column of smoke has started to disorganize itself, where the lines of intention and association are already swirling incoherently in what appears to be a pattern only to those who insist on patterns, who cannot imagine the absence of pattern— or the dependence that implies.

Malebranche admitted such a dependence. With every breath he took. He inhaled by the grace of God. And then, only by the grace of God, exhaled.

I cannot believe that far. But I am soothed to imagine such a life, calmed by the realization that there have been such men.

Would there be any point in my going to see Macrae? Would I be doing anything other than torturing myself?

17

LANSBERG is gone. Fired, or, more likely, maneuvered into some impossible position in which the only honorable choice he could make was to quit. To deprive himself, in other words, of a package of unemployment benefits—severance pay and the right to collect unemployment insurance. How many other jobs are there like this one, after all?

Cosgrove would have been well aware of how much money he'd be saving if he could get Lansberg to throw in the towel.

A memorandum from the publisher adressed, rather cozily, to "All hands," as if we were jolly shipmates, announced the departure of Sidney Lansberg and, in the very next paragraph, his replacement—Harris.

The dingbat king!

I sit at my desk and try to decide how this affects me. Or, even more to the point, what my reaction is. I never much liked Lansberg. I thought he was an exploiting bastard, which he was. But I understood that he had once been something better than the editor of our vulgar rag, and that whatever indignities he heaped on our heads, his own was even more weighed down with the redolent filth of Cosgrove's business.

And that we had, each of us, made our own choices—Malebranche or no. We were each responsible for our own fates.

Malebranche waffles on this point, talking about how we ought to pursue the good, how we ought to "make good use of our freedom."

I don't believe this. I think the idea of freedom is a snare and a delusion, just another indignity, and perhaps the worst of them.

Anyway, Lansberg is out of here, and well out, assuming that there is still some hope for his immortal soul. That such a thing exists.

Harris is my friend, right? Life will be better now.

But I know better. Our friendliness, our having worked together, will be counted against me. He will resent favors he thinks I may have done him, expecting that I shall expect more favors from him. Embarrassed, too, as he ought to be, at having leaped over me and all the others, through no particular virtue of his own but because of dumb luck.

It will bother him that we are all aware of the fortuitousness of his promotion.

Cosgrove, on the other hand, will delight in that knowledge we all share—of the arbitrariness of his decision, which is to say, the great scope of his power!

I open my desk drawer, as if I hope to find some similar passport to success and promotion, something like that scrap of paper with the dingbats. I am surprised to find something else—a large paperback anthology of Chinese poetry. And there is an inscription on the title page: "Think of Yüan Chen! And think of me, too. Yours, SL."

Lansberg's farewell.

Or part of it, anyway. The dinner was another piece of his general good-bye gift. And his approval of my trip up to see Babcock.

Not that these gestures turn him into any kind of decent fellow. It is not inconceivable that he picked me out as a representative of all the underlings here, one arbitrary vessel for his little act of contrition. Or just enough to leave me wondering whether I hadn't misjudged him all these years. In other words, to bug me.

But even so, even with the worst possible spin I can put on it, there was still some gesture he was making toward me, some degree of concern with what I think of him.

Perhaps, like a Catholic, he was making a deathbed confession. They believe in that.

Lansberg isn't Catholic, though. Neither am I.

That was at the heart of the absurdity of the whole damned series on the relics of these martyrs he'd forced me into doing. That neither one of us believed in saints or relics. Not at the beginning, anyway. I have no idea what I believe in now.

I have lost my faith in skepticism and am willing now to allow all sorts of remote possibilities. I am perhaps becoming as gullible as any of our readers. As I believe Lansberg must have known, from the very beginning, would happen to me. In which case, his assigning me the series would have been either a heartless experiment or a huge practical joke.

But who's laughing now? The tables are turned, as in our headline of this week.

PIT BULLS

EAT MOBILE HOME

That grotesque pronouncement was Lansberg's swan song.

Good night, sweet prints. And flights of angels sing thee past the rest room.

Adieu, St. Denis!

I've found a poem in the book that Lansberg marked—either for me, if he brought this copy to give to me, or for himself. It is a poem by Po Chü-yi (772–846), who was a buddy of Yüan Chen's.

Parrot

The day's chatter at last subsides,
But at midnight, he fidgets on his perch.
Caged that way for his gaudy plumage,
His heart is embittered because he understands.

At twilight, he thinks of his nest and of going back;
In springtime, there are the mating calls of other pairs.
Who will smash his cage, who
Will set him free to flight and song?

I realize that it doesn't make any difference at all which of
us he had in mind when he ran his pencil down the margin.
"Embittered because he understands"! That is the modern martyrdom. His and mine and Harris's too, I have no doubt.

In the evening, I call Stephanie. I am contrite. I should have
called her sooner. I say that. And ask how she has been.

"All right," she tells me. "A little edgy, maybe. I have the
weird feeling that there's some freak who has been driving by,
parking, looking at the house, and then driving away. Or maybe
it's just some drug deal going down. Or maybe the freak is
interested in the house across the street. But I worry about it.
It's the same car, and I've seen it three or four times. Nobody
gets out. Nobody gets in. It just stops, parks for a half hour or
so, and then goes away."

I am tempted to confess. But I worry that she's going to be
offended.

"Have you thought of calling the police?"

"There's no crime. Anybody can come and park for a while
on a public street."

I admit that that's true, trying to sound as regretful on her
behalf as I am relieved on my own. I ask her if she feels like
company. Dinner maybe.

"Sure. Why not?"

How easy it is. But isn't that exactly what I've expected all
along and have most feared?

We make a date for the following evening.

At three in the morning, I am awake, having wrenched myself
out of another dreadful dream. In this one, I am at a gallery of
some sort, a large, modern, classy place with white walls and
indirect lighting. I am covering an opening of a new exhibit.
And the works on display are *objets trouvés*, which is a kind

of prank lazy sculptors have dreamed up to play on the unsuspecting public. This sculptor's work has a certain energy, or at least ambition and nerve, for the pieces are quite large and fascinatingly ugly. Great hunks of twisted metal! Only gradually do I realize that these are wrecked cars he has put on display. And even at that, I don't get the point, or not at first. I am more and more uneasy, but I wander around like the rest of the guests, who are standing around enjoying themselves, gobbling canapés and swilling champagne. I am unable to explain what is making me so miserable until I see at last, among the pieces on display, the car in which Pam and Leah were killed. Not just a car like that, but the very one. It becomes clear to me what the artist was doing, what the point of the show is—that all these cars are wrecks in which people have died.

And then I feel the anger building in me, the rage I am obliged to hide, because I am there on assignment, managing editor Harris having dispatched me to cover this grotesque event. I am to heap scorn on the dumb nobs who are in the room with me, looking for something striking to put into their entrance halls or their living rooms, but I am also to convey their grisly thrill—or the photographs will.

I try to run, but that is difficult in the familiar, thigh-deep tapioca of dream exertions in which I can hardly move even though I make every possible effort, can barely breathe, am sweating. . . .

I am sweating, as I discover when I wake up. To a not very much better reality.

Still, it's a little after three. I'm halfway through the night, which is farther than I often get before the first interruption. Or intermission?

Anyway, I open the anthology again, because it is there on the night stand. I am not going to attempt to read the poems, which take too much concentration for this hour of the night, but I will content myself with a diverting look at the biographical notes in the back of the volume. Gossip, the easy stuff. Brief lives, lives that have, because of the constrictions of the format, the same cartoon vividness as those of the saints.

I have actually heard of some of these people, of Li Po and Tu Fu, at least—who were a generation or two earlier than the ones I think of as my guys, Yüan Chen and Po Chü-yi. Po Chü-yi was the earliest popular poet in China. He is described as having been surprised in finding, on his travels, poems of his that had been written out on walls of inns and monasteries. And singing girls who knew his songs would demand a higher price.

Which he paid, without letting them know who he was? In my version, that's how it would have been.

In 807, he was appointed to the Hanlin Academy and given the title Commissioner to the Left. Whatever in hell that means, he apparently took it seriously, criticized government policies, and defended his friends who had incurred the court's disfavor (Yüan Chen, among them). As a result he was sent out to remote posts, which seems to have happened a lot back then in the middle T'ang.

And now?

I switch off the light and close my eyes, wondering what horrors I will devise for myself this time around.

I am in a slum of some kind, an awful building. I have been there for some time, having been involved in something shameful, something so bad I don't even define it for myself. But I am leaving, or I at least intend to leave. I am packing up the few things I brought with me. I thought there were only a few things, but there seem to be a vast number of shoes. I am down on the floor, putting these shoes into a large suitcase. There is a pair of red boots, a woman's boots . . .

What woman has been here with me? To whom do the worn boots belong? What was the point of this sordidness if I can't even recall it now? I hurry, wanting very much to escape from there, but I am woefully clumsy, and it takes a long time for me to stuff these shoes into the suitcase. It is worse than running through the tapioca, even more frustrating because I seem to be more to blame for my dreadful ineptitude.

I wake again, almost amused by this one. At any rate, it is less a horror than most. I don't even bother to turn on the light.

I just lie there waiting to drift off again.

Since Pam and Leah were killed, every night has been like this, with five-act Elizabethan tragedies of blood in constant repertory. I am the sole season subscriber.

In the morning, I drag myself out of bed. I ache all over, as if I'd been pummeled. Which is what has happened to me. My jaw is tight from the grinding of teeth.

But there are worse nights. Sometimes, I wake to my own screaming.

Which is one reason for my having kept on with the job. It is a place to go, an excuse for leaving the house every morning. No matter how dreadful, it is better than what I leave behind. Other people's desperation and suffering are at least diverting.

Harris has already moved into Lansberg's office. And has brought in paraphernalia with which to claim the space—a jade plant, a photograph of his wife and children, and a quite large reproduction of a particularly upsetting Soutine painting showing a sheep carcass in a butcher's window. The Soutine is an interesting choice, some sort of comment on his life or our organization or perhaps his general world view. Or perhaps it is designed to be provocative—Cosgrove will certainly notice it eventually and may worry about it.

A way to test Cosgrove's resolution, perhaps?

We have a weekly story conference, just like all the others except that the personnel have changed slightly.

Only at the end does Harris stake his claim. He announces that we are going to address the concerns of our readers more attentively. Which sounds reasonable enough on its face but has rather unattractive hindquarters. What it means is that he wants to pander more, to lower our already subterranean standards so that we feature more of the supernatural stuff, more reports about dreams and lottery numbers, more stories about witchcraft and spiritualists. What lives have we all lived before this one?

"I'm not just talking Shirley MacLaine," he tells us in peroration. "I'm talking Shirley MacLaine's *maid*!"

Words to live by!

Maybe, by his perverse lights, Cosgrove was right after all.

There is no point in getting exercised about it, though. It was all waiting to happen. Cosgrove, Lansberg, Harris, and I are all dancing out the steps that were there on the floor like the Arthur Murray footprints, not merely waiting for us to weigh them down but occasioning our feet.

In which case, one may smile like an Eastern sage, mildly amused by whatever happens but never actually involved. The secret of the lotus is to float, a white purity on the generally filthy water.

I float through the day. I do a piece I actually like about four brothers who chipped in on a lottery ticket that won, and then, in their wrangling over the proper division of the prize money, killed one another. It is a classic story—see *The Treasure of the Sierra Madre* or *The Jungle Book* or "The Pardoner's Tale." It is actually pleasant to see what happens to it as it gets adapted to our spare stylistic exigencies.

> And thanne shal al this gold departed be,
> My deere freend, bitwixen me and thee.
> Thanne may we bothe oure lustes all fulfille,
> And pleye at dees right at oure owene wille.

The poor sods! The two thieves set upon the third and kill him, and then they drink the poisoned wine and they die too. And the pardoner, as crooked as any of us here at ABC, brings his sermon to a close and goes into his pitch for the indulgences he's selling.

(No, I don't have this committed to memory. But when I look it up later in the afternoon, I know where to look. And I recognize it right away.)

The question is how Harris will take it. I have nowhere referred to Chaucer or Kipling or even B. Traven. But he'll know what I was thinking. And he'll approve or disapprove. And let me know what he is thinking or keep his thoughts to himself. But no matter how he responds or fails to respond, I shall have some sense of what the weather is going to be like for the coming weeks. Perhaps even the climate.

I put the finished piece in Harris's box. And I go to lunch—the lean pastrami on a hard roll and a diet soda at a place nearby called Uncle Belly's. I am not worried. Curious, I think, is a better characterization. And when I get back, I am rather pleased to find that there's a note on my desk. "See me. H."

How quickly he has assumed the manners of middle management! I have my underling's stratagem, however, and in conformity to its dictates I saunter, nonchalance itself, down the hall and into his office. "You wanted to see me?" I ask, all easy smiles.

"Yes. Close the door, would you?"

I do so, thinking that the "Close the door" is ominous and that the polite "Would you?" is even more unsettling. But my face remains confident and serene. I'm affability personified.

"I've read your 'Pardoner's Tale.' "

"I figured you'd make that association, yes," I tell him. For a brief moment, I entertain the zany idea that he might even want some reference to Chaucer put into the story.

"But where's the old man?"

"What old man?"

"In the Chaucer, there's Death. Or the Devil. A menacing old man who sets up the whole thing. That's what people believe in. That that much bad luck has to be destiny! You were at the meeting this morning. I want juice."

"Two brothers shoot two brothers and then drive off in the truck where one of the murdered guys drained the brake fluid. That's not juicy enough?"

"The Devil made them do it!" Harris tells me, leaning back in Lansberg's chair.

"Are you serious?" I ask.

"You haven't accepted it, have you? That Cosgrove picked me and that you're still out there in the same chair you were sitting on last week. That still bothers you, doesn't it?"

"No, not at all."

"You're not a good liar," he says.

"You'd have been bothered if I'd been the one who was promoted. But I'm not. Can't you believe that?"

"No," he says. "I can't."

"Well, I don't see what I can do to convince you," I say, the smile still there as if we are a couple of high-school kids in a bull session.

He is as aware as I am of the unreality of our conversation. He, too, feels the need for a more definite gesture. He takes my copy from his desk pad and rips it showily in half. Then in quarters.

"Write it again," he says. "Put the Devil into it."

"All right," I say. "Is that all?"

He is disappointed. I am skating on thin ice, but I'm enjoying it. He knows that too and it troubles him. He rocks back in his chair. "I don't know," he says. "I was really expecting that you might quit."

"Well, I haven't," I tell him. "And I won't. Do you want to fire me?"

"Not really," he says, "but I suppose I have to."

"Why?"

He nods. Have I missed something?

"Why?" I repeat. Not pleading, but after all, I do have a right to some explanation, don't I?

"Because I can't trust you. I just don't believe that you don't resent me."

"I do now," I tell him. But I'm still smiling even as I get up and leave.

I empty out my desk and put my stuff into a carton and a wastebasket, which I can use as a container. And I try to analyze what happened. What could I have done differently!

It wouldn't have mattered. There's nothing I did or didn't do that would have had any effect. It was all in Harris's head. Or in the mind of God. It was all settled, from the moment Cosgrove found the paper with the dingbats in Harris's drawer.

I'm not sorry to be free of this. I'm just worried about how I'll spend those hours between the time I wake up and the time

I go to bed. It was a mindless job, but that was what I liked about it.

Quite conceivably, Harris has done me a favor, although that wasn't his intention. If that is so, I hope the cynic was right who said that no good deed goes unpunished.

It wasn't a bad story!

That was what was wrong with it.

18

IF I hadn't called Stephanie before I'd been fired, I would have called her right afterward. To let her know. To ask her help? Her sympathy? For her reaction, at any rate. One needs some-one to turn to. To turn to.

Yes, I know. That's tautological. (Or untaught and illogical.) But say it over often enough and it begins to twitch with some sort of meaning. Ah, ah! Not too much, or it loses its meaning and turns again into nonsense.

Ha ha!

That's a crossword puzzle word. A sunken fence. There are a lot of them in crossword puzzles, hahas, and adits, which are mine entrances.

Aha! A haha!

Eh?

A haha!

Ah!

One could go on that way. As people do, who have nothing else to turn to. Or nobody else.

It was a good thing that I'd already made the date with Stephanie. I didn't have to call her and tell her of my disaster, beg her to soothe my wounds, grovel, abase myself. I could imagine myself referring quite casually to the contretemps of the afternoon, and her generous concern not unmixed with admiration for my virtually nonexistent stoicism.

I didn't really believe it would be like that, but I could choose to imagine it. Or, just as easily, I could imagine Stephanie in bed. Stephanie and me in bed.

St. Agatha is generally represented by a pair of breasts on a dish. Agatha was a third-century Sicilian martyr whose legend is characterized even by the hagiographers as "worthless," but which must have had a certain charm, as evidenced by its persistence over the centuries. It was popular with that class of people to whom one might refer in crude shorthand as being like . . . shall we say Shirley MacLaine's maid?

At any rate, Agatha—which, in Greek, means noble—was a girl of noble family of Catania who was pursued by a fellow named Quintian, a man of consular rank. She rejected him, either because she didn't like him or because he was a pagan and she was a Christian. He denounced her as a Christian, whereupon she was turned over to the Bureau of Pornographic Fantasies—a governmental institution that recurs often in Western Civ. She was carried off to a brothel, was stretched on the rack, had her breasts cut off, and was finally rolled over hot coals until she died.

She is represented as carrying pincers or, alternatively, holding her breasts out in front of her on a salver. In second- and third-rate paintings, it wasn't always clear what those mound-like objects on the dish might be, and they were taken by some to be loaves of bread—so there is a ritual of blessing the loaves on her day, which is February 5.

She is patroness of—bizarrely enough—nurses.

It is a thoroughly nasty story, not quite redeemed by its virtually incoherent primitivism.

And why do I think of it? Because lust and aggression are unpleasantly mixed in us all? Because I am trying to find daytime correlatives for the horrors of my nights? Because one breast is much like another?

Impaled on the spikes of a haha, one's mind wriggles.

Meanwhile, I console myself by doing my laundry. It is soothing to hear the reassuring slosh or the hum of the machines as, inside, the drum spins like a Tibetan prayer wheel. Cleanliness is next to godliness after all.

Or less confidently, as long as you're doing your laundry, all hope is not yet utterly lost.

I drive to Stephanie's. I have showered and—for the second time today—shaved, which makes me feel a bit silly, like a teenager getting ready for a hot date. But why not? It is pleasant to think of crawling into bed with Stephanie and just staying there. She can get out of bed from time to time to get food or bring in the mail. But aside from smallish ventures to the bathroom, I'll just lie there like an infant in a crib but with the pleasures of sex instead of the shit-smearing little kids take such delight in. Like that Honeymoon Couple in their hotel suite all those years, those anchorites of the flesh.

What's scary is that it is actually possible. What with the money from the drunken bastard's insurance company for Pam's and Leah's deaths and with what Stephanie has from Roger's pension. At least from the financial point of view, it is perfectly plausible.

I am, nevertheless, ashamed of myself for having had such a thought. It is as if I am an innocent bystander and the thought has waylaid me, not doing me any actual bodily harm but humiliating me, as street toughs in unsavory neighborhoods can sometimes do with their taunts and insults.

But the house is paid for. Her house, that is. And what I'd save on my mortgage payments and insurance and taxes if I moved in with her would be substantial. We could live forever, doing absolutely nothing and never touching capital. It's the American dream!

Or, more accurately, the capitalist Nirvana.

Dare I mention this fantasy to Stephanie? Of course not.

But I propose a kind of dopey bargain with myself. To atone for my shameful vision of an endless Oblomovian wallow, I might admit to having been her night-stalker, that fellow in the car.

That's actually funny—that I am coming to see her at least
in part to guard her against myself.

Or maybe it's not so funny. There is a persuasive sound to
it. Absurd, but not funny.

She welcomes me perfunctorily, which pleases me. The
pecks we exchange on the cheek are just what I want. Any
more enthusiasm would be malapropos. Or anyway, silly—like
my second shave. We are both too knowing, too grown up for
effusiveness. I actually prefer this all but domestic greeting.
She is wearing a khaki skirt and an aqua turtleneck pullover
and is neat and presentable but hardly done up. Which is also
right.

"Drink?" she offers.

"Sure," I say. "To celebrate."

"Oh?"

"My freedom," I explain. "I was fired today."

"I'm glad you're glad about it."

"It was a terrible job. To get fired from it is about the best
thing that can happen to someone."

"Better than quitting?"

"Oh, yes. If you quit, there aren't any benefits. If you're fired,
you get severance and then the unemployment insurance kicks
in. It's a bonanza!"

"Or a sabbatical."

"That too."

"All right, we'll drink to it then," she says. "Gin?"

"As Pushkin said, 'One gin.' "

"What? Oh! That's awful," she says.

She shakes her head and goes to the kitchen for the ice. I sit
down and look around trying not to be too proprietary. It is
pleasing to imagine myself in this house, to yield myself to
choices that have already been made about styles and fabrics
and colors. The Strattons didn't have me in mind. But here I
am. As perhaps here I always was, lurking in the mind of God,
waiting for this room to be readied. As it was waiting for me.
As my place may be waiting for that unimaginable family who
will want it, furnished, just as it is, as if it had been done for

them rather than for us. The terrible faithlessness of objects!

"Very dry martinis," she says, having brought glasses with ice from the kitchen. She pours gin from the bottle on the cart. "No vermouth? None?"

I shake my head. We raise our glasses to "Uhuru! Freedom!"

"If you say so," she says. "What happened?"

I tell her about Lansberg getting fired and Harris getting promoted. Although it happened in the reverse order, this version is easier to follow and closer to the truth. And I describe Harris's suspicion of me and its inevitable consequence. "The odd thing isn't that I don't care. It's more than that," I explain. Or at least I try to. "I can't understand why I hadn't quit long ago, why I kept getting up every morning and getting dressed and going there . . . I didn't like it. And after Pam and Leah were killed, I didn't even need the money. But I kept doing it. I guess I was afraid that if I stopped, the world would stop. Everything would fall apart."

"You're not worried about that anymore?" she asks.

I shake my head. I am thinking about my daydream of living here, of just moving in and taking over at her husband's desk. Putting his sharpened pencils to use at last. Or leaving them alone and just going to bed for thirty years or so.

I am tempted to tell her about this persistent idea of mine, but I resist. Instead, and in accordance with that bargain my conscience had offered, I tell her that I can reassure her, at least, about the freak in the car.

"Oh, yes?" she asks, perking up to attention.

"It was me," I tell her cheerfully.

She is not amused.

It wasn't a prank. And I'm not a freak. I try to explain to her that I hadn't intended to impose on her, that I took an odd kind of comfort in being there, being near her, but I was reluctant to bother her because it was late at night.

"You could see that my light was on," she says. "You knew I was awake."

"Yes."

"So?"

"It was still late," I tell her, knowing, even as I speak, how feeble it sounds.

She shakes her head, a pitcher rejecting the catcher's sign. She'll go with the fastball. "I think you were doing what a lot of men do. Getting close and pulling away. You're not sure what you want out of this, are you?"

I am, like Verlaine, dismayed to be too well understood.

"The fear of intimacy and commitment!" she continues. "There was a Donahue show about it. Or maybe it was Oprah."

"I wouldn't know. I don't watch them."

"There are degradations you haven't even imagined, Buster. And daytime television is one of them."

"Sufficient unto the daytime is the evil thereof?" When in doubt, joke.

She smiles. I have the sense that it may be all right, after all.

"You'll have to make up your mind. You can't just come up here and jump my bones and then take off and not call, not be here. Or only be here in ways that do me no damned good at all. Sitting outside in the car, for Christ's sake!"

"I was afraid . . ." I begin. But she interrupts.

"I know that. That's obvious. And it's also obvious that you've got to decide what you want. And whether you want it enough not to be terrified. Or to ignore that you're terrified. Not that I can imagine what in hell there is left that can scare either one of us after what we've already been through."

"That's just it. What we've been through is enough so that I don't trust myself. Or you. Or anyone else. Or anything at all!"

"So? That only makes it more important. You've got to decide what you want to do. You can't hide at that terrible paper anymore."

I shake my head.

"It's your life. You can live it any way you want. Or not live it at all."

"That's true."

And then, after a pause, she looks at me and says, "You're

not ready for this, maybe. Maybe I'm not ready either. I don't know."

"I understand," I say, even though I don't.

"Do you?"

"No," I admit.

"I'd been looking forward to this evening. I really was. I took a bath with my nice bath oil. I smell good and I'm smooth all over—or as smooth as I get these days. But it's not enough." She stops.

"It's not?" I prompt.

She shakes her head. "We've both got a lot on our plates," she says. "But we're like people in adjoining beds in some hospital ward—we may have the same kinds of wounds, but we don't necessarily share anything. There isn't any connection."

"Isn't there?" I ask. I feel like a parrot or an idiot, but for the life of me I can't think of anything smarter to say.

"What do you want?" she asks me.

I hesitate, and then, feeling dumb, I blurt out the truth. "I've been imagining . . . I've been trying to imagine what it would be like to move in here with you."

She laughs, a single odd bark. That she then stops is, I suppose, something. She just looks at me without any expression, or not with anything I can read, mere curiosity, perhaps.

"That's what you were thinking about out there in the car?" she asks after what seems quite a long time.

"Out there in the car. And at home," I tell her. "A lot. Is it such a crazy idea?"

She shakes her head. "It is if you just sit there out in the car like that."

"And now that I've told you?"

"I don't know," she said.

That's also something, a kind of progress.

"I'm not certain about it myself. But it keeps occurring to me. And it does seem attractive." I don't want to sound too eager.

"I'll have to think about it," she says after another long moment. "We both will."

I am encouraged. It's better than I could have hoped. "And

about tonight?" I ask, reckless, enjoying the giddy feeling of pushing things a little farther than I should, wondering whether the evening might not be retrieved.

"We're not going to fuck, if that's what you mean. But it's not wasted. Nothing is wasted."

I'm disappointed, of course. Laid off again. Or, actually, not. "Dinner, at least?" I ask, wanting to show that I'm a good sport, a good boy.

"Why not? But tonight, it's my turn to get the check."

"Okay" is what I force myself to say. I manage a smile, too.

"We can celebrate the end of your career in the yellow press," she says.

"Freedom!" I say, raising my glass with the last of the gin.

"Is there any such thing?" she asks, but she drinks what's left in hers.

19

YOU can't just play around with these saints. You can't diddle with them—as Stephanie thinks I have been diddling with her. What is necessary is that you trust in them, really believe in them. Pray to them, even.

"O, St. Anthony, help me find my fountain pen!"

I remember a kid from the second grade who seriously advised me that this was what I should do. Pray to St. Anthony.

It didn't work. I never found the pen. It was one of those Estabrook fountain pens with the moiré stripes. In blue. The point was broad—2668, I think. The pens used to sell for two or three dollars.

You can find them now in antique shops, but they're a lot more.

The kid's name was Nicholas something. He said it would work, if I believed. Which was nice, because if it didn't work, then it was my fault rather than St. Anthony's. He was hedging his bet, maybe, because he knew I was Jewish.

On the other hand, I suppose that if I had believed, if I had been able to take the great Kierkegaardian leap and trust to St. Tony's intercession, it is quite possible that, in some trance state, I might have been able to reconstruct what I'd been doing, where it was I might have lost it, and then go there and look under some radiator or behind those stacked auditorium chairs where it had been kicked.

Or not. It could have been stolen, after all. And therefore in the bailiwick of some other saintly spirit altogether.

Nicholas Something. Italian. It ended with an *o*, I'm pretty sure. And began with an *M*?

I could pray to some saint who looks after failures of memory. Or, not knowing who that is, I could just think about it until I get a headache—in which case Teresa of Ávila and Aedh Mac Bricc will take over and look after me, one or another of them. (Do they rotate, on some on-call schedule like hospital interns?)

Teresa we have heard of, but Aedh Mac Bricc is somewhat more exotic—a fellow who died in 589 after a life of extraordinary marvels, transits through the air, and miracles of healing, including the relief of a bad headache of St. Brigid.

Was it by the laying on of hands, I wonder? Or was there no need for any such vulgar external display? Maybe it was just a matter of belief. (His? Hers? Of both together?)

Belief is exactly what I lack. Which is nothing to be proud of. It is by no means evidence of a cranky self-reliance or dislike of superstition. I long for superstition. I have the feeling that too great a reliance on rationality is only another kind of superstition.

To follow the teachings of Malebranche is absurd. But at the other end of the spectrum, we have Isaac Newton's silly partisan, Pierre Simon Laplace, another eighteenth-century philosopher and mathematician, to whom the workings of the universe were nothing more or less than the innards of some incredibly large and efficient computer.

Cause and effect, right? But Laplace is now more a figure of fun and an object of scorn than Nicolas Malebranche.

Nicholas Marsicano?

Marciano? Malfitano? Something like that. It is written in invisible ink with a pen that is long gone. I can remember that big box in the school's musty lost-and-found closet with its burden of gloves and sweaters and galoshes and such assorted detritus.

I assumed that these objects were as bereft as their former owners. Part of me still thinks so.

In politics, it turns out that the extreme right and the extreme left meet—as Hitler and Stalin did, agreeing about the necessity for central planning and control. And in philosophy it seems to happen in some such way too—that there is a confluence of the streams of thought of Malebranche and Laplace. Whether you prefer to nestle in the simplicity of God's Will (Malebranche's idea) or the complexity of the world's huge numbers of variables working together and defying us to sort them out (LaPlace's notion), there is still a gloomy resignation that nothing much is knowable. Bits and fragments, here and there, may tease us. But the whole thing? Or even any considerable portion of it? It defies the intelligence.

Which turns inward.

I like to think of those great thinkers lying in bed, as I have been doing, staring at the ceiling and all but unable to move, weighed down by the burden of the unknowableness of the universe.

Look, Kant held his socks up with strings tied to his pants pockets because he hated garters. And they didn't have elastic one-size-fits-all socks back in those days. So he had to improvise.

It's the most engaging thing about Kant, to imagine him wandering around Königsberg with those strings running up the sides of his legs. And then, back home, he lay in bed and stared up at the ceiling, thinking about synthetic a priori judgments and categorical imperatives.

Things happen. You can't help it. You don't know what's going to happen but you know that something will. And you probably ought to be as decent a fellow as you can, decent to other human beings, at any rate, whatever is happening and whatever you know or don't know about it.

That's Kant, in a nutshell. Kant made simple. That, and the idea that you should, whatever happens, keep your socks up.

What shall I do about Stephanie? About myself?

I'm damned if I know.

Damned if I do, damned if I don't. So, at least I give a damn. Give a shit! Give a fuck? (I gave at the orifice!)

I could lie here for weeks and nothing would happen. I'd eventually have to go out to the market—Publix or Piggly Wiggly—risking the contingencies of their parking lots to replenish my stock of bottled spaghetti sauce and frozen melon balls. And pay the bills. Turn into a low-level recluse. Or a giant cockroach. Or a fruitcake, if that's what Malebranche's deity has in mind for me.

This little Piggly Wiggly stayed home.

I knew what was wrong with me. I knew, all right.

I understood the problem all along. I didn't have to be any kind of genius to figure out that if I lay in bed for days at a time and didn't have any physical reason for doing so, I was, more than likely, depressed. And I didn't have to be an adept analyst of the human soul to hazard a guess as to the likely reason for my depression—which wasn't just the deaths of Leah and Pam, but the way recent events had triggered my bomb. Or set off my psychic booby-trap.

Oh, poor booby!

My getting fired. My conversation with Babcock, and just as important, my realization that he wasn't the one I should have been confronting—that it was Macrae I should have been talking to—that was what did me in.

Lump all that together and what it came out to was an overwhelming feeling of powerlessness. Which accurately represents how I felt. My inability to do anything because I was not persuaded that anything I could do would make any difference.

Did the depression arise from the powerlessness, or was it the other way around?

Ideas flickered across my mind, possible courses of action, even sensible proposals . . . I could have called Lansberg, for instance. He was no dummy, and he had lots of free time. I could have settled that business one way or another . . .

But that was irrelevant.

I could have called Harris—called him at home, at three in

the morning, to offer him fire insurance. But I didn't. Not because it was probably illegal but because I didn't care enough. Harris wasn't the one I hated.

There was no way for me to get to Macrae. To go through the same business that got me in to see Babcock wouldn't have worked, in the first place, because they'd have figured out who I was. (Macrae wasn't important enough a criminal for my story about being a reporter for ABC to be plausible.) And even if there had been some way I could have figured out, some maneuver or impersonation that would actually have worked, I knew that there wasn't anything he could have told me. He, too, would turn out to be inadequate, disproportionate, trivial . . .

A Malebranchian instrumentality.

I felt powerless because I had been unable to foresee, to protect, to prevent, to save them. Unable even to die with them.

As I was still unable even to manage the smallest detail, like cleaning out their closets.

I could have seen some therapist, of course. But I wasn't going to do that. Because a part of me was simply unwilling to take that easy medicine. I didn't want to have my anguish analyzed away. Or "resolved." Or whatever it is that they do. I didn't want it undermined or diminished.

The one thing I could do, that was within my power still to accomplish, was to lie there and suffer.

I was not so stupid that I couldn't understand that.

It wasn't much, but it wasn't nothing.

I'd have felt better about it if I had voluntarily chosen to do it, though, instead of just falling into it the way I did.

It was Harris's and Cosgrove's gift to me.

Which was why I didn't want to call Lansberg, either—because he'd have laughed at me. And rightly. But that didn't change how I felt. It was as if there were a moral weight holding me there, an actual weight on my chest.

I liked it there. I liked those terrible programs. *The Morning Show.* And Phil. And *People Are Talking.* And Oprah. And Sally Jessy . . .

Or, worse yet, worst of all, *Wheel of Fortune*. And *The $100,000 Pyramid*.

It was cruel and unusual punishment, but that's what I liked about it. Did I dare to imagine that we were on our way to becoming a nation of penitents? That there would be processions through every main street and across every mall with flagellants beating at their flesh? That there would be crucifixions, the way there still are in the Philippines—with real nails in the hands. With Dick Clark as the emcee.

Compared to this drivel, ABC had been a university press!

I couldn't call Stephanie. That would have been a moral failure. I couldn't tell her what I didn't yet know myself. I couldn't suggest what the state of my heart and soul might be and how little she could therefore expect from me. I had agreed to that and was bound.

But she wasn't. She could, out of some kind of charity, or recklessness, or selflessness, have called me. Or simply out of curiosity, which would have been my weakness in her position.

I looked at the phone and willed it to ring. I prayed to St. Valentine. I put my trust in Malebranche's destiny that it has all been foreordained and will work out.

I was tempted to rely on that because it didn't require much. It allowed me to lie there and feel the bed floating through Henri Bergson's *duré* of space-time with the same exhilaration and at the same breakneck speed as anything Mario Andretti ever experienced.

Whatever I did, the universe aged, the atoms of uranium decomposed, the clocks ticked, the planets spun, and the system did what it was destined to do from the first big bang and bright light.

I stared at the phone—as I was destined to do. And it didn't ring.

It was waiting, perhaps, until I gave up. Only in answer to my despair would it bring its relief. Any dumb screenwriter knows that much. The hero is hanging by his two hands from the cliff. The dirt around one small plant's roots gives way and one hand loses its hold.

Now? Now will he be saved?

No, not yet. Figure something else to turn the tension's screw a little tighter. The other hand slips a little and now it's only a couple of fingers.

Now? Ring?

Not even now. But if I stopped thinking about it, gave up and adopted a Buddhist's perfect indifference?

That might have worked. And if it didn't, I'd have been in good shape anyway. The trouble is that perfect indifference is not so easy to achieve. That's the Nirvana they pray for, the Nothing that is virtually the same as the Christian All.

I went to the kitchen, where gratification was reliable, and opened the freezer. That tiny beast that dwells at the heart of each of us can be bribed at least for a little while. Its rages and griefs can be temporarily assuaged. I found that out the week of Pam's and Leah's funeral. All it takes is melon balls. Preferably in one of the little round green Pyrex bowls.

And Lo, the poor Indian. And Behold, the other Indian.

A solution. An answer. An irresistible prompting. The answer to my prayers. All prayers are answered—most of them with silence, but that's a kind of an answer. Or else with some nearly irrelevant reply like this one.

Along with the circulars from eager roofers and the bills I tossed onto the desk, there was a letter from the Crime Victims' Advisory Panel, Herbert Kronenfeld, Esq., Executive Director, advising me, in mimeograph—it must be the last mimeograph machine left in the state of Florida outside the school system—that the hearing for JAMES MACRAE for MOTION TO REDUCE SENTENCE would be heard at GLADE COUNTY CT. HSE.

If I wished to make my views known, wanted to appear or to present evidence of the continuing injury I had suffered because of the criminal action of the aforementioned, I was invited to write or call the Crime Victims' Advisory Panel, which would advise me how best to present this information to the court. *There is no fee of any kind for this service!*

Their free advice was worth every penny, I was sure.

I remember how good they were the last time I dealt with

them. They called me up to tell me that there was a Victims' Compensation Board that would give me money for the funerals. It was a part of what the state did to compensate victims. All I had to do was make a telephone call to a number in Tallahassee . . .

Silly me. In the wrecked state in which I then found myself, I thought there was something starkly decent in this gesture by the state. I called the number. I gave my name and the address and the names of the deceased, both names, and the police precinct in which the crime had happened. And God only knows what other information. The young woman on the phone said, with an aggrieved sigh, that would mean filling out two forms, although, having given all of this information on the telephone by long distance, I couldn't imagine that there would be anything left to fill out on the forms themselves.

Eventually these thick envelopes arrived that wanted only slightly less work than a corporate tax return or a public stock offering. And, among other things, there was a request for my 1099s or, alternatively, my income tax returns for the previous two years. Which prompted another call to that Tallahassee bureaucrat, who was annoyed at me for not having known that you have to be indigent to qualify. If you made more than $14,440 in either of the two previous years, you don't get burial money from the state.

"Why didn't you tell me this?" I asked.

"Why didn't you ask?" she asked.

I thought of calling the Crime Victims' Advisory Panel to complain. To tell them that they'd wasted my time and energy. That their assumption that all victims of crimes were indigent was unwarranted, a kind of bigotry, actually.

But I thought better of it. I figured I'd never hear from them again. Nor they from me.

After all, I had nobody left.

But a piece of paper arrives from an absurd bureaucrat's underling, and my life is different, for I know I shall go to that hearing. I never went to the trial. It didn't seem to have anything to do with me. I wasn't a party to it, certainly. The dispute was between the People of the State of Florida and James Macrae. I had no standing. Or interest.

But, of course, I did. And do. I am curious to look at this man, to see how he is different from Babcock, say. Or Adolf Eichmann. Or Adolf Hitler. One looks at those faces in history books and tries to puzzle it out, but there is no solution. The disproportion remains. That unprepossessing little face? That joke mustache? That prissy little mouth? And all those millions dead.

Not that the numbers matter. Each individual is a universe.

But I will go to the courtroom. And look at him. I cannot imagine not going. What was, only a couple of days ago, an idle conceit—of my coursing through Bergsonian space-time—is now inescapably true.

Putting it another way, I have a sense of having been aimed, like a character in a novel, where there is a plot hustling me along. Tricks and turns, perhaps, but a conclusion looming, and the sense of it getting all the stronger as the number of pages in the reader's right hand dwindles down. Malebranche had such a sense, the idea that there was an Author who could write whatever He liked.

It is possible to debate which is the aesthetic that governs that author's exercises, or that can be inferred from what he has actually done. It can be suggested—as the various religions suggest—that he is a novelist of manners, a sentimental romancer, a satirist, a player of intricate games. But to deny that there is any such tendency in the real world is to deny that there is any meaning at all in life.

Which is a logical possibility, but not one that comports with the experience most people have had at one time or another of how their lives go. There is a sense one has, now and then, of weight, of significance.

I have sometimes felt that my encounters with Stephanie were freighted in that way. I looked into her study, her late husband's study, and I could see myself sitting at that desk. That desk and that chair were yawning for me, as much as that bed, surely.

And Stephanie must have been aware of this, too. Or bedev-

iled by it. And her hesitation, her balking, was an expression
of her distaste for a solution that was too easy and too neat.
The novelist ought to have figured out that something else had
to happen. There had to be some resolution, of which my pair-
ing off with Stephanie could be the emblem but not the means.

From time to time? But what about the times in between?
The way we live most of the time has no such weight! I can
anticipate my readers' objection (for if I am in a novel, there
must be readers, at least theoretically the possibility of readers).

And the answer of course is that most of the time we are
minor characters in somebody else's novel. We don't have a
range of possible actions wide enough to register on our fairly
crude nervous systems. But when we get to some passage where
what we do makes some sort of difference, moral or aesthetic,
where we can even affect the plot . . . Ah, then, it's a different
story!

We can feel it, the way we can feel snow coming in the
winter. The sky is steely and odd, but it isn't the look of
the sky or the quality of the light so much as the density of
the air. The pressure has dropped and our blood flows and eddies
a little differently. Or maybe it is the fluid in our semicircular
canals. But there's something. We can feel it.

And something happens.

And then? We turn a new page, as we say, but are we altogether certain that it's merely a metaphor?

Less fancifully, I find myself roused to what may not amount
to "Action" but is undeniably a series of small actions. I have
to get out of bed—if only to check on my shirts. For an occasion
of this gravity, I am not going to wear polyester, but a pure
cotton shirt, as an invocation to my father, who believed in
natural fibers. But cotton shirts have to go to the laundry, and
I'm not certain whether I picked up my last package of shirts
or only thought about it. There's a shirt in stone or bone or
ecru or whatever that indeterminate shade is called this season.
That's the one I want, and it's not in the shirt drawer. So it
must be at the Old Boston Cleaners. (Is there a similar place
in Boston with this city's name?)

Which means I must get dressed. And, as long as I'm taking that decisive and forthright step, I might as well shower and shave.

If cleanliness is next to godliness, are ablutions ablaut oblations?

It certainly puts a new face on things.

Not, of course, that I have the faintest idea what to expect from this encounter with the killer of my wife and daughter. I am content to let the author worry about it. I will behave as it is my destiny to do. All I know is that I cannot possibly stay away.

I can't even tell anyone I'm going. I know that any friend in whom I confided would urge me not to go. Why inflict this on myself? Why put myself through it—for nothing? And what can I expect to happen, what good can come of it?

I know what they'll say. It isn't worth sitting there with the phone at my ear just to hear them say their lines.

But as long as I'm going to the cleaners, I might as well take the stuff that I've been collecting to take in—a couple of pairs of pants that need to be cleaned and pressed.

Life lurches into gear.

20

THE courtroom could not have been better designed if a Hollywood set decorator had done it for a satiric director of particular cruelty—modern, even *moderne,* but at the same time shoddy. The construction was a disgrace, substandard materials everywhere proclaiming not only the insolence of office but its corruption and incompetence. The plaster at one end of the ceiling and down one wall was already flaking. There was a leak somewhere, and water must have been coming down from the roof for quite a long time to get down three stories to this one, where the courtroom was. The rooms above it had to be jungles of mildew and rot.

The building couldn't be ten years old, but the tang of defeat and decay was as vivid in the air as anything the Austro-Hungarian Empire could have offered Kafka in those baroque cubbyholes from which he excogitated our nightmares. I stared at that blotch in the plaster and tried to think what Eastern European country it most resembled.

My mind wasn't exactly wandering. On the contrary, I was keyed up, my nerves jangly and my perceptions almost painfully sharp. Because I had spent most of the previous month alone, in the house, mostly in bed, there was an even greater exaggeration of everything I was to see and hear and smell and think. Colors were garish. Engines roared. Horns blared.

Daumier caricatures jostled Grosz grotesques—looking all the more peculiar in their tropical suits and straw hats. I could hear their gold chains clanking, Marleylike, as they walked.

I took a seat in that dismal courtroom and waited while a clerk shuffled papers. There were various lawyers and bail bondsmen and plainclothes detectives, recognizable as a distinct class, and then, in uniform, bailiffs and several deputy sheriffs whose job it was to accompany their charges out from and then back to the holding cells somewhere in the dank bowels of the building.

There were a few other people whose connection with the proceedings here was harder to guess. Witnesses? Relatives of the perpetrators? Or, like me, victims and their survivors? Unsure of ourselves and suspicious of one another, we avoided the exchange of any but the most furtive glances, as if we were ashamed of ourselves, not only aggrieved and victimized but disgraced too.

At length, the indolent activity in the front of the chamber seemed to focus itself. A clerk called out, "All rise," and the judge appeared from a side door.

"Be seated," the clerk called, and the activity resumed, the exact nature of which was impossible to guess.

These weren't trials but only motions, parts of other proceedings, other trials that were not yet begun, or had been suspended, or, as in Macrae's case, had been concluded long ago. There was no jury present. These were questions of law for the judge to decide, or at least to take under advisement. Actual decisions were in the indeterminate future, by which time that plaster flaking would have grown from a likeness of Serbia or Montenegro to a relief map of the whole of Eurasia. Once in a great while, the judge said something decisively. "Motion denied." Or "Motion granted." But it was difficult to see what effects had been produced by these pronouncements. There weren't even corresponding smiles and frowns on the faces of the lawyers who had won and lost. And their clients, the principals, were not identifiable. Perhaps they had not bothered to show up.

I had begun to wonder whether I was in the right courtroom

after all. Or, if I was, whether I hadn't made a terrible mistake, expecting that a court appearance somehow meant an actual, physical appearance. But there was no one I could ask for information. The only thing to do was wait and listen and look around. What became clear after a while was that there were two categories of cases. One involved litigants who were not at present incarcerated. These the judge disposed of first. Then came the other cases, which he had lumped together for the convenience of the sheriff's department so that the prisoners could be brought up and led back in some orderly way. Or maybe the reason for the delay was that the prison van had been delayed.

In any event, there came a time when the quality of attention in the room changed, but without getting any more serious or dramatic. Indeed, one of the reasons for making these motions, as the judge suggested, was that it was boring in the penitentiary and the court hearing was an occasion for a long bus ride. And a shave and a haircut, it seemed, as well as the opportunity to wear a suit and tie rather than the denim prison uniforms. A lot of the court's business that morning—most of the time, for all I know—was trivial, even frivolous. (Which was fine with me. I was happy to know that their chances were remote and that the judge was not particularly receptive to their complaints. I was hardly sympathetic to them, myself.)

In fairly brisk order, a variety of thugs, villains, and malefactors came into the courtroom. They were not shackled or handcuffed, but there were two guards escorting each of them, and there was a uniformed state policeman who had appeared at the doorway, armed with an automatic rifle. Was this usual practice? Or did it mean that one of the prisoners had been judged to be especially dangerous? I had no way of knowing.

The clerk called out the name of each prisoner as he came before the bench, which was reassuring, because I had worried that somehow Macrae might be brought in and hustled out without my knowing it. When I heard the clerk call out the first name and then the next, and realized that this was the usual procedure, I stopped fretting about that—and immediately began to worry that something else would go wrong, or had already done so. Had Macrae changed his mind? Had his hearing been postponed? I had been foolish in deciding not to call the Crime Victims' Advisory Panel. I just hadn't wanted to talk to them. I didn't have any use for them and thought that, somehow, it would be unlucky to let anyone at all know what I had in mind.

(Even myself? Yes, that too.)

Now that I was in the courtroom, I was convinced that I had been stupid. At least they could have given me the number in the courthouse of the calendar clerk or whoever it was with whom I could have confirmed that Macrae's motion was to be heard and that he would be brought to the courtroom for the occasion. I had nothing to go on but that mimeographed form letter.

Names that I don't remember, and faces of varying degrees of submissiveness, defiance, resentment, or blank depression. A rainbow coalition—except that it was a rainbow in an oil slick. And who in the courtroom had these people beaten, robbed, embezzled from, burned out, raped, or murdered? I could not read the expressions of the men and women to my right on the spectators' benches. I was all but certain that I'd made some mistake, got the date wrong or the room number wrong, or that the clerk in that damnable Crime Victims' Advisory Panel had mistyped something, when I heard the clerk announce "James Macrae" and saw a tall lean man in a blue suit nod in response. He was the man. He had acne-scarred skin and a bald spot like a monk's tonsure in his lank brown and gray hair.

Harmless was the word that flashed into my mind. He would have been pitiable, except that I had no pity to spare for him, having used it up elsewhere. I'd have preferred someone more formidable, somebody who approached positive evil, who was in some way proportionate to the terrible wreck he'd made of our lives. He even had a slight stammer: "Yes, Y-y-y-y-your Honor."

So much for my elaborate fantasies of revenge. There was no satisfying gesture that could any longer be imagined, because this poor excuse for a human being, this runt, this scarecrow wasn't a suitable object for it.

Like Eichmann, he was a disappointment.

On the other hand, there are photographs of bacilli and spirochetes and viruses, little insignificant creatures, that do disproportionate damage. Not that they are moral vehicles, creatures that can be hauled into court, or held accountable.

I felt very odd. Light-headed. Giddy and, yes, on the verge of some sort of dreadful hysterical laughter.

To protect myself—I didn't want to get cited for contempt of court and thrown into the cell next to Macrae's—I got up and left the room.

And then? Then what? I couldn't go back, couldn't possibly go back to look at that blistered plaster and watch those functionaries shuffle papers, while Macrae stuttered and stammered his way through the joke of the hearing. But I couldn't walk away, either. Couldn't leave the building or even that corridor, its linoleum already sun-faded, its walls painted in those shades of lime and bile that are made for institutional use only. I leaned on the sill and looked out of the window at a dying palm tree in the center of a patch of yellowing Bermuda grass.

What else had I expected? What good could have come of it? Or what transaction could there have been of any reality or importance, whether good or bad?

I must have stood there, not waiting, not patient, but merely unable to order my feet to function, either to go back into the courtroom or to carry my body toward the elevator or the stairwell. Rooted, like that tree, as wooden and pathetic as the tree, I stood there. Or leaned there.

As it was my destiny, apparently, to do.

And then I heard a noise behind me. And it was Macrae, flanked by his two escorts, the uniformed deputy sheriffs.

"You're James Macrae," I said.

"Who w-w-w-w-wants to know?"

"I am the husband of the woman you killed. And the father of the little girl."

He looked, I think, or maybe only hope, panicky. As if he

had learned, in prison, that anything unexpected is threatening. Or maybe he always knew that. Maybe he'd learned that at his father's knee, out in the woodshed. Or his mother's lovers' knees, geting the daylights whaled out of him.

I have no idea. And don't care much.

But I do think it was fear.

He looked to his left and right, as if he were checking to see that his escorts were still there. Not that he was thinking of running, but their presence was his main security, his only real protection. Emboldened by the fact that they had not abandoned him, he looked at me and said, "Give me a b-b-b-b-break!"

"How do you live with yourself?" I asked.

He had no answer. Or didn't feel compelled to offer it to me.

The three of them turned the corner of the corridor and stopped at an elevator marked "Official Use Only." The deputy sheriffs hadn't said anything. There was no reason for me to stop trying.

"Do you ever think about what you did?" I asked.

"I didn't m-m-m-m-mean any harm," he said.

"You think that changes anything?" I asked.

He may have shaken his head no. Or he may just have been looking from side to side, to make sure the guards hadn't been bribed, weren't going to stand aside and let me stick a knife in his back, or gouge his eyes out, or do whatever it is that people in prison do when they're sufficiently annoyed.

The elevator door opened. The guards took him into it. I could not follow, not being official. But I could ask him some stupid questions.

"Do you think about them? Are you sorry?"

"W-w-w-w-whatever you w-w-w-want . . ."

And the doors closed.

Back on my back. Back to bed.

I was again reduced to the condition of a sentient vegetable. Or, this time, truly reduced, because this mood made my earlier state seem almost blithe. I no longer bothered to distinguish among the television programs but kept the machine on now only for its babble of noise and colors, as if it were an electronic fish tank. I looked at it sometimes, but without comprehension, seeing what a cat sees. At night, its eerie glow suffused the room. It was my night light. Or votive candle.

All my books seemed to have been transformed into foreign languages, Turkish or Hungarian. I opened them and stared at the pages but could not make sense of their sentences. I let them fall, and eventually kicked them under the bed as I made my way to the freezer for my melon balls. I was soothed by their pale greens and golds, but I indulged myself only sparingly, for I was no longer confident of my ability to organize another trip to the supermarket.

Mostly, I stared at the ceiling, watching its wash of changing colors from the television screen—a succession of delicate pastels much better and much more interesting than anything the program directors contemplated. I waited for my mind either to function again or to give out entirely.

That would have been a kind of blessing.

The trouble was that with Macrae, there was just nothing to think about. A miserable, deplorable, contemptible, totally insignificant nexus of inadequacies. Had he not stuttered and had that odd little bald spot, there would have been nothing at all for me to remember. I could not summon up his face . . .

A man kills your wife and daughter and isn't vivid enough for you to remember him. What does that mean? What does it say about the quality of your love for them?

Babcock was much more satisfying. Although also contemptible and deplorable, he was at least interesting. He was glimmeringly aware of the disproportion between himself and what he'd done. And if he wasn't ashamed of himself, at least he had the good grace to be afflicted with that apologetic little cough, that "heh-heh."

It didn't have much moral weight, but it was an agreeable adaptation, like the viceroy butterfly's markings that mimic the malodorous monarch, so that the birds avoid it too.

Isn't it also true that by having killed so many people,

Babcock has acquired a kind of stature? Or, no, it was probably
the simple fact that I never knew any of his victims. I was free
to react, or at least to notice some of his idiosyncrasies.

It may be the case that Lansberg's assignment was the best
thing that could have happened to me, a kind of therapy my
guardian angels had devised for me and directed him to have
me undertake. When there was no longer any need for it, or
good in it, the entire arrangement was canceled. Which was
why Lansberg was fired. And why Harris fired me.

Ah, Malebranche!

I wonder if it was Malebranche's initial that was keeping me
from remembering the name of the other Nicholas, my class-
mate in the second or third grade. He sat in the seat directly
to my right. And we had a certain compatibility, finding the
same kinds of things funny and having sometimes to work
strenuously at not laughing out loud, which is difficult for one
person to do and twice as hard for two. But I couldn't think of
any other initial that seemed more promising. And St. Anthony
was of no help whatsoever. Hadn't been then and wasn't now.

There are certain subtle connections I have been considering,
probably insignificant, but then, who is to declare that this is
full of meaning and that isn't? If Malebranche's thought has
anything to it at all, then the universe is a text we may read
any way we like, figuring that it's all authorial and therefore
all subject to analysis.

Which is what we do anyway, right?

What I've been thinking about is the possibility of some sort
of connection among Babcock's victims, other than the simple
coincidence of their all having been in that parking lot at that
moment.

Laura Bowers booked plane tickets for Babs Theodore, mis-
tress to Ron Hapgood, whose wife Amanda was a part of
Babcock's bag, as Laura was, herself.

Meaning?

Very likely, nothing at all. It would be amazing if, in a city
of this size, there could be assembled a group of eight people
with no connections of any kind whatever. Hasn't some math-

ematician worked out a proof that you only need four intermediaries to connect any two people in the United States
through their networks of friends and acquaintances?

It is through those connections that jokes radiate out from
New York and Los Angeles in a kind of jungle telegraph so that
they're yuking it up in Des Plaines and slapping their thighs
in De Funiak Springs within six days.

Nonetheless, it's interesting. It is also interesting that Hafiz
Kezemi was enrolled at the school where Roger Stratton was
a member of the faculty. It's perfectly possible that Kezemi
was enrolled in one of Stratton's sections of bonehead English.
(I could check, I guess, but what would it prove? What would
I find out? Even if there are no records, it would still have been
possible for Kezemi to have been assigned to one of Stratton's
sections, but to have dropped out, because of a scheduling con-
flict, or because of some instant antipathy either of them might
have felt for the other. Or both might have felt at the same
time. And there'd be no record of such an encounter, however
tantalizing!)

And Springer's father sold Porsche automobiles. One of
which was parked outside the compound of Ambrosio Márquez
Martínez. Did Ambrosio own the Porsche? Did he buy it from
the agency where Springer worked?

(I have no reason to suppose that Springer sold Martínez that
particular car, but I have no reason to think otherwise. I'm only
entertaining possibilities. Or letting them entertain me. The
work in the library or in the laboratory is not the grand enterprise that scientists claim, but a rather vulgar consultation with
the poor dumb stuff of the world that can't speak for itself and
is all too likely to be misunderstood or betrayed. There was
something stupid but lofty about the medieval attitude toward
natural philosophy: that the best thing to do was to sit—or
kneel, or lie prostrate—in a bare room and meditate, waiting
for some sort of inspiration, some enlightenment. That, or look
it up in Aristotle.)

If these deaths were not so much crimes but rather acts of
nature, comparable to the fatalities of an epidemic that hit
town, wouldn't there be some such series of questions the

epidemiologists would ask? Wouldn't they look for connections, however tenuous?

Ah, they all had their film developed at the same shop—
some dopey thing like that!

A plausible idea for a show for *Quincy*, perhaps?

I wonder if we aren't all in reruns. There may have been free
will the first time this episode played, in some other version
of the universe. This time around, the only question is where
the commercial breaks will occur.

Or maybe this isn't the universe but a rough draft, a prelim-
inary model the creator devised and then discarded.

Do you suppose that that's Wink Martindale's real name?

I'm afraid it might actually be. That's the worst case, after
all, isn't it?

What could his parents have been thinking of? Could they
have had some inkling, right from the beginning, how he'd
wind up? And how did they bear it?

This is a perfectly normal thing for a depressed person to
think about. It is a strategic displacement. When one's real
problems are overwhelming, one's mind finds ways to distract
itself with irrelevant worries like this. Or just retreats to a
smaller and smaller circle, cutting off its connections with the
outside world because they are painful.

I remember a party I went to a few years ago for the sixtieth
birthday of a cousin of mine, and his father was there, my uncle
Saul. A natty dresser, Uncle Saul looked fine. He was a little
overdressed, maybe, wearing a blue suit and a white shirt and
a dark tie. That's how he and my father always dressed. What
was impressive was how he wandered around my cousin
Harry's living room, coming up to people, grabbing them by
the shoulder with a still vigorous grip—he must have been
eighty-six or eighty-seven then—and confiding in the ears of
the guests the wisdom of his long life. There was a moment
when he held you like that, and then he'd nod and say, "Fuck
'em!"

That's what he'd learned. Or that's all that was left when
the rest was washed away.

Ecclesiastes for our time!

When my mind is not wandering toward Uncle Saul or Wink
Martindale, I speculate about other kinds of connections that
there could be that I haven't even imagined, between Babs
Theodore, say, and Ambrosio Márquez Martínez—both of
whom, let us suppose, could have stayed in the same room of
the Rockresort Hotel at Caneel Bay, although probably not at
the same time.

It doesn't mean a thing, but it is still interesting, like the
back of a piece of needlepoint. That's not what anyone is supposed to examine, but we do, don't we, to get some idea of the
character of the craftsman? Has he or she taken pains? Is there
that neatness and authority in the work?

If we look that way at a wall hanging or the covering for a
pillow, should we not also examine the world to see how it is
made and what it says about its maker?

It is possible to turn the television set on but keep the volume
down because the telephone has rung—a consumer survey to
which, bizarrely enough, I reply, calmly and politely, distin-
guishing among my likes and dislikes of dishwasher powders
and liquids—and then to turn the radio on, letting it play the
classical music station I generally listen to. And then, forget-
ting that I've done these things—I've picked up a book, stared
uncomprehendingly at the pages and let it drop—it is possible
to look at the television set again and make sense of the arbitrary sound track, which seems rather clever actually. A
dreamy Brahms background to a soap opera episode? Why not?
There are lovers on the screen. No dialogue those desperate
hacks in New York could have devised would match the
Brahms Quartet that is now welling up as they stare into one
another's eyes. Unlike most soap opera episodes, this is effective, almost moving. The music is sweet and sad, which is
right for this mutual enchantment that can't last. It has its
ephemeral reality they will remember forever, that may come
back one day to haunt them, as music can come back, or to
accuse them, to remind them what they should have done,

how they ought to have lived.

But the soap opera breaks off for a commercial. And the musicians saw away at the Brahms on their instruments, in what is now rather nasty parody—for whose life hasn't had its Brahmsian moments, and whose life hasn't then descended to the bathos of One Thousand Flushes?

The coincidences of sound and sense are random but unavoidable. As are those of the lives of Babcock's unhappy band. And they mean nothing. Or anything.

W-w-w-w-whatever you w-w-w-want.

Fuck 'em!

There is another connection, of course. When I go to a store, Piggly Wiggly or any other, I feel myself to be a possible victim. I look around for the glint of sunlight on gunmetal. I listen for any sharp crack. I hear the backfire of some truck engine and actually hit the dirt—which produces alarmed looks from passersby—am I crazy? An epileptic? Just drunk? There are a variety of interpretations, but the reactions are more limited in range. The passersby walk around me, looking down at me with pained distaste.

Perhaps that's why we are the way we are. In India, the victims of misfortune get charity, not much but enough to live on. They are a nation of beggars. We are less indulgent to suffering and take a tougher position. Let them help themselves! As they do, of course. So we are a nation of thieves.

Ashamed of myself, I get up, brush myself off, smile in order to demonstrate to any eyes that are not averted that I'm okay, and go into the store, where, at the checkout counter, I find Harris's new issue of ABC's weekly woes and wonders.

INFANT BORN

WEARING ANCIENT

EGYPTIAN AMULET:

HAS SHE LIVED

BEFORE?

I wouldn't have included the question, which ought to be obvious even to our—their!—dim-bulb readers.

Besides, the other question that comes to mind is even gamier and therefore more attractive from the purely commercial standpoint: why was this woman using an Egyptian amulet as an IUD?

If that was the case, then it's interesting, if only because, at least this time, it didn't work.

A service piece, then?

Why do I torture myself this way?

I torment myself with nightmares in which I'm back there—the worst punishment my unconscious can devise. But clearly, it feels some prompting to punishment, its infliction or, more probably, its endurance. There is no hell except for what we have invented, recognizing the need for one, for others and for ourselves.

I am not Babcock. Or Macrae.

I'm not, I had nothing to do with it, didn't know until it was all over and the telephone rang with the terrible news.

But who believes that? Who can maintain the Buddha's serene indifference that allows one to see things clearly, or lacking that, Malebranche's strength of character that can by sheer force jettison all causal connections and fling itself upon the mercy of God's whims? If I could do either of those things, I'd be truly free. But a part of me is still persuaded that there is a rationale, some pattern, some basic meaning to the important things that happen to us in our lives. It's what novelists have been telling us for two hundred years—although, when you come down to it, they are just a gang of high-class ABC sensationalists.

If there is cause and effect in the world, then there must have been a reason for Pam and Leah to die, or even for them to be killed in that awful brutal way.

I can't find it in their lives and characters. (Their deaths couldn't possibly be of any use in correcting or chastening them, anyway.)

So the point of those terrible deaths must have been, must be, to punish me!

Ah! A ha-ha! And I am impaled upon it. I writhe in anguish.

A contestant spins the wheel. If she gets a dollar exactly, then she gets a thousand-dollar bonus and a free spin, and if she gets a dollar on that spin, she gets ten thousand dollars!

And the chorus wails the *Messe des Morts* of Jean Gilles.

Grotesque and heartbreaking! Or it would be if it meant anything, but it doesn't. Just a coincidence. The station's director of musical programming has not consulted the *TV Guide*, has no idea that he is competing with—or, actually, complementing—*The Price Is Right*.

Only in the mind of God could there be any connection.

If I believed.

If the point of their deaths was to punish me, then I am punished. But then I am also guilty, guilty beyond all possible atonement or punishment.

This is what we do to hold on to cause and effect.

We are all abused children who, nonetheless, cling to their parents, make up excuses for them, lie for them, and even love them.

Jean Gilles's music suggests how grief ought to be—restrained, courtly, almost fussy in its grace. The record liner tells me that Gilles was trained at Aix at the choir school of St. Sauveur where he studied with Guillaume Poitevin, served at the choir school at Agde for two years, and then went to the Cathedral of St. Étienne in Toulouse, where he remained for the rest of his life. Which wasn't much. He died in 1705 just after his thirty-seventh birthday.

St. Étienne was almost certainly the proto-martyr.

But it could well have been another Stephen. Stephen the Younger, perhaps? A martyr who perished in Constantinople in 765 during the iconoclast persecution that had been renewed by Constantine V. This Stephen, a hermit monk on Mount St. Auxentius, was banished to the island of Proconnesus in the Sea of Marmara—I guess you have to be a real pest as a hermit-monk to get yourself banished like that. He was the foremost defender of the veneration of religious images and, however he did that, he seems to have been an effective irritant. After three years on that island, he was brought back to Constantinople, hauled before the emperor, and questioned.

He produced a coin and asked the emperor if it wouldn't be wrong to treat its image of the emperor's face disrespectfully. And would it not be just as wrong to stamp on the image of Christ or of his mother, or to burn it? And then to make his point more vividly, he threw the coin onto the floor and stepped on it.

It is not surprising that he was hustled off to jail—to a cell not much worse, I imagine, than the one from which he'd started on Mount St. Auxentius. Except that it was more crowded. According to the account before me, there were three hundred other monks there in jail with him, and for eleven months they kept a kind of monastic life together.

This could not have been what the emperor or his advisors had had in mind. And they were shamed into an action that, apparently, the emperor hadn't really wanted to take. He ordered Stephen to be "battered to death."

Poor St. Stephen! Or, rather, rich St. Stephen! To have such faith, to care so strongly, to stand up not just to Lansberg or Cosgrove but to an emperor, and to suffer so for a cause. For a reason!

Having no such beliefs, I would be willing to dance on an emperor's face, or a president's, or the flag, or the cross.

But Stephen knew that Jesus' death had been for him. And had saved him and all mankind from death's sting by offering a new and eternal life that, presumably, he is enjoying even now. Beaming down from some comfy cell in one of Heaven's quiet backwaters.

It's kitsch, but does that mean it isn't true? Who can say what eternal taste is like? Maybe God sits around in his bathrobe watching Wink Martindale and eating melon balls. Judging from what we see around us, not on television but in what we flatter by calling the real world, the odds are not good, are they, for high art? Think of what people love. Those roadside stores that sell commemorative plates of *The Honeymooners* or the

Challenger crew or the two dead Kennedy brothers! Those sac-
charine choirs on the Sunday-morning religious shows that sing
"Bridge Over Troubled Waters."

Not Jean Gilles, surely, and those elegant turns of his.

But that's beside the point, isn't it? The style of the thing is
almost irrelevant. Think of the words that the singers are actually articulating. It's a Mass. Gilles believed! And if he did
not give witness in as bloody a way as St. Stephen the Younger
(that is what "martyr" means, after all), his music is a kind of
testimony. That I have been ignoring. Or rejecting.

For I cannot believe. I am a Jew, but also a humanist. A
secularist. A skeptic. A rationalist . . . All those things those
rabid preachers inveigh against. And the rabid rabbis used to
inveigh against—think of Spinoza! Those crazed sermons on
television are mostly a comfort to me, however, for if they
were right, they wouldn't need to carry on so.

They could still be right!

What if I'd prayed to St. Anthony? And what if I'd then found
the Estabrook, there in the lost-and-found room? Or back in
my classroom, under the radiator by the window, where someone had kicked it, quite innocently perhaps, after I'd dropped
it? What then?

Would I have converted? Would Nicholas have triumphed?

At least Christianity addresses the grief I feel, the despair,
the terrible guilt! If Jesus died for us, then our obligation is
already so great as to defy calculation. And our losses are diminished. If I could suppose that I'd see Pam and Leah again,
that we'd be reunited in Abraham's bosom, or Jesus', I'd be
consoled. I'd miss them, but it wouldn't be so total, so terrible
a loss.

I don't believe any of that. I can't. It's all twaddle. Pap! Pop!
Poop!

Matthew, Mark, Luke, and John batter the bed that I lie on.

Oh, but St. Stephen! Either St. Stephen. Stoned to death. And
battered to death.

And Jean Gilles, under all that ornamentation, is saying:
"Lord Jesus Christ! King of Glory! Free the departed souls of
all the faithful from the pains of hell and from the deep pit:

deliver them from the mouth of the lion that hell may not swallow them up, and that they may not fall into darkness; but may holy Michael, the standard-bearer, lead them into the holy light, which you once promised to Abraham and his progeny."

That's me. That's us! Oh, God, oh, God.

"May eternal light shine upon those, Lord, with the saints forever, because you are merciful. Grant them eternal rest, Lord, and may eternal light shine upon them, with the saints forever, because you are merciful."

Oh, God.

What I sometimes feel is anger, as if at an enormous practical joke. It's like those trick window displays that hide the glass and make it seem that all you have to do is hold out your hands and you can scoop up the jewelry or whatever else is the bait of the shopkeeper's trap. But the glass is there, all right, and you can't have it.

With heaven, too. It's a great idea, a tempting vision, real enough to take us in, to fool us, and then, when you give yourself over to it, there's the thick pane of glass, bulletproof. Foolproof.

This was a sufficient explanation, I always thought, of anti-Semitism. The fact that we didn't believe was unsettling enough, threatening enough, to make the Gentiles cranky. And of course they took it out on us. This seemed so obvious as not even to require confirmation from my parents.

Also in bad taste. One could not allude to the delusions of Christians, who were like people with some deformity—actually believing that stuff!

On some science-fiction planet, suppose two races of creatures, one of which took it as an article of faith that three times nine equaled twenty-nine. Never mind why. They believed it. *Credebant quia absurdum.* And from time to time, it really screwed up their engineering and their bookkeeping. But some saint or emperor or pope had decreed it, and as a matter of religious conviction and patriotic pride, they maintained it, in spite of all its obvious inconveniences. And this other race of creatures, an oppressed minority, just didn't buy it. Three times nine? Yeah, twenty-seven. Right! Obviously! So what?

So the twenty-niners don't like it. And they take out their embarrassment and resentment by tormenting and hounding and killing the infidels.

So what if their music is nice? They're still jerks. Assholes. Assholes to the twenty-ninth power!

But the pains of hell? The deep pit? The mouth of the lion? With what can I fend off those terrors?

It takes courage to look into that maw and not imagine a kindly personal God, a sweet fellow whose eyes follow you wherever you go. A dad. Or a pal and brother! (And if you add the Holy Ghost as a connection, and then deny that the three you've now got are any more than one—you're almost on my supposititious planet, aren't you?)

It is possible, however, to rage at the church and still to love its saints. The church was always the establishment, but the saints were the poor man's friends.

The saints, of course, were mostly dead. But they were nice people, sweet, pious, willing to put in a good word . . . if you believed that stuff.

You weren't alone. (Or, if you were, it was your fault.)

The saints couldn't do much to help you. If they'd had any real power, the kings and the church biggies would have gotten together to fight them off, or take them over.

As it was, the saints were just what the establishment needed as an escape valve when the pressures of their own depredations and oppressions approached the limits of what the system could stand.

And the urban poor and the peasants out in the countryside, who weren't so stupid as they looked, probably figured this out. But having done so, they loved their saints all the more. For they realized that these saints depended not on any official support but only on their own fragile and illiterate allegiance, their own ephemeral love.

Hating the church, hating two thousand years of oppression

from Christians, I am still drawn to St. Stephen the Younger, the enemy of iconoclasts, venerator of images, and persistent pest. He simply would not defile the icons, the images in which he believed and from which he had taken comfort.

I read in the *New York Times* a report of a study by Dr. Mardi Horowitz (if I were making this up, do you think I'd have the nerve to invent such a name?) of the UCSF medical school about grief. "Some troubled mourning can approach the bizarre," the article says. "One man kept his dead father's broken cameras hanging in his clothes closet for fourteen years so he could glimpse them while he dressed in the morning."

Oh, St. Stephen, pray for us.

Later on, in the same article, I read through my tears that there is an observation by Dr. Vamik Volkan of the University of Virginia (again, a truth beyond anyone's fabrication), whose grief therapy "makes use of a common phenomenon in those with problems in mourning: the possession of a special object that links him to the dead person, such as a piece of jewelry. . . . These objects are symbolic tokens jointly 'owned' by both the mourner and the deceased person."

Pray for us, St. Stephen, now and at the hour of anyone's death.

What Dr. Volkan does is to ask the mourner "to bring in the linking object and explore its symbolic meanings."

Close, but no cigar. The cameras only work if they are glimpsed that way between the hanging suits and sport coats for that brief moment each morning. I know that intuitively. As would any of St. Stephen's votaries.

Oh, St. Stephen, help me. Pray for me, St. Stephen. Bless me, St. Stephen. Pray for me, Stephen, pray for me, Stephen, pray for me, Stephen, pray . . .

The doorbell rang.

It was Stephanie.

"Jesus!" she said.

She shook her head. "It stinks in here," she said. "It literally stinks. Go take a shower. I'm going to air this place out. This is terrible!"

I looked at her uncomprehendingly, stupefied. One doesn't expect such direct answers to one's prayers.

She took charge, which was not difficult. I hadn't the heart to argue or even to try to talk much. I nodded but that wasn't enough. She made me say it. Out loud. And I did, repeating the details of the arrangement. The deal was that she'd come back in three days. In the meantime, I had to get rid of all this shit! Clean it out. Throw it out or give it away.

I hadn't the heart to argue. I supposed I could keep one or two things. Broken cameras or some equivalent. But the rest? Out!

"And then?" I asked.

"And then, we'll see," she said, promising nothing.

21

AND?

And! And! And!

The tyranny of "And" is that no matter how complete and final a stop one puts to a sentence, there is always the slovenly possibility of an "And" to extend beyond the period, beyond all possible endurance or sense, the grammatical involvement.

An innocent little connective. A syncategorematic term—which is how the medieval semioticists thought about language. Categorematic terms were those for which there were categories—objects or actions or qualities. Brown. Dog. Runs. But "The"? or "Away"? Those were syncategorematic, showing connections among the categorematic terms but without categories of their own.

Syncategorematic—sounds like a saint in that drawl the upper-class English affect. Like St. John, when it's pronounced Snjn, with hardly any vowels at all.

And?

The heart keeps beating and the diaphragm keeps bellowing the air in and out. The guts keep on working. And the cardiac valves continue their iterations: And then. And then.

No reason for it. Or even aesthetic justification. The heart has its destiny (which sounds like a title of some dreadful novel for women by some woman who uses three names). The liver has its destiny. And the pituitary gland. Even the pineal, where those Rosicrucian rays converge with the wisdom of the ages.

Everything does.

A door opens. A door closes. These are the events that mark our lives. It was not absolutely miraculous that Stephanie was at the door, had been standing there for quite a long time actually. That was capable of satisfactory explanation without resorting to supernature. She had been thinking about me, worrying about me, concerned that the smaller shock of having been let go at ABC would be enough to bring down what remained of me after the earlier and greater disaster. She had been expecting me to call, to continue my petty pestering. It was my silence that had been eloquent enough to get her to drive down to find out how I was.

But for her to have arrived at that particular moment? There is no way to account for that. An unimportant coincidence? And was it an unimportant coincidence that when the Israelites reached the Red Sea, there just happened to be a tidal wave, perhaps as a result of some earthquake somewhere? And that when the Egyptian host showed up, the water all surged back?

We can, of course, dismiss these happenings as random conjunctions, agreeing that if we can't explain them, there is nothing else to do with them. But one of Freud's boldest strokes was his refusal to dismiss trivial things like slips of the tongue—to which we have now given his name. He took these accidents seriously and understood that the mysterious workings of the soul are betrayed sometimes by these coincidences and lapses.

Are the workings of the universe any less complicated? Can we take them any less seriously? Is it not arrogant to insist on our rationality in the face of hard but irrational evidence?

At any rate, and by whatever mysterious or miraculous process, perhaps even in answer to my desperate prayer, she arrived. She stood there and rang my doorbell. At the very moment of my shreddiest despair, when my despair had reduced itself to the repetition of a phrase that was, like an old etching plate, beginning to drain of meaning.

But then, my unbelief was also drained away. I was an idiot, or at least a little child. "Suffer the little children to come unto me."

Her appearance was providential. That she was wearing a turtleneck sweater and a khaki skirt and a pair of white Reeboks instead of long white robes was a stylistic anomaly that struck me. But I didn't say anything about it. I allowed her to take charge, do what she wanted, however she wanted. It was, after the *coup de foudre* of her ringing the doorbell at that instant, a matter of unremarkable detail that I should eventually find myself translated from that house to this, from that life to this.

This room I am now writing in is one that Roger Stratton arranged and equipped for his work in retirement—his next collection of poetry or whatever else he was going to write. But was it not all along intended for me to move into?

The noise of typing that Stephanie hears reverberating around the house can't be any different. The production of sentences goes on, words without end, amen.

We are subdued, perhaps, she and I, but not gloomy. We make jokes, rather a lot actually. Sometimes there is even laughter at them.

Not the laughter from before. Before Babcock and Macrae. But laughter.

I work. Which gives a kind of point to my life. And to hers, too. It was her chosen career to be a provider for some writer. She isn't even that crazy about writing. If she were, she could read books, or write them if she really wanted to bother doing that. But it's writers she likes. The way some people like Dandie Dinmonts or Rottweilers. Or Burmese cats.

She's a fancier. I am a fancy.

Which is both more and less cogent than reasons would be. It is sufficient. And comfortable.

And from it, in the long run, could come whatever it is that people mean when they talk about love.

The wish to die when the other person dies? And you can't? And can't understand why not?

Nothing has changed, and yet there are changes. It is a process like the dry heaves. Eventually, the impulse or stimulus or whatever it is exhausts itself. And there is at last a respite.

It isn't the same as robust good health, but you can get up from the bathroom floor, bid at least a temporary farewell to the tiles with which you have been so intimately associated for what seems like quite a long time, and you stagger back to bed.

It's not much but it's progress.

I saw a report, this evening, of another mass murder— in Arkansas, in Russelville, where Gene Simmons has tied Charles Whitman for second place in the bloodbath sweepstakes with sixteen victims. Most of the victims were his relatives. Most of them were wearing overcoats, which the police interpreted as evidence that they were killed almost immediately upon arriving at Simmons's house, for a Christmas party. "The gifts are still under the tree and packed in the closet as though they didn't have a Christmas at all," the sheriff said.

I'm not makng that up.

Seven of the bodies were found in a four-foot-deep grave 150 feet from Mr. Simmons's house. The bodies of two other children were found in plastic garbage bags in the trunks of two abandoned cars.

And?

I am saddened by this. Numb, I guess. But not utterly destroyed. I watch the reports or read about them with dolorous incomprehension. But I don't connect with them. Their disaster doesn't touch me.

This is what we have agreed to call sanity.

I work. I am able—as you see—even to incorporate this grisly tidbit into my work. Work and love will keep us going, as Dr. Freud so wisely observed. If you can work and love, you are doing okay. However hateful that may be to you. However contemptible it may be of you to be able to do.

You go on. You get up.

And?

You have coffee and rye toast with light cream cheese. Or that new bran cereal with all that bran in it, as much roughage as driveway gravel. It keeps the guts going.

And? And?

You go into the study, the study that has been waiting for you all along, since the beginning of time, perhaps.

Just like this except for a woman's silver Cross ballpoint pen you keep on the desktop but never use.

And a little green man.

And . . .

David R. Slavitt is the author of many novels, among the most recent of which are *The Hussar and Salazar Blinks*. He has also written several volumes of poetry, including *The Walls of Thebes* and *Equinox*. He has had a grant from the NEA for his translation of *Ovid's Poetry of Exile*, has been a film critic for *Newsweek* and has taught and lectured at a number of universities.